HENS DANCING

Also by Raffaella Barker

Come and Tell Me Some Lies
The Hook

RAFFAELLA BARKER

HENS DANCING

'Me and Bobby McGee', words and music by Kris Kristofferson and Fred Foster © 1969, Combine Music Co, USA. Reproduced by permission of EMI Songs Ltd, London WC2 0EA.
'Sorrow', words and music by Bob Feldman, Jerry Goldstein and Richard Gotte © 1965 Grand Canyon Music Inc/EMI Partnership Ltd. Worldwide print rights controlled by Warner Bros Inc, USA/IMP Ltd, reproduced by permission of IMP Ltd.

First published in Great Britain in 1999
by REVIEW

An imprint of Headline Book Publishing

First published in paperback in 2000

10 9 8 7 6 5 4 3

ISBN 0 7472 6221 7

Printed and bound in Great Britain by
Clays Ltd, St Ives plc

Designed by Peter Ward

Headline Book Publishing
A division of the Hodder Headline Group
338 Euston Road
London NW1 3BH

www.reviewbooks.co.uk
www.hodderheadline.com

For Esmé

with love and squalor

HENS DANCING

February 14th

Seven Valentine cards have been delivered to the house this morning by the postman and not one of them is for me. Three are for Giles, who is eight and therefore at an age where the bolstering effect of a Valentine card goes un-noticed, two are for Felix, six, who is in a big rage that anyone has dared to be so sissy as to send him any; and two are for Charles, forty-one, who had not planned to be at home, but an airport strike prevented his business trip to Paris.

'How did they know I'd be here?' he murmurs, a smirk of smug spreading over his face. He drops the one his secretary always sends him without opening it, and looks at the other. It is not from me.

'The postmark is smudged. Can you read it, darling?' he says to me, and hating to miss an opportunity for one-upmanship, adds, 'Did you really not get any cards? How odd.'

Scrutinising his envelope, I drop it in the washing-up water.

'Oops, sorry, Charles, it's a bit soggy now.'

He looks at me with loathing. I smile sweetly.

Breakfast is an orgy of martyrdom on my part, as usual unnoticed by spouse and offspring, who according to age and inclination are reading their valentine cards/the *Beano*/the cereal packet. I clear away, deliberately not asking for help, and return to bed. The telephone clicks a couple of times and I know better than to pick it up. Charles has a sixth sense for an overheard conversation and will insist he's simply checking in with the office. I think he's having an affair, and am shocked to find that I don't care. Even being five months pregnant doesn't make me care; in fact it cushions me from any feeling towards Charles stronger than mild dislike. So glad the hysteria and throwing things phase has passed.

After an hour or so of luxuriating with *Regency Buck* (my second-favourite Georgette Heyer; I have just finished my namesake and favourite, *Venetia*, for the seventeenth time), I am renewed and can face the day, so rise again with a view to gardening. Downstairs the boys hover in an aimless fashion, kicking things and playing 'Greensleeves' repeatedly on the piano. Their father is still on the telephone. They need fresh air.

'Come on, I need help, you two,' I urge. 'Please will you come and clip the yew hedge with me?' Giles continues to play 'Greensleeves' in various keys. Felix shoots at me with a bow and arrow but misses and loses his arrow behind a painting which is propped against the wall, still waiting to be hung.

'Do we have to?' he whines, hurling himself backwards onto the sofa. 'I hate outside, it's really cold. I want to play cowboys in here with Dad.'

'Dad is going outside too,' I say firmly, as Charles sidles towards the serenity of the drawing room with his newspaper. He glares, but complies. Felix is won over by the discovery of a magnificent pair of secateurs in the conservatory. Thus armed, he takes a stepladder to my token topiary, a gloriously sculpted ten-foot-tall chicken, and prepares to strike. Charles is passing at this moment, and although he fails to register the chicken crisis, he wants to use the stepladder, so Felix and his flashing blades are diverted to ground level and a less precious bush. Giles, having condemned me as 'really sad' for asking him to help, is forty feet up a tree, shouting instructions to the rest of us about where to find the wheelbarrow, the rake and all the other garden implements he can see scattered in the long grass, relics of last weekend's attempt to get the children to help outside.

'Mummy, you've completely missed that spade; go back ten paces and then a little to the right and you'll see the trowel as well.'

It is pointless to ask him to come down – he won't, and an unseemly shouting match will ensue from which he will emerge victorious and possessor of the high ground – literally. Can't help wishing that instead of encouraging him to think of himself as one of life's commanders his school would exercise a few more Victorian dictums. 'Seen and not heard', 'polite to elders and betters', 'helpful and courteous at all times' could all be drummed in to great effect. Sour-lemon thoughts are interrupted by his appearance from the tree with a spray of cherry blossom, a joyful hint of pink in its tiny buds.

'Happy Valentine's Day, Mummy,' he says.

February 14th – one year later

Woken by the doorbell instead of The Beauty, and dash down to find the postman, grinning, with a handful of cards.

'Happy Valentine's, love,' he says. 'You're a bit popular, aren't you?'

Leafing through them in the kitchen, am relieved that he did not notice the names on them: four are for Giles, which seems excessive to me, two for Felix and one for The Beauty. None for me. Can't help remembering last Valentine's Day. Improvements since then include having become mother of The Beauty (now eight months old), and having shed faithless husband (divorce now three weeks old), but still no Valentine cards. So much for the glamorous life of the divorcée.

Spluttering and growling noises similar to those made

by a small lawnmower announce over the intercom that The Beauty has woken and will require breakfast. So will the boys, now clumping downstairs uttering the usual litany of, 'Mum, where are my shoes? Is there any tuck? Can we get a Nintendo 64?'

Felix freaks out when presented with his cards, 'I hate them, I don't want anyone to send me Valentine cards. They're for girls. You have them, Mum.' He hurls his spoon into the porridge saucepan and porridge rises like a tidal wave and slops onto the Aga hotplate.

'But one is from Dad,' says Giles. 'Look, it's definitely his writing.'

Felix is placated by this, but I am irritated. The school run mother of the day arrives and the boys depart like a mini tornado, hairbrushes, biscuits and pencil cases whirling around them, closer and closer until they vanish into rucksacks. The Beauty waves regally, bouncing on my hip as we let the hens out and throw them a few scraps. The air is steel-cold and heavy on the lungs; the hens, plump in ruffled feathers, groan and cluck a bit then troop back into the henhouse. They are protesting against the weather, and none of them has laid an egg since October.

February 17th

Odd communication from Charles asking me if I want to sell my shares in Heavenly Petting. He will give me a mark-up on their value. Instantly suspicious as Charles is the ultimate nipcheese, so send his letter straight to Maurice Salmon, my lawyer.

Heavenly Petting began life in an old electrician's workshop on the Bedford Road in Cambridge, and came into being because Charles was keen on shooting and wanted to employ a taxidermist to stuff various bird corpses. While investigating taxidermy, Charles became morbidly obsessed with dead animals, and quickly recognised a business opportunity. As he had never liked live animals at all, I couldn't take the idea seriously, but he persevered, working day and night to build his first crematorium, before moving out into the local streets to chat up the old ladies who lived in the terraced houses which fanned out from Cambridge into the fens. His first client was a blue budgerigar called Billy. Charles charged Mrs Day seven pounds for Billy's funeral service and a cardboard box containing his ashes. The funeral service comprised handing Mrs Day a piece of paper with Billy's name, type and age on it, then standing with her in the whitewashed workshop for three minutes listening to a tape of Albinoni's *Adagio*.

'We will bring you the ashes a little later. We like to

check up on the bereaved to make sure we have done all we can to help,' Charles gravely told her, patting her hand as she dabbed her nose with a mournful mauve handkerchief. Mrs Day tottered home to an empty cage, immaculate, as she had scrubbed it to keep herself busy before the cremation. Charles scooped a spoonful of ash out of the incinerator into which he had chucked Billy's little body some time earlier, filled a household matchbox he'd painted blue that morning and arrived on Mrs Day's doorstep before she had had time to make herself a cup of tea. She couldn't bear the empty cage, she said, so Charles offered to take it away. He sold it for ten pounds the next day and hey presto, Heavenly Petting was launched and running at a profit on its first transaction.

That was ten years ago. Charles had just left the army, I was pregnant with Giles and we wanted to live in the countryside. My grandmother had left me some money, and with it and some of his own, Charles bought his first incinerator and the inaugural premises of Heavenly Petting. I found the house and Heavenly Petting paid for us to live in it. And still does.

February 20th

Felix is off school with a horrible rattling squeeze-box chest infection, and is lying on the floor in the drawing room watching something unsuitable and eating marshmallows. I have a deadline and the tight-eyeball feeling that comes after a night of trailing in and out of children's bedrooms administering cough mixture in increasingly large doses. Just wondering whether to ring my mother and persuade her to come over, when her car creeps up the drive, engine at full throttle and windscreen wipers wagging furiously. Felix rushes to the kitchen window in time to see her execute a series of bounces across the yard before parking.

'Why does Granny always drive like that?'

'I don't know, you'll have to ask her. Actually, don't. I think she's concentrating so hard that she forgets to change out of first gear.'

Granny is my salvation and I am in no mood to carp at her motoring skills. She enters the kitchen, her arms full of books and a half-drunk bottle of red wine corked with a twist of silver foil.

'It's so cold at home, the gas bombs have run out and I forgot to order any wood, so I thought I'd come here. Egor is in the car.' She pauses expectantly. I don't like Egor, he is a halfwit, and, being a bull terrier, is also a potentially lethal weapon.

'Good, he can stay there,' pops out before I can stop it, but luckily is eclipsed by Felix, dancing up and down and begging, 'Let's get him in, please Mum. I want to see him chase his tail.'

I relent and escape to my study, leaving my mother and Felix exclaiming with delight as Egor spins in tiny circles like the melting tigers in *Little Black Sambo*.

February 21st

A savage wind is rattling the windows in my study and sending little gusts through the gap beneath the door into the hall, so that the papers, which are supposed to be in orderly piles on the floor, are rising and floating about at knee level. I have been working in this room for most of the ten years we have lived here, and I still don't have any drawers or bookshelves.

The Beauty, splendid today in pink tights and lime-green pinafore, is loving the swirly paper display and whisks about in her Popemobile trying to grab tax returns and their attendant threatening letters. The Popemobile is a mixed blessing. It was lent by a friend and it is loathsome to adults, being plastic with raucous bells and squeakers. The Beauty especially adores the telephone bit and is practising opening her mouth wide enough to fit the whole receiver in. All this is fine: the worrying bit is her mobility. She vrooms backwards through the house at several knots per hour without having any route planned, and becomes strident if marooned. I'm not sure why she can't go forwards, but she can't. She can't crawl either. Apparently babies with these walkers don't bother with crawling. I am pleased about this, as it means she can't fill her mouth with dog food, paperclips, used chewing gum and all the other things I haven't swept off the floor. Instead she drives around the house and appears just where you weren't expecting her, breathing heavily and cackling with triumph as she espies you. It gives her an air of independence beyond her years, or rather months, and makes her very cocky. She needs a helmet.

February 24th

Pancake Day starts badly. I have forgotten to purchase extra milk, lemons and so forth. Much smoke and slopped batter on the Aga results in truly inadequate trio of splodgy pancakes.

'You're meant to have lemon and sugar with them, Mummy.' Felix glares at his plate as I trickle golden syrup over it.

'I know. I'm sorry. I'll go shopping today and you can

have proper pancakes when you get back from school.'

The Beauty is still in her pyjamas for the school run, and a new tooth is causing much misery. She moans sadly as we head towards the supermarket after dropping the boys, and falls asleep within a hundred yards of its car park. Asleep, she is transformed to cherub, the rosy cheeks caused by teeth giving her a Renoir complexion and her lashes a dark sweep beneath porcelain-blue eyelids. Cannot face waking her, so drive once round the car park to give myself the sense of having been there, then swoop on towards home. Will have to purchase everything from the village shop and any roadside stalls I pass. Remember this as the way of life when The Beauty was brand-new. Could never be bothered to get out of my car; it was too much effort to wake the sleeping Beauty. Shops became impossible unless I could leave her in the car outside and still see her from inside. This ruled out all supermarkets, and most high street shops. Bought everything on account and had it sent, even Giles and Felix's uniforms. Food was either literally home-grown or from side of the road home-grown stalls. Very good way of life, with no boring twilight time in supermarkets. Much cheaper too.

Leeks, marmalade and a pot of crocuses are the stall haul today, no good for pancakes, so I leave The Beauty in the car outside the village shop and purchase the rest. Hope these pancakes are more successful than the last.

SPRING

March 1st

The wind of the past week is unabated; a pink plastic bucket has just bowled past the window and two cockerels have hopped onto the sill for shelter and are staring in at me. Their wives huddle in the flowerbed below, having scratched out a couple of really nice little hen-sized hollows with scant regard for my plants and bulbs. Hens spell death to a garden, and my bantams were carefully selected for their prettiness and also for their small talons. They are all called Mustard, Custard and Flustered for ease of identification. They make a big effort to keep things trim with beak and claw in the borders, and have clipped back the wallflowers to stumps, so I don't think they will manage to flower this year. It doesn't matter; the wallflower display was pretty paltry anyway. I am planning something more splendid for next year, and have ordered six packets of wine-dark *Cheiranthus* Ruby Gem accordingly.

I used to buy ready-grown wallflower plants in late autumn from an old man who sold them from a trestle-table on the roadside in front of his cottage. He always wore a collar and tie for gardening, and even in high summer he kept his jacket buttoned up and belted with binder twine for double security. Last year he gave me three ornamental cabbages to go with the wallflowers, and we were on excellent terms. His garden was a delight all year round, and he was like a benign Mr McGregor in it. He painted his terracotta flowerpots pale blue and had a compost heap as brown and square as an Oxo cube.

But when I drove by after Christmas there was a 'For sale' sign on his cottage. It went a few weeks later, and now the shaggy hedge has been clipped, the rose bushes shorn and a smart red estate car is parked where once there was a stamp-sized lawn. A silver climbing frame gleams on the vegetable patch, and the cottage has been repointed and tidied like any other. All traces of the old man have been hurled into a skip and driven away to a dump. I hope he died quietly in his sleep, or keeled over into oblivion in the garden during a double-digging session. It is unbearable to think of him now in some grim old folks' home in Cromer, tethered to a chair and staring into the sea.

March 5th

The Hallidays, wonderful glamorous Rose, godmother to The Beauty, and her husband, Tristan, are coming to stay and I want everything to be perfect. In preparation I sally into the garden in the manner of Vita S-W to pluck some appropriate offerings for their bedroom. The air is dry and bitter, the friendly barn owl swoops past, his feathers ivory and cream against a white sky. He flits over the hedge and continues to search for afternoon tea in the water-meadows, flying low and following the contours of the ground like a miniature warhead. The garden is a disgrace. Everything small and delicate in front of the house is mud-splattered, and otherwise there are only daffodils, but none of the wild, ragged double ones, just those that remind me of children's plastic windmills in their chrome-yellow neatness of trumpet and petal. I toss one or two of these into my basket and march on, sighing and squelching in new ankle-length red wellingtons. Felix ambushes me to discuss his pocket money.

'I need to buy some Warhammers on Saturday, how much money will I have when you give me all the pocket money you owe me? I've got seventeen so far.'

'Seventeen what?' I am wondering whether the red wellingtons were a mistake, but have no concrete evidence against them. Felix digs into his pocket and shows me a few pennies.

'Seventeen of these,' he says. Not enough for so much as a Warhammer arm. Weakly, wrongly, considering that I have just rejected them for lack of beauty, I agree to pay him fifty pence if he picks a vast quantity of daffodils. He hurtles off to oblige, and I am tempted to give up my search for a decent bunch for the Hallidays' bedroom. A few anemones are gasping and lying flat on the ground in the manner of fish out of water, but mainly the garden is twiggy in anticipation of buds. I drag a lot of sticks into the house and plonk them in vases. They almost look Japanese. Felix's daffodils do not.

March 7th

The Hallidays arrive bearing armfuls of exotica. A black hellebore, a jar of lobster bisque, *confit de canard*, organic sun-ripened-on-the-vine tomatoes and the books that the children have been longing for but which I have been too mean to buy. We are all wildly overexcited at seeing one another and I realise just how feeble my twig displays are when Rose produces a peerless posy of gold-lace polyanthus. Immediately consume half a walnut cake and three pots of tea with Rose. Due to my excitement at seeing her, my brain cannot register the fact that she does not want milk in her tea. The table becomes covered with unwanted cups of pale tea as I solicitously pour yet more milk for Rose. Meanwhile, Master Halliday, who is one and a half, is conducting a top-secret excavation in the food cupboard. He emerges, beaming, at his mother's side and she and I scream. He is smothered in blood. Mercifully we see the bottle in his hands.

'Oh, God, it's cochineal,' says Rose, then she blanches. 'Look at the floor.'

The beautiful, warm, expensive, sweet-chestnut floor is splashed with crimson. He seems to have toured every corner and we have not noticed. I laugh like an idiot; Rose leaps into action, dons rubber gloves, finds a scrubbing brush and some detergent and becomes immersed in pink foam. The next half-hour is a scene from a *Carry On* horror film. Rose and I scrub, wipe, sigh with relief and sit down, only to jump up shrieking again as more bloody blobs appear. Cochineal is on our shoes, under our nails, over the table and most of all on Master Halliday, now known as Vampire Baby. Rose is far more concerned about the floor, but I want to see if we can turn him back into the perfect specimen he was, or if he is going to stay gruesomely pink for ever. An hour later he is slumbering sweetly, and, thank God, *not* pinkly, and Rose and I collapse onto the drawing-room sofa as wrung out as a couple of old dishcloths. We are now supposed to sparkle, pre-dinner, and be vivacious. A drink is called for. And another.

March 10th

The evenings are slowly becoming lighter, but the air still breathes a chill through the yard when I go out to lock up the hens. The wind is high tonight, pulling at branches and wrapping around the roof, but it is mild, and, on ground level, quite still, so I decide to take the rotund terrier Rags down the lane a few yards to stretch her legs before bed. Moonlight illuminates the way, then is eclipsed by gusting cloud. I kick at an old black bag, a darker shadow in a dark corner by the hedge, and scream as it rises and lurches past me. Rags comes to the rescue with a flourish, yapping and growling at the swaying, ink-dark form. Cloud blows off the moon, and in the half-light I make out the bony shape of a calf's back humping away down towards the road. Two others hurtle past me to join their leader. Heart still racing, I return home to telephone the farmer. Should really herd them in myself, as I know where they belong, but it is nine-thirty, and I will miss vital classic serial on the radio if I do. It is *War and Peace*, in twenty parts. Blissful and agonising, and essential as bathtime entertainment for me, being a million miles from childcare and domestic toil.

March 14th

The Women's Institute market supplies instant satisfaction in the form of trays of gaudy primulas for me to dot around the house and plant in the garden. Much needed, as we have reached the most squalid phase of the year now, when weeds are revving up to choke the borders and no plants have yet emerged from beneath the ground. The house is just as bad, filth exposed by the harsh glare of March sunshine. Fingerprints like a tide along every door, and most furniture creaking and shedding infinitesimal quantities of sawdust every day, like a tree's deciduum at dusk. Only notice this when hoovering, as one sweep beneath a chair leaves a very obvious path between kerbs of dust. Must don a mob cap and do some work avoidance. Spurred on to housework by the arrival of three different brochures in need of copy. My job is to write it. This week I must sift sense from pages of computer-speak to make an interesting and readable booklet for Belhaven Conference Halls, for Tremendous, a new outsized clothing catalogue, and for Heavenly Petting's new mail-order funeral service. Can hardly contain my excitement and yearn to get down to it. But first, the cupboard under the sink has become a hotel for slugs and snails. It needs my attention.

March 16th

The Beauty and I are in west London preparing for a meeting with an intimidating and groovy magazine editor. As I try to wipe traces of The Beauty's breakfast off my only decent shirt, I rack my brains for things I can say I want to write about. A human biology poster on my host's bathroom wall offers inspiration, and I plan an article: 'We are all obsessed with the value of our houses, but do we realise how much our internal organs are worth?' It could be illustrated with a picture of Kate Moss with arrows and prices pointing to different valuable bits of her insides. Downstairs, the house we are staying in, which belongs to my friend Lila, is enveloped in incense and weird fluting and groaning noises are issuing from the CD player, creating an ambient atmosphere for her private yoga class. I tiptoe down and out with The Beauty, and catch a glimpse of Alaric, the hirsute Californian teacher, hitching up his Y-fronts so the waistband shows above that of his trousers as he prepares himself for a new position.

The Beauty enjoys the magazine meeting very much, and destroys three copies of the latest issue while grinding her teeth and cackling. The editor disarms me by being friendly and approachable where I expected hauteur and disdain, and by being dressed in a delicious skippy skirt which I covet. I am delighted with the whole occasion and sweep out feeling it has all gone superbly, until I catch sight of myself in a mirror as I pass a beauty salon. My cheeks are puce, as if I have been drinking port since crack of dawn, or have reached the hot flush stage of life.

Can't help contrasting my appearance with The Beauty's majestic loveliness today. She is stuffed, for the last time, because it really is too small, into an emerald-green Indian dress with mirrored and embroidered bodice. Setting off the outfit is a small mauve horse she has pinched from Lila's spoilt daughter Calypso. She has not let go of this horse since breakfast, believing that possession is nine-tenths of the law, and this is now her horse. I am on her side. I shouldn't think Calypso will notice, but if she did, she would not *dream* of giving one of her sackloads of toys to The Beauty or anyone else.

On the way home we strike a blow for helpless femininity in the multi-storey car park. No amount of jerking forwards and backwards on my part can extract my car from its space. The iceberg-dark walls begin to close in and panic also, and I imagine spending the night in this morgue with only a few rice cakes as sustenance. Salvation appears, in a dark suit with a mobile phone and briefcase. He has just parked his own sleek car without any trouble. I rush to accost him before he vanishes onto the street.

'I can't get my car out of this car park. Please can you do it?' I beg, and he beams happily, as men do when faced with female frailty, and obliges. I am profoundly relieved that he is not a New Man, and head for Norfolk in a cheerful and grateful frame of mind.

March 20th

Nits have staged a comeback. A posse is installed on Giles's head, smaller ones grouped behind the ears, grading up to the crown of his head where the field-marshal nits, creatures on the scale of an insect Arnold Schwarzenegger, have settled. Felix has them too, and as usual I start scratching as soon as I spy theirs.

I am an old hand at nit work, and am expert on different methods. The doctor used to give us highly toxic lotion which a) didn't work, and b) has since been condemned as brain-damaging. We keep away from orthodox cures now and have adopted a series of treatments through discussion with other infestees. Tea tree shampoo and conditioner is the current success story, combined with vigorous use of a nit comb, although here opinion is divided. My mother, despite insisting that my brother Desmond and I have never had nits, swears by the plastic comb, while Lila snorts in disbelief at the idea and waves her metal-toothed one as if it is a magic wand. We use both, and it is gratifying in the same awful way that picking spots is gratifying, to see the nits lying helpless on the comb and then to guillotine them with a sharp finger-nail.

I forget to de-nit myself and remember on the way to the hairdresser. Arrive there in a welter of embarrassment at what they may find. Mercifully Emily, my usual coiffeuse, is in a trance of gloom and stares at the ceiling without speaking once during her twenty-minute assault on my hair. This technique does not make me looked groomed and expensive, but at least it saves me the hideous humiliation of being outed as a nit carrier.

March 29th

Easter Sunday, and we have lunch with my mother. Roast lamb, mint sauce, apple crumble. This has been Easter lunch ever since I can remember, and is the high point of my mother's culinary calendar. We find her painting her fingernails alternate red and blue stripes.

'It won't be ready for a bit,' she says, 'probably an hour. Go and see what you can find in the garden.'

She has a large carrier bag behind her back, and as we follow the children outside, she surreptitiously reaches into it, replenishing stocks of miniature coloured eggs on garden seats and steps. 'Come back, you've missed some,' she calls to Giles, now vanishing into undergrowth at the bottom of the garden. Then she turns to me.

'I've hidden a few miniatures and a couple of packets of Silk Cut as well. Just to make it fun for us geriatrics and The Gnome. Come on, let's go and find them, it's time for a pre-lunch drink.'

The Gnome, my mother's lodger, emerges from his caravan, called from his star maps and astrological calculations by whoops of triumph from outside. He is particularly Hobbit-esque today, with ink smudges on his face and a short brown suede jacket with brass buttons and a belt. All he lacks is a pointy hat. Felix crawls out from under the caravan step and charges towards the Gnome's front door.

'Oh, no, dear child.' The Gnome is so softly spoken that his voice has been recorded and used to signify conscience and also dew, on local radio productions. I can never believe that anyone can hear him, but somehow they do. The Gnome smiles, bestowing watery good tidings on the boys.

'Don't go in there, it's just a mess. Here, the Easter Rabbit asked me to pass these on.'

He holds out two toffee apples with long brown felt ears. Felix and Giles thank him and vanish behind the caravan. My mother beckons to him.

'Come in for a drink, or rather out. I've put a table down by the stream.'

The Gnome looks pleased, and follows us down a winding path to the tiny fairy stream, where my mother has arranged three small chairs and a table. Water chatters over blue and brown pebbles in the one-foot-wide ripple of river as it makes its way through the garden. A pink jug and bowl lie on the bank, and a small pair of pink wellington boots. My mother sinks into one of the chairs and lights a cigarette.

'It's really for The Beauty, but we may as well sit here for a minute with her and see how many of those miniatures we can spot. They've got ready-made Bloody Marys in them.'

The Beauty, like an empress, sits by the water's edge, chewing chocolate and wiggling her boot-clad feet. We, her subjects, drink Bloody Marys straight from little cold bottles, and absorb spring birdsong in the pale sunshine.

April 1st

Suspicions should have been aroused by the arrival of Giles and Felix by my bedside.

'Hello, Mummy, we've made you some tea.'

Dear little tousled children with pyjamas on. Kiss them as I struggle into wakefulness, and do not even mind that it is six-thirty and still dark, thanks to British Summer

Time, because I am touched by their kindness. Nestle against pillows with darling sons on either side. Both very smiley. Sweet. Sip daintily at my tea.

'Euugh! Who on earth taught you to make tea? This has got salt in it, you twits.'

'Ha, ha, April Fool.' They dance around my bedroom squealing and laughing. 'Tricked you, tricked you. We wanted to make an apple-pie bed, but there weren't any apples.'

Become helpless laughing myself, and with their Exocet instincts for a weak moment they wring a promise of apple-pie-bed instruction from me.

'Then we can do it to Daddy, next time we go to stay.' An excellent notion.

April 8th

Vivienne and Simon, local farmers and stalwart friends, arrive for tea with three pigeons, a pair of ducks and a mother hen with chicks.

'Happy Easter,' beams Simon, kissing my cheeks on the threshold, leaning in through the back door and swinging a pigeon from each hand.

Giles has been up a tree overseeing the nest-building activities of various small birds. He slithers down, having spotted the pigeons, and helps Simon mend the holes in the wire netting of the henhouse.

'They can all live together in there,' pronounces Simon, 'but we'll have to get rid of some of those young cocks. You've got more than you have hens, you know.'

'Venetia, don't let him bully you. He loves killing things, and will find any excuse,' Vivienne intervenes, as Simon marches towards the henhouse with a broom in his hands.

'I'll leave it until dusk, then they'll be in the house. It's easier when they're asleep.'

I am unkeen on this cold-blooded murder. 'Can't I just give them away?' I plead.

'Don't be feeble,' says Simon briskly. 'No one wants cockerels except to eat, so you may as well eat them yourself.'

Fortunately, the execution is forgotten in a sudden flurry of activity. A car's wheel bowls into the yard, hotly pursued by my mother's car.

'Does she not know where the spare tyre lives?' jokes Simon. It transpires that the wheel has fallen off the car.

'It happened just by your gate. Thank God. I could have been on the superhighway.' My mother clambers out of her seat and stands in the yard, huddled around a comforting cigarette.

'She means the main road,' Felix whispers to Vivienne.

My mother continues, 'It just kept rolling, and I thought it was better to stay with the wheel than to stop. Odd that the car didn't tip up. I was rather impressed by it. I suppose they balance them in case of this sort of thing.'

'I don't think car manufacturers expect the wheels to fall off their vehicles,' says Simon drily, his voice wafting from beneath the car, where he is examining the axle.

April 17th

The financial struggle is exacerbated by the non-arrival of Charles's usual cheque. When I telephone him, he says that he forgot to post it this week because he and Helena were skiing. However, he will send it now. Then he coughs and says, 'And maybe to help finances, you might have Helena's aunt to stay tomorrow night. She's bringing her bloodhounds to Norfolk for some filming. The film company will pay you.'

Even though they are related to Helena, I cannot resist the idea of film-star bloodhounds and agree to have them. When I put the telephone down I am irritated to realise that I accidentally let the skiing holiday through without comment.

April 18th

The bloodhounds arrive with Val, aunt of the poison dwarf Helena. They leap, with sinewy grace, from a brand-new Range Rover, at precisely the moment that Rags returns from her excavation of the rubbish bags at the bottom of the drive. She launches herself at the nearest one, her absurd, clockwork yaps ricocheting off the door panel. The bloodhounds retreat in horror, but the larger one is too slow: Rags leaps and embeds her teeth in its voluminous and probably very valuable lower lip. It yowls and runs to its car for comfort with Rags dangling from the mighty jaw. Luckily Val thinks it's funny, otherwise we could be facing a vast bill for trauma and surgery to the film star.

Felix and Giles throw sticks for the bloodhounds and Rags dashes to and fro yapping, determined not to be left out. Val comes to life wondrously at the offer of a gin and tonic and I pump her for *Hello!*-style information about the famous people she has met. She can only remember films by the animals and doesn't know who anyone is.

'Oh, yes, they used Jane Bentley's horses for *Sense and Sensibility*, and three of my pugs. Chris Dowell was the lucky one on that – two hundred white doves she took down there and they never got them out of their cages. She got paid two grand just for being there.'

'But did you meet Alan Rickman?'

'Who? Oh, you mean the bloke with the black-saddle horse. No. . . he didn't look much once he got off the horse. I'd be hard put recognising him, to be honest.'

There is evidently no point in pursuing this line with her, so I try a different tack.

'Could Rags do film work?' Val laughs more than I feel is necessary at this, and I am hugely relieved when she asks if there is a local pub she can eat in. I offer to babysit for the bloodhounds and am accepted. Wonder if I can charge extra for this service.

April 21st

Garden work is badly needed right now, or the whole thing will bolt and be gone for the summer. I do wish I had not sown so many seeds. The conservatory is littered with trays: they are in the cold frame and perched in the back kitchen where Sidney, the cat, instead of using them as a litter tray as one might expect, sleeps in them, crushing the struggling seedlings straight back into the dirt from whence they came. I must plant them to save them from suffocation by cat.

I array myself in an anorak caked with plaster and dog hair and an orange bobble hat and step gingerly out into the elements. I do not look fetching and have picked a bad day for gardening; dirty grey clouds spit rain in flurries and the bullish wind pushes me around. I would give up, but my mother has taken The Beauty for the day, and I must seize this opportunity to have uninterrupted access to soil, compost, rose thorns and other items unacceptable to a baby. I am sidetracked, as I wheel numerous seed trays towards the borders, by my short red wellingtons. They are on my feet, but I keep glimpsing them out of the corner of my eye, and they make me uneasy. I am pretty sure that they look absurd, and even foul. Still, no one can see me, so it doesn't matter and I won't wear them again. I plant a row of black pansies and the sun rushes out from behind a cloud, the wind drops and a waft of spring warmth envelops me. Spreading my arms wide, I throw myself on the grass and gaze up at the infinite blue.

'Mrs Denny?'

I must have closed my eyes and gone to sleep. Opening them now, there is a face where there had been sky. Slate-grey eyes laugh, but a polite and serious voice says, 'I'm looking for Mrs Denny.'

'Oh yes, that's me.' I must get up, but how? He is still looking at me from beneath dark, arched brows.

'I'm David Lanyon,' he continues. 'You rang me last week about some work on your bathroom.'

I don't in fact hear him say much of this; I am wrestling with rosy embarrassment and trying to get up without showing my pink face. Am convinced that my mouth was open when I was asleep, and I may have been snoring. Glimpse a wide grin, and buy time for myself by pretending to pull a thistle from the grass.

'Yes, yes. It's in the house. Do go and have a look at it.' He doesn't go. Instead he holds out a hand to help me up as though I am a thousand years old.

'Will you show me where it is?' I probably seem antique to him. He is about my age but not careworn and wrinkled by responsibility. Can't help staring at his unlined countenance, his straight nose and then at his trainers which have silver ribs and are very unrustic. Suddenly realise that once again he has been speaking and I have missed it.

'. . . Could be the best way to approach it for now, if you agree.'

'Oh yes, I agree absolutely,' I start to gabble. 'I'm so glad we agree about that, and everything.'

He looks surprised. 'But I haven't shown you the prototype yet.'

'No, but I'm sure it will be lovely.'

Thankfully we have now reached the bathroom, pausing on the way for me to shed boots and awful exterior layers in the hall. Underneath not much better. Why didn't I notice that my shirt is missing most buttons when I dressed this morning? How can my standards be so low? Must reform and refine my wardrobe immediately.

I show him into the bathroom with a flourish of my arm and just stop myself making a trumpet-call sound. It transpires that he wants to build a majestic bathroom with cupboards and so forth, completely free, if I will allow him to have it photographed for publicity and for his brochure. My only cost will be paint when it is finished. This is fantastic. I agree, and wildly say I don't even need to approve the sketches. He shakes my hand fervently and capers about saying what perfect proportions the bathroom has. After he has gone I begin to regret having relinquished any control, but cannot think of a way to unsay it without seeming rude and untrusting.

April 23rd

Lie about groaning for most of the morning due to hangover. This was caused by an evening alone with a bottle of wine and a mirror. Not a good combination. At eleven p.m. Kris Kristofferson and I were alone together and he was reminding me that:

> *Freedom's just another word for nothing left to lose,*
> *And nothing ain't worth nothing if it's free.*

Copious weeping on my part as I faced the terrible drunken truth: I am doomed never to be attractive to anyone and will never find a fling, let alone a boyfriend, again. I am old and mouldy now and have missed my chances. At midnight I was juggling the household accounts and failing to find funds with which to go to health farm and/or buy cashmere cardigans. At twelve-fifteen I noticed that the wine was finished and the fire was out, and took myself to bed to sleep off self-pity.

The children have ice cream and Rice Krispies for breakfast because I am enfeebled and there is no milk. Not my day for the school run, so thrust them into another mother's car with scarcely a kiss and retreat to the security of the Aga rail. Dump The Beauty back in her cot as soon as decently possible after breakfast, where she wails loudly and causes my head to whirl and bounce horribly. The hangover retreats but not the cause of it, as I can see only too clearly in the bathroom mirror when I finally decide to brush my teeth. Distracted from detailed survey of my skin's dry rot and subsidence by the door-bell. It is the postman, with a fat pile of letters, probably all bills. He could easily have put them through the letter box, but has chosen to summon me and is now smiling fondly, as if at his favourite football team, at my droopy nightie and crimson toenails.

'You're late,' I snarl.

A mistake, giving him the opportunity to reply, 'But you aren't up anyway, are you?' He winks, then turns back to his van and drives off whistling and revving the engine. This is all very trying and sends me huffing and muttering back to my room. I am not at all cheered by the postman's interest in me. I do not wish to have a Jack Nicholson/Jessica Lange empathy with him. I nestle back against the pillows for further wallowing and watch *Teletubbies*. An excellent programme. The Tubbies are all skipping about singing, 'Telescope, telescope'.

They give me the boost I need. I telephone Mo Loam's Temple to Beauty in London and book myself an appointment. The earliest available one is in six months' time, and an hour with the high priestess slapping unguents onto my face will cost £120. I put the telephone down with that shaky, nauseous guilt feeling that comes with wanton extravagance. Feel sick for a while before realising that it will cost the same as half an hour with my lawyer. Plainly a bargain.

April 26th

Spring pours in through every window on a tide of blossom-scented air. One of the hens, Custard, or perhaps Flustered, has hatched three chicks and they bowl about after her, tiny blobs of apricot cotton wool beneath the apple blossom. The Beauty is very taken with them, and makes her way towards the orchard any time she is not under close surveillance. Her new shuffle, on her bottom with rowing action from her legs, is speedy, and I am constantly having to leave the telephone dangling from its rubber spiral, or damp laundry spewing from the washing machine, to follow her as she scoops herself down the drive with Rags. Giles offers to look after her this morning, but becomes engrossed in Billy Whizz; The Beauty eats three geranium heads and is sick.

'She's been sick, Mum.' Giles wanders off, reminding me unpleasantly of his father. The Beauty takes advantage and vanishes. This time I discover her with Felix. He is attempting to climb a small flowering tree with her, but has not yet got far up it. He is doing well. The Beauty is wedged into a fork in the branches and squeals and claps with delight as Felix climbs up past her then reaches down to lift her onto her next perch. There she rests, a vision of rustic charm, in her green jersey with ladybirds on it, waving a fat hand at me from behind a spray of apple blossom.

Mustard the cockerel is in attendance. He is a control freak and polices the garden daily to make sure that all is as it should be. He likes to find The Beauty in her pram under a tree, and hops onto the handle to cast a beady eye over her as she sleeps. Sometimes he cannot resist spoiling everything, and crows mightily from this vantage point, startling The Beauty awake and causing her to yell. This morning he is not pleased to find her flitting about in treetops, and perches himself at a cautious distance on the swing to watch while emitting a ghastly slow groaning noise.

April 27th

What was to have been a lazy Monday morning due to the boys having the day off, is shattered by the shrilling of the doorbell and pounding on the door at seven-fifteen. It is David Lanyon and two carbuncled henchmen, one with a bobble hat, one without.

'Hi, I hope you don't mind, I've brought Digger.' He gestures towards the garden where a muscular black Labrador is aiming a jet of steaming urine at my green tulips. David is a shining example of health, optimism and clean laundry; he has on a washed-out red guernsey and jeans faded to the point that I always long for mine to reach. He chats to the boys, who are hanging around in the hall in their pyjamas. Giles and Felix bond with him instantly.

'Mum, have you seen David's trainers? They're excellent. Can I have some?' His helpers are less fragrant, and look like a couple of Scaven Dwarves from the boy's Warhammer armies. I begin to feel utterly invaded as they tramp in and out with toothy saws, rolls of cable and sagging metal toolboxes. David's car, an old Red Cross Land Rover with logo still intact, is reversed right up to the door to speed the unloading process. The postman arrives, and even though he only has one thin card reminding me of The Beauty's vaccination dates and the door is wide open, he finds it necessary to ring the bell and express concern.

'Hope nobody's been badly hurt,' he says, and I smile as disdainfully as I can with sheepskin slippers, bare legs and a helping of Ready Brek plastered over my shoulders.

'Not yet, but that may change.' My taut, brooding delivery is faultless, and he drives off very alarmed.

later

The bathroom is a cross between a potential Little Mermaid's sea palace and Stig's dump. Sticks of MDF and little piles of sawdust lie among the stacks of castellated wood and odd lengths of gleaming copper piping. Plastic tubes, sand, insulating foam and baskets of mottled shells fill every spare inch, and there is no way anyone will be able to use the room for at least a week.

The two Dwarf Warriors have gone, David is teaching Giles and Felix how to slow-bowl on the lawn and The Beauty is having her bath in the kitchen sink. This is huge fun. She puts a green flannel on her head and delivers her mad, squeaky laugh. As I lift her out, Digger trots past the window with a blur of feathers in his mouth. Wild rage surges. I scream, 'You bloody bastard shithead dog.' The Beauty's face crumples and her mouth becomes a square of misery.

Am heading out to kill Digger when Giles runs in, breathless. 'Don't worry, Mum, it isn't a hen, it's a pheasant from the meadow, David just got it with Felix's catapult. It was such a cool shot, I wish you'd seen it.'

I joggle The Beauty about and she begins to coo again, so sanity can now return. 'How did you know what I was thinking?'

Giles giggles. 'We could hear you swearing from the other side of the garden. You must have left The Beauty's intercom outside. David said I should run and tell you before you burst a blood vessel.'

'What a disgusting image.' I turn crossly and flounce upstairs to give The Beauty her bottle. When I come down half an hour later, Giles and Felix are watching a video of *Calamity Jane* and David has gone. I settle down on the sofa in time to sing along with Doris Day to 'Take Me Back to the Black Hills of Dakota'.

May 1st

Dawn finds me crawling around in the garden with bits of wet grass on my face, having washed it in dew for increased possibility of great beauty. This is an economy drive, and virtue propels me about beneath the apple trees which are bowing and quivering in arctic winds. I could be paying large sums of money to a mail-order beauty company whose boast is that their products 'give the complexion the glow of a country walk, the texture of a sun-drenched apricot'. I can't wait to achieve this loveliness, and am convinced that nature can do as well as Agnès b in assisting me.

May Day is traditionally riven with ice storms and hailstones of record-breaking proportions and today is no different. I do not linger in the orchard, but dash inside to a mirror. A red nose and mud-strewn cheeks are the only sign that I have been involved in a beauty treatment, otherwise the usual pallor prevails. My skin looks nothing like a sun-drenched apricot: the economical rustic beauty treatment is wanting. But I did try. Virtuously, I write a plump cheque to Agnès b make-up and post it off. Within twenty-eight days I will achieve the longed-for apricot look with the assistance of Super Silk tinted moisturiser. Until then I shall avoid being seen in strong sunlight. Pretty easy, if this freakish and foul weather continues.

May 4th

Terrible cabin fever this week, caused by the work in the bathroom. All day drills whine, saws rasp and hammers bang until I am forced out into the garden to escape. Have therefore achieved a lot of weeding and no work. Weeding is second only to hanging the washing out in my tally of chores that give job satisfaction. For me, the washing line is as good as any piece of contemporary art. Indeed, when married I could always irritate Charles a lot by telling friends of my plan to take a washing machine, a line, some pegs and a few days' laundry down to Cork Street and set myself up as a one-woman show. I still think it's a good idea, and often expand my thesis. A narrative statement could so easily be found in the separation of whites (innocence) and darks (death). The coloured wash can represent anything – sin, love, family life, fertility or joy; even a disaster such as colours running can be turned on its head so that all the grey vests symbolise politics or our cultural identity or something similar.

Whenever I start thinking about this again I am reminded what a brilliant idea it is. Promise myself that tomorrow I shall take photographs of my washing line and send them to Charles Saatchi. Increasingly, planning and fantasy are replacing any social life in the evenings. It is six months since Charles lived here, and even then he was only around at weekends because in the week he was in Cambridge at the head office of Heavenly Petting. I realise, with horror, that I am no longer civilised. Have not spent ordinary, companionable evenings with a husband or similar creature for years. I don't know how to any more. Quickly telephone Rose to discover what she is doing now, it being mid-evening. Reassuringly, she is eating Twiglets and will be having cereal to follow. Tristan is apparently watching a programme about war and weaponry and has not said a word to her since he came home from work.

'Have you had a row?'

'Oh, no, he just doesn't speak most of the time.'

'Have you fed him?'

'He made himself a foul-looking jam and peanut butter sandwich and then said he didn't want any supper.' She yawns. 'I'm going to bed now, actually; Theo is getting more teeth so I'm bound to have a bad night with him. Let's speak tomorrow when they're all out of the way.'

It does not sound like much of an improvement on my evening. Immeasurably cheered, I ring off and get back to my plans for the laundry exhibition.

May 9th

Heady, scented day makes chores impossible.

'Let's go for a picnic,' says Giles. We arrange to meet my mother in the bluebell wood and become carried away with picnic fare. While I am dressing The Beauty, Giles makes forty-two egg sandwiches and Felix climbs onto the Aga to finish stirring the custard for the rhubarb fool. He then adds the rhubarb and pours the whole lot into a blue bowl and places it carefully at the bottom of the picnic basket.

'You can't take a china bowl,' I shriek. 'It weighs a ton and it'll break if—' I bite my tongue. Felix's eyes are strained with tears.

'You *always* make it in this bowl when we go to the bluebell wood. And Dad *always* used to carry it so it didn't matter how heavy it was.'

I grit my teeth, recalling Charles's vile and draconian discipline on picnics, when the boys were supposed to carry rugs and keep up with his ex-army speed-march through glades we should have dallied in. He carried the basket, so insisted that he could decide when we stopped, resulting last year in a picnic nowhere near bluebells but overlooking a gibbet. Felix, of course, has forgotten all this.

'We'll manage it,' my best Brown Owl voice booms from somewhere, and we bustle on again, leaving the awful gap which I cannot fill for them behind us.

The scent of bluebells and wild garlic hits us as we approach the wood through a tunnel of cow parsley. Giles has run far ahead, but Felix saunters just in front of me, his hands lost in the froth of cream flowers. Rags is wild with excitement in the adjacent field, her ears appearing sporadically above speartips of young corn as she bounces in pursuit of rabbits.

Just as Felix starts to dawdle, we round a corner and walk into a scented sea of blue framed by beeches, their leaves neon green above soft silver trunks. We spread our rugs, and it is impossible not to crush a thousand flowers in doing so. The boys throw themselves down on their backs and stare up at the sky. The Beauty, released from the backpack she loathes, copies them, waving her feet in the air and catching her toes with her hands. I lie back and sigh, releasing all tension as taught by Alaric the yogic, and experience a moment of perfect calm.

'Hi, chick, how're you doing?' My brother Desmond leaps from behind a tree and into my tranquillity, an urban troll with sideburns and a leather jacket. I groan, sit up and an explosion of hot breath erupts in my ear. Egor, my mother's bull terrier, bounces through the bluebells followed by my mother, bearing three helium balloons with acid-bright Teletubbies on them, and a wine box.

'What a perfect day. Hello, my darlings.'

'Mum, why are you carrying those balloons?'

'Well I brought them for The Beauty, and then I

had a brilliant idea.' She lights a cigarette and puffs triumphantly. 'I realised that if I tied them to the wine box it wouldn't be so heavy.' She produces three plastic beakers from her pocket and struggles with the tap on the box for a moment. 'And do you know, it really worked.'

Desmond stretches next to us and reaches for a beaker. He has a black eye, much to the delight of Giles and Felix, and the mauve and yellow bruising blends fetchingly with the bluebells.

I open my mouth to comment, but my mother hisses, 'He's too stupid and annoying to speak to. He's been banned from the pub. He's going back to London tomorrow and the band are playing on Tuesday evening, so he's going to be teased quite enough then.'

Desmond is in a rock band called Hung Like Elvis, and is also a session musician, specialising in making recordings for commercials. This career suits him to a tee, enabling him to work infrequently for large sums of money which he can then spend in the pub and on his vinyl collection. He is also a rabid football fan, and is keen to brainwash Felix and Giles into his team's support club. Today he has brought each of them an Arsenal item: for Giles a backpack, for Felix a hat.

'Totally cool,' shrieks Felix, unwrapping his hat from its polythene bag and chucking the rubbish on the ground.

Giles is a little more restrained. 'Thanks, Desmond. Did you see the match on TV last night?'

While Desmond is occupied, I grill my mother further: 'Were you there as well? What was the fight about?' Notice that she is behaving uncharacteristically. She is pale, and has a straw hat jammed down over her eyes, but even so she winces in direct sunlight. She has left her wine untouched, slopping a crimson stream onto the bluebells, and is drinking Felix's Lucozade in noisy gulps. Of course, she has a hangover.

'No, but I was very stupid.' She sighs and shakes her head. The Beauty, who can't take her eyes off Granny, squeals and claps. 'Very stupid,' repeats my mother. 'I stayed up far too late with the Foxtons. The Gnome brought them in and then went off to write a sonnet inspired by the stars or a comet he's seen through a telescope on a mountain in Pakistan. I don't know; anyway, he wasn't there. And I soon discovered why he scuttled off.' She pauses, sips her wine, shudders and begins to look normal again.

'They want to make a sculpture and put it in the Wilderness, just outside The Gnome's caravan. They want to do the skeleton of a giant pig. It sounds hideous, but I felt so sorry for them. Now I don't though. It's bad enough having The Gnome there without a dead pig arriving.' She lights another cigarette, and stops looking quite so undead.

Desmond butts in: 'She hasn't been to bed. She stayed up with those oldsters quoting Latin all night. No wonder she looks rough.'

My mother coughs and groans colourfully, 'No, no, I did go to bed, but it was light by then.' She breaks off to shake her head sorrowfully at The Beauty, who is still rapt and gazing with her head on one side. 'Poor Granny,' says Mum with feeling, 'poor old Granny.' I pass her an egg sandwich and feel positively ancient and also depressed that none of this excites any emotion within me, save relief that I wasn't there.

May 10th

Dusk has fallen. I am businesslike in yellow rubber gloves and the horrible red wellingtons, planting out the ranks of sweet peas I have grown. They are slightly depressing. I don't understand why some are the picture of health, yet others look like heroin addicts, long, pale and trembling with yellowed extremities. I plant them alternately and hope that the healthy ones will improve their etiolated companions.

The Beauty retired hours ago and is sound asleep with her green-velvet kangaroo's ear resting against her nose and her thumb in her mouth. This set-up was quite her own idea, and is instantly effective. As soon as the kangaroo ear touches her nose she is asleep, and if it strays in her sleep she reaches out to bring it closer. The downside of this form of baby hypnosis occurs if we go away and forget the kangaroo. It has only happened once, and would have been terrible had I not realised just as we were driving through Norwich. Another kangaroo, identical in every aspect save colour (the new one is blue with red triangles, the old one green and purple), was purchased and The Beauty did some delighted heavy breathing.

She is dreaming of bouncing around in the velvet pouch, but her brothers are less satisfactorily occupied. From my stooped toiling in the garden I can hear pauses and thuds as Felix makes a teddy-bear stepping-stone path around his room. Now and then cuddly toys leap from the window and Felix's muffled voice follows: 'Sorry, Mum, that was a dud. It didn't work as a stone.'

From Giles's window I hear what sounds like an elderly and lugubrious woodpecker at work, but is in fact Giles knocking in his cricket bat. Knocking-in and boxes are things I did not know about cricket. Man's stuff which I would rather Charles had to deal with. Knocking-in is a mini Labour of Hercules, requiring you to thwack your bat with a cricket ball for a total of six hours. The idea is that this will stop the bat splintering to matchsticks when it first confronts a bad ball on the pitch. I can't help wondering why the manufacturers don't do this bit. I would happily pay extra for a mechanical Swedish masseuse to do the job, and it would be much more effective than the efforts of a small boy and his mother. In fact, it would be a perfect job for the poison dwarf, Helena. She could be hitched up with some paddles on her hands and tied to the factory conveyor belt. Must remember to suggest it as a nice little earner next time Charles comes for the boys.

The box, on the other hand, is nothing like a box but is the same as an oxygen mask except that it covers a different area.

'It will be jockstraps next,' I say to Giles with a stupid snigger, when I go to turn his light out. He sees nothing funny about jockstraps and looks at me severely.

'I know, otherwise your willy flaps out from your shorts like a hose. That happened to Paul Bilton last week.' Still not the flicker of a smile from Giles, and his blue eyes are fixed on my face so I am not allowed to either. Whatever happened to lavatorial humour? Such base thoughts are interrupted when I reach to close the curtains.

'Giles, Felix, quick! Look! Deer. Rags is barking at them.'

Giles, Felix and I are in a line on Giles's bedroom windowsill, hanging out of the opened top of the sash. Beyond the garden wall, a veil of green has crept across the field which was bare earth a few weeks ago. Enjoying tender ears of young corn by the mouthful are two red deer, one with antlers big enough to hang a coat on, the other delicate and almond-eyed like Bambi's mother. Clockwork yapping from their feet reveals Rags's presence, although she is invisible in the fading light. We all want to be nearer, and run downstairs and out through dew-soaked grass to the wall. The deer lift graceful necks and look across at us but do not move. Giles climbs over the wall and tiptoes to pick up Rags, who is dribbling with excitement and wriggles madly to escape. Still the deer stand, nibbling corn and blinking at us, as green leaves and grasses turn grey and ink, and birds swoop low as the darkening sky swallows the last pink drops of evening light.

May 13th

It is Wednesday. David the carpenter and Digger the dog reappear after a long weekend and both look sheepish. As they should. There is a Pompidou Centre arrangement in the bathroom, and the two henchmen have not been along to clear it up as David promised they would when he left on Friday to join a party of friends for a weekend in Bruges. Apparently he has been wined and dined by a handbag designer who owns a *petit château*. I am in sour-lemon mode and it sounds to me like a particularly shallow and silly feature in a glossy magazine. Cannot resist saying so.

'But isn't that the sort of thing you write?' David asks blankly.

'Certainly not. I write brochures for corporate entertainment.' Hope to sound lofty, but fail. David ignores me and goes into the kitchen to put the kettle on. This is the final straw. Not only is he destroying my house, and spending glamorous weekends in the manner that I should like to be spending them, with people I am sure would be my friends if only I knew them, but *now* he's helping himself to my kitchen. I huff about for several minutes, ostentatiously filling the dishwasher. David, a stranger to the placatory gesture, leans against the Aga watching me with narrowed eyes. Become sick of this oafish appraisal.

'It's rude to stare,' I snap, wiping the table.

'I wasn't looking at you, I was thinking,' he says absently, and is clearly still elsewhere in his thoughts. He starts to leave the room, but turns, hearing me slam saucepans into the sink.

'You know, if you find this all too much, it might be better if we call a halt to it,' he says. 'It seems to wind you up having us here.'

Sensation of being winded, and overpowering desire for the new-look bathroom.

'Oh, I don't mind, really,' I laugh, 'it's fine. I'm really excited about it.' He pours coffee, rolls a cigarette and lights it.

'Well, try not to let it get to you,' he recommends, then adds, 'Are you all right?' I am fine. To me, the smell of coffee and new roll-up is heaven. I remind myself that I gave up evil toxins when my husband left. Have to leave the room to prevent myself snatching both items from David and consuming them. The Beauty wakes. She and I agree that Cromer is where we want to be and depart. As we head down the drive in a spin of gravel, I glance in the rear-view mirror. One of the Scaven henchmen is looking up at the bathroom window, from which David is lowering a sheet in the manner of a stork delivering a babygram, except that the baby is my loo. My banshee shriek upsets The Beauty and we have to listen to the garage hits on Vibe FM all the way to Cromer to cheer her up. She has acquired this taste from Giles, who makes the school run even more of a trip from hell than it has to be by forcing us all to share the sounds of vile local radio station Vibe FM. If I make a bid for Radio Four, he sighs and tuts like a bank manager all the way to school, except that his remarks would not pass muster in Barclays or Lloyds:

'Oh, Mummy, sixty is so *slow*, we'll never get there if you drive like this.'

This line alternates with, 'When can we get a decent car?'

May 14th

Giles's joy knows no bounds this morning. We pause at the first junction on the way to school and Carmel and Byron Butterstone flash by in a mink-coloured slink-mobile.

'Let's see if we can keep up with them,' I joke. 'They always go at about a hundred miles an hour because they're always late.'

'That means *we're* late,' Giles points out. I catch a glimpse of Bronwyn Butterstone's helmet of groomed and sprayed chestnut hair and the hint of a sage silk shirt and become consumed with rage – either road rage or wardrobe rage, I'm not sure which. Steeling myself until my knuckles are white, I grip the steering wheel and, hissing to myself, 'I'm sure she's had plastic surgery', I put my foot down and we shoot off in pursuit, Giles a mound of giggling flesh next to me.

'Mummy, you look so funny,' he gasps in pauses, and then explodes again. A mile on I conclude that the winsome Bronwyn Butterstone can audition for Brands Hatch; I, however, cannot.

'Mum, I feel sick,' croaks Felix in the back, while The Beauty crows and shrieks with pleasure at this new, improved version of her favourite amusement ride, The School Run. A nicely positioned tractor prevents ignominy, and we follow the Butterstones into school nose-to-tail. Very pleasing, except that when Byron and Carmel get out of their car they are unaccompanied by sweet wrappers, crisp packets and Rags the terrier.

Felix and Giles stuff litter into my hands and aim covert kicks at the dog. 'Just go, Mum,' hisses Giles when I reach to embrace him.

Arrive home to what looks like a Council of War on the Scaven Warrior front. My mother, the henchmen and David are sitting in a circle in the garden on various bits of my bathroom, drinking mugs of tea and swapping roll-ups for straights. My mother's specs have broken, and one arm is rising straight up from her head. She looks as if she is chief Mekon for the day and also Scaven High Priestess, due to the flowing nature of her coat, which has no sleeves, just ragged holes.

Digger and Egor the bull terrier sniff one another but the wrong message is transmitted. Egor mounts Digger, and my mother can't control her mirth and snorts tea out of her nostrils. Rags rushes to join in and a dogfight explodes as our neighbour, a Christian, approaches up the drive. I have identified her as a Christian by the fish logo on the back of her car; it is the same as the one on Felix's godfather Gawain's car. Gawain is not a Christian, he got it under false pretences by sending off to the Christian Union to fool the police into thinking he was a godly teetotaller.

The Scaven Warriors jump about kicking the ball of

tumbling dog, while my mother and I clutch our sides and can't stop laughing. Have noticed that this seems to be a genetic failing in crisis, and Giles has it too, and probably The Beauty, who is clapping and cackling on the doorstep. She stops, though, spouting instant tears and yelling, when the Christian squats down in front of her and holds out a friendly hand. The Beauty recoils and raises her shoulder, shrugging off the proffered hand. The dogfight subsides, thanks to David's well-placed blow with a length of overflow pipe, and birdsong erupts, loud and implausible, around us. The Christian coughs and speaks.

'I wonder if you could come and get your duck? She's had ten ducklings and they are all over my vegetable patch.'

Am sick of animals and their fecundity. I wish Simon would come and cull them all. My mother breaks off her conversation with David, in which they have been saying vile things about Rags.

'How lovely to have ducklings, would you like to give them to me?' The perfect solution, as my pond has dried up and is just a muddy pit. I agree at once.

'What a brilliant idea, and you can help me catch them.'

Armed with a red candlewick dressing gown unearthed in the barn, we set off with The Beauty to catch ducklings. My mother hobbles in an embarrassing fashion, having broken the heel off one of her shoes in the dogfight. The ducklings are milling about in a bed of euphorbias and look as though they are clockwork as they whirr along behind the duck.

'We'll head them into this run, then you can throw that thing over them,' says the Christian. It sounds foolproof and simple. It is a fiasco. The mother duck flies straight out of the run and then zooms up and down quacking at her trapped children who keep appearing out of the sleeves and around the edges of the flung dressing gown. Moments later the euphorbias are quivering again, with anxious duck noises emerging. Suddenly the mother duck breaks cover and, head held high, quacking encouragement, she leads her fluffy string past us, through the hedge and out into the water-meadow.

'They're going to the stream. I doubt if many of them will survive to return with her this evening,' says the Christian in a voice of doom, and she looks at me as though it is my fault. My mother also looks at me reproachfully.

'We'll try again tomorrow, then.' I try to keep good cheer uppermost in my voice until we are out of hearing. 'Why did you look at me like that? I couldn't help it.'

My mother shakes her head. 'Far too hasty in your approach – it's always been your trouble.'

I decide to let this deeply provocative remark go, and ask instead, 'So what do you think of the bathroom?'

'Oh, they didn't show me; we were talking about

sculpture. David seems to have a much better idea than that pig thing for my Wilderness. He wants to make a bacchantine temple.' She bends to smell a branch of apple blossom at the bottom of the drive. 'How lovely spring is,' she muses.

I take deep breaths to prevent the sour-lemon words within me from coming out. I succeed. Instead of saying, 'Typical, trust him to see what you're made of,' I say, 'That sounds splendid.'

'Anyway, I've asked him to come and have a drink tomorrow evening so he can see the garden. You can come if you like.'

'How kind,' I smile, and my mother gives me a sharp look.

'It'll do you good to get out without your children. When is That Man having them, anyway?'

'He's coming with the poison dwarf to fetch the boys on Saturday. They're taking them to Centre Parcs for the night.'

My mother snorts. 'God, how pukesome. Still, a weekend off. I'll have The Beauty, you can go to London and have fun, or do whatever you like.' She sees me trying to think of an excuse and raises a hand. 'It can be payment for the ducklings if you ever catch them. And think of the bliss of escaping from this junkyard of bath stuff.'

May 16th

Life is a bed of rose oil and I am blissed out after aromatherapy, and only a third of the way through my weekend at heavenly health farm. My friend Rose is joining me this evening for a couple of lettuce leaves and a celery stick, and I have not a care in the world. Even Rags is taken care of; David is house-sitting for me and will get on with drawing up the plans for the plumbing system, which presently resembles the Minotaur's labyrinth sans string and Ariadne. But anyway, I just don't care.

Everyone here wears sorbet-coloured tracksuits, and some sportier folk even have tinted sun visors. I can see three oldsters, backs curved like commas, arms bent into marathon-runner mode, trotting in a little line around the gracious and groomed gardens as I write. One in mint, one in peach and one in plum. Musing as to why the particularly nasty palette of colours for shell suits are always given edible names, I photograph the line as they stagger past. Proof, should anyone require it, that it's not all sybaritism here. No, no, no.

Am feeling so on top of the world, I can't keep still. Book myself into a cranial osteopathy session, remembering the beatific effect this invisible treatment had on The Beauty when she was born. Charles and my mother had been withering in their condemnation of alternative therapies, and when I summoned the cranial osteopath, Charles left for two days. He said it was as a protest; I now realise it was to go and frolic about with pygmy Helena.

Anyway, Yvette arrived, a true exponent of hippy culture with batik T-shirt, more or less see-through, droopy tits (of course) and yellowed toenails. I was determined not to be put off by her appearance, but Felix, who had popped his head round the door, vanished downstairs yelling to my mother, 'Quick, Granny, there's a witch in Mummy's room and she's putting a spell on the baby.'

By the time my mother had bustled up, huffing fury at me and Yvette, the treatment was over. The Beauty, who had been yelling, was languid and sleeping, and has scarcely cried since, unless in protest at perceived poor treatment. Even my mother admits that there was something in Yvette's magic. All she did was rest The Beauty's tiny head in her hands. Truly cosmic; I can't wait for it to happen to me.

May 18th

Nature has gone wild during my two days away, and this morning I saw three wild orchids among the many primroses on the roadside, a joyful gathering of flag irises in a meadow and also a jay. It was dead, unfortunately, but I was nonetheless delighted to see it and add it to my bird count. So far I have heard more than I've seen, including cuckoos, woodpeckers and assorted owls. Since cranial osteopathy I am convinced that my senses have improved, and I am now much like the six-million-dollar man except in muscle power. It is as if I have been put through a car wash and had all the detritus scraped off everything. Even breathing has become a joy, with spring scents mingling and hitting me in the lungs. I am becoming a nose. I mean this in the perfume sense, not physically, thank God, although Giles told me the other day: 'You'd be really pretty if your nose wasn't so big, Mum.'

This morning's olfactory experience includes a hint of grass cutting, a suggestion of apple blossom, a waft of cow from the field and, best of all, an overriding scent of wet paint. David is finally at the decorating stage with my bathroom. With my new improved eyesight I can tell that I do not like the colour he is using, and despite his insistence to the contrary, I know it is not the one I chose. I wanted Plover's Egg, and I think he has used Dead Mouse. He insists there is no such colour as Dead Mouse; I am sure there is, though. These colours prove their smartness by having eccentric, call-a-spade-a-spade names. There is String, Ox Blood, Cold Cream White and the enigmatic Dirt, but I wish they would be a little bolder and have Phlegm and Fungal Brown as well. And

I would especially like to be able to get hold of Eyeball White for the bathroom ceiling, which needs a blue-white tone to lift it a bit.

May 20th

Felix and Giles return. Charles rings the bell, and I open the door to one former husband, smirking slightly, and two piles of merchandising. 'The way to a boy's heart is via the shopping mall,' I quip.

Charles jangles his keys. 'We had some time on our hands yesterday after the boys did well with an early reveille and run.' He allows himself a flash of a smile as I gape in astonishment at this insight into quality time with Dad.

Giles and Felix are not listening, but are burrowing in their shopping bags. Charles coughs self-effacingly and continues.

'They said they hadn't any clothes, or trainers, and from what you sent with them it seemed true.' A needle of resentment jabs at me. 'Don't criticise my packing,' I hiss, a line so babyish I wish to bite off my tongue. The boys push past into the house and there is Charles's car with the crown of Helena's head just visible in the passenger seat. I turn to him in reproachful surprise.

‘Oh, Charles, you should have bought her a little cushion while you were shopping.’

He hardly pauses, but swipes right back as he marches to the car. ‘I’ll be in touch about next month: I thought I’d take the boys to Wimbledon, I’ve got tickets for centre court.’ Fifteen, Love to Charles. I slam the front door cursing, and am almost sent flying by huge, hugging boys.

May 26th

Thrilling sense of freedom caused by sitting on the train to London reading *Hello!* and being surrounded by other ladies, many of them quite antique, with packets of sandwiches and sensible shoes which say that they, like me, are on their way to the Chelsea Flower Show.

I, however, do not have sensible shoes. By the time I have negotiated the tube as far as Sloane Square and lost half an hour in a delicious ribbon shop, I have two blisters and a throbbing big toe. Trailing an exquisite bundle of pink and yellow satin, which I plan to sew round the edge of a cardigan in the manner of top fashion houses this season, I head for the nearest shoe shop and arrange myself for purchase. Very shaming moment when I remove the silly slingbacks I had thought appropriate when dressing this morning, and find aroma of Emmental clinging to my feet. Rub them on the shoe shop carpet and move to a different squeaking leatherette chair. How does anyone buy summer shoes? Summer feet are clammy and puffy and have red areas and also grass stains on their soles. They are hideous. They do nothing for the flimsy, strappy shoes so fashionable this year. Regretfully, I opt for a pair of clumpy mulish sandals as worn by biology teachers. These will get me through the flower show in comfort, I tell myself, and turn resolutely away from the shocking-pink kitten heels which beckon and tempt from the shop window.

By the time I have crossed the King's Road I am in agony, and at the entrance to the flower show I am forced to remove the new instruments of torture and go barefoot. I now have seven blisters bubbling on my feet. With savage pleasure I hurl the nerdy cripplers in a bin and hurry into the floral vortex of Chelsea. So glad I paid for them with Charles's money out of the children's account, so have not just wasted £80 of my own. Surely I can now go back for the kitten heels, as I still have no shoes? This uplifting thought carries me barefoot into the throng of well-behaved frocks and hairdos and little notebooks with neat notes.

Two hours later I am sagging beneath piles of catalogues, and the inside covers of *Devil's Cub*, my Georgette Heyer of the moment, are dense with illegibly scrawled names of flowers and cryptic notes. On the train going home, assisted by a gin and tonic, I decipher 'Heterosexual Lord Bute trailing clouds of perfume', and give up. Maybe 'heterosexual' is 'heliotrope', or 'hemerocallis'. Or maybe it's a colour code. I don't know, and what's more, I just don't care. For on my feet beneath the Formica table lurks a pair of perfect pink kitten heels. Even the blisters don't hurt any more.

SUMMER

June 1st

Chaos of clothing carpets my bedroom as I attempt to find something to wear. I am going for a drink with David to celebrate the near-completion of the bathroom. Initially refused David's kind invitation, issued just after an outburst on my part at Digger, whom I caught burying a newly bought loaf of bread under the yew chicken. Having stubbed my toe kicking him, I marched round to complain to David, and felt lame and crabby when he spoke first and asked me to go to the pub. Giles overheard me saying rudely, 'Sorry, I can't. I'm busy', as I stood, arms crossed, leaning on the door of David's ambulance with Digger cowering within. 'Yes, you can,' Giles interrupted. 'Jenny can babysit. You shouldn't make up excuses.' Tried to tread on his toe to shut him up but he skipped out of the way, leaving me red-faced in front of David. Had to say yes to diminish embarrassment.

Jenny, who has a gold tooth, hennaed hair and a flourishing business growing coriander and basil in poly tunnels for local supermarkets, arrives with her boyfriend. He is called Smalls. 'It's a nickname,' Jenny explains, unnecessarily. Smalls turns out to be one of David's henchmen, and as well as looking like a Warhammer, he is an avid collector of these oddities. Felix and Giles cannot wait to get me out of the house so that they can leap into pitched battle with Smalls and a cohort of wild woodland elves. The Beauty doesn't need me either. She is fast asleep in her cot, exhausted by the arrival of three new teeth this week. Despite being redundant, I hang around at home making myself late and telling Jenny dozens of ways to deal with The Beauty, should she wake: 'But of course she won't, this is just in case.'

Take short cut to unknown pub selected by David, and become very lost. The Wheatsheaf, East Bessham is somewhere in a valley fringed with bluebell woods, and I soon stop worrying about the time and am enchanted by my route down narrow roads which tunnel through banks scattered with pink campion and buttercups. The evening light is a luxurious gold after a day of energetic sunshine, and I take deep breaths and revive from children's bedtime and am glad that I bothered to wear my ironed skirt and not jeans. Just becoming parched and anxious when the pub appears in front of me, separated from the road by a little stream and enhanced by branches of fragrant lilac waving pinkly over the garden wall. I park the car and dawdle across a peeling blue footbridge, noting its rustic charm and its excellent credentials for the Troll and Billygoat game with Felix. Once within the pub walls I quickly find David on a cropped lawn playing boules with a gang of men. I pretend to be interested in rules and scores for a few seconds before saying brightly, 'Let me get you a drink,' and diving into the bar.

At the bar, I become panic-stricken by the thunderbolt reality that I am out having a drink with a man. On my own. What will we talk about? He is bound to think I am pursuing him. Am I pursuing him? Why have I come? What shall I drink? I'm starving. Will I look deliberately suggestive if I have crisps?

The barman has been patiently waiting, but begins to shift from foot to foot and roll his eyes. I take a deep breath and order the first drink that enters my head. 'Two Pimms, please, and some prawn cocktail crisps.' David appears next to me and is drawn, as I am, to silent contemplation of the lengthy procedure of the Pimms' creation. The barman must be about to do his cocktail exam. Everything is going in – strawberries, lemon, cucumber, orange, apple, a glacé cherry and finally a pink paper umbrella. On the bar, surrounded by pints of Guinness and halves of cider, the Pimms are lush and outrageous, like a couple of dolled-up transvestites on a commuter train. I am thrilled with my choice of drink. I hand one of the confections to David with a flourish, along with a pink foil packet of prawn cocktail crisps.

'Shall we sit outside, or have you finished the game?' Have regained my nerve, am full of renewed poise, and am looking forward to my drink. Another boules player is at the bar now, and his face is a mask of severity as he gazes at David with his pink drink. David's lime-green shirt seems to me the perfect backdrop to the cocktail, and, emboldened by the first gulp of Pimms, I say so, loudly.

David puts his glass down on a low table behind him. 'I think I'll have a pint as well as this,' he says hastily, and the boules player unbends visibly and turns back to his cronies.

I drink all of David's Pimms as well as my own, and eat both packets of prawn cocktail crisps. I am thoroughly enjoying myself and can't believe I was nervous. I share my feelings with David.

'I am so glad Giles made me come out, because now I realise that it's no big deal to go for a drink with a man.' He looks taken aback for a moment, but rallies.

'Would you like another drink?'

'Yes, I'd love one, and shall we have something to eat? I'm starving.' Am vaguely aware that protocol would have preferred him to say this, but he hasn't and I have, so what the hell. He reaches for the menus from behind the bar, and passes me one.

'Go ahead. I won't. I thought you might have eaten with your kids, so I had something earlier, but don't let that stop you.'

My stomach shrivels like a slug with salt poured on it, and I feel blushing embarrassment rise in a tide up my neck and onto my face.

'Oh, God, I can't. I'm not hungry at all, actually, I forgot I'd had those crisps. I'm full, in fact. Completely full.'

David is grinning. 'Only teasing. Come on, let's order quickly before they close the kitchen. I'll have a steak sandwich, what about you?'

Can only just bring myself to say, 'Me too, please.'

June 2nd

Am enjoying a most satisfactory morning, having spent half an hour scraping dried Weetabix and worse off The Beauty's high chair. It looks lovely now, and she is in it, dressed for success in shocking-pink tights and leopard-skin miniskirt. Have never seen anything as delicious as this miniskirt, which is made of soft felt and is full like a tutu. It came by post this morning from Rose, accompanied by a card announcing her arrival. Decide to go and get her room ready to avoid doing any work for a bit longer.

I have a setback with the joys of morning upon reaching the spare bedroom. Sidney had peed on the pillows, and even more insultingly, padded little black raspberry footprints over the crisp sheets to reach his lavatory. I fling open the window and hurl the gross, damp pillows out, shrieking, 'Urgh, bastard cat. God, I loathe you.'

Muffled echo of the 'Urgh' noise comes from outside, and I peer out to see David and Smalls, who have just arrived in the ambulance, with the pillows which must have landed on their heads. Quickly step back from the window and hope they haven't seen me as I can't be bothered to explain.

The morning improves again when a large delivery lorry hums up the drive with my order from a poncey garden catalogue. The company is called Haughty Hortus, which I think is nearly as good a name as Teletubbies. I have bought a Vita Weeder, which is a chic trowel, and a glamorous fork called a Daisy Pusher. Their arrival necessitates a morning in the garden. The Beauty enjoys this, and almost eats her first worm. Well, I hope it's almost. The worm is wiggling from her mouth as she sucks it in like her favourite pasta. I yank it out as soon as I notice, but cannot tell how tall, or rather long, the worm was before it went in. She sobs bitterly at the loss of her worm, and I am about to cave in and give it back rather than have to go inside and find more wholesome bribes when Sidney the creep arrives. He slinks over to The Beauty and insinuates himself like Shere Khan. She pats him vigorously, cooing and a little breathless, with a fat, spent tear wobbling on her cheek. He departs. Regretfully I down my top new tools and return to the house to find elevenses for The Beauty and to say thank you to David for taking me out last night.

Having greatly enjoyed most of the evening except for the moment of salted-slug stomach, am now keen to find other people to go for drinks with. Telephone my mother to ask if she can think of anyone. She suggests The Gnome, and I am underwhelmed. Get off the telephone and find The Beauty mimicking me. She is sitting in her toy car under the kitchen sink, babbling sweetly into her pink plastic mobile telephone.

June 9th

The bathroom is finished. Vivienne appears as David is taking me on a guided tour of its beauty spots and areas of perfection. We are admiring the copper pipe which runs from the high cistern to the loo when she opens the door.

'Gosh, this is wonderful, isn't it? Venetia, did you know that there is a black Labrador mounting Rags on your lawn?'

I am out of the mermaid's palace in a flash. 'That creep, Digger. I think Rags is on heat. Who let that filthy brute out? I shut him in your car, David. God, I wish you wouldn't bring him here.'

All this is wasted breath. David is demonstrating the power shower to Vivienne, and anyway couldn't care less what Digger does to Rags, as he won't have to bring up a litter of freak pretend-Labradors with terrier-length legs or worse. Fortunately, Rags has protected her virtue and is sitting firmly on her tail looking apologetic; Digger saunters down the drive with garbage investigation rather than carnal matters on his mind. Vivienne appears in the garden with The Beauty, fresh and twinkly of eye post-rest, and David; I am sidetracked by noticing that all three of them are wearing purple T-shirts and look like the perfect family in a cereal advertisement. On reflection, Vivienne's wild red hair makes them a bit too avant-garde for cereal; perhaps a new car commercial is more the look. David is giving her the full programme of events now the bathroom is officially open.

'. . . And we're going to use it to photograph this mate of mine's handbags. He designs them, and has a backer who will pay for the location and give me some of the pictures.'

I am not sure about all this, and wish Rose had not gone suddenly to Spain instead of coming this weekend to advise me. I must be looking especially blank, as David suddenly breaks off and turns to me.

'I thought you would like it, Venetia. And don't forget, part of the deal was that I could use it for photographs. You'll really like Rob, anyway, and it'll be good for you to get to know a new crowd. You never know, if you chat Rob up enough he might give you a free handbag.' I open my mouth to tell him he is a patronising git, but he has already turned back to Vivienne, who is becoming very excited.

'*Who* did you say was coming? Robin Ribbon? Oh, I've read about his designs, I'd love one. Venetia, you are lucky.'

I find her words unaccountably red-rag-like: 'Well, I don't want one, and I don't want to meet any sodding handbag-makers. You must be mad, David, if you think I've got time to deal with all this sort of nonsense. God, I left London years ago to get away from handbags and all that they stand for.' My outrage gathers momentum. 'And how am I meant to show off that bathroom properly if you aren't here?'

'Why won't I be here? I'm not going to leave you to deal with something I've set up.' Exasperated, scowling, David runs his hands through his hair. The Beauty leans towards him from Vivienne's arms to pat his shoulder. She then reaches for his hair and grips a few locks tightly in one fist. David tries to detach her, but she continues breathing heavily and gripping. He grabs both her hands, and clasping them as if pleading with her, says simply, 'I don't want to put you through any hassle, it'll just be a bit of fun.'

Awful how unused I am to dealing with genuinely

thoughtful men. Feel guilty, and supress lemon-faced emotions in a rush of hospitality.

'Shall we all have some lunch to celebrate you finishing it?' The Beauty catches my effervescent mood and suddenly launches herself from Vivienne's distracted embrace and hurtles, arms and legs whirling, towards the floor. David neatly catches her and she pulls his face towards hers and peppers his cheek with her first kisses.

June 11th

Felix, The Beauty and I arrive at school having dropped Giles at the more senior entrance, and are met by a huge poster announcing the Concert with Cake Sale this afternoon. Had, of course, forgotten all about this dainty entertainment, and will now have to forgo lunch with Vivienne and afternoon of gossiping and dawdling at her house. In the school cloakroom the smell of antiseptic smarts from the loos and mingles with a puff of the headmistress's scent as she rustles past with a pile of egg boxes and a grim, determined expression. She smiles vaguely at Felix and I realise that we have failed to brush his hair. The Beauty adores school and settles down, growling happily, to remove books from shelves in Felix's classroom. Felix and his friends assist her and she holds court delightedly, her gingham bloomers causing mirth among her admirers and huge pride for her.

On the way out of the school with The Beauty, I enjoy a five-minute interlude with two other school mothers. We talk about our children, their starring roles in the forthcoming concert and how many cakes we are baking for the sale. All is a big lie on my part. My cakes, although often surprisingly delicious to eat, are low on physical charms, and I have no intention of making any for the school at any time in case I am humiliated by their not being bought. As for the concert, Felix is still on 'Old MacDonald' after a year of piano lessons, and shows no promise at all. I never make him practise because both of us hate it so much, and we have begged the teacher to let him give up. She just smiles kindly, and says, 'Have you tried bribery? He must persevere, he's doing so well.' Another big lie.

Disaster lurks in the car park. I bid farewell-until-the-concert to the other mothers and move towards the car. Rags is leaping up and down in the front seat, whining and scratching as if she has been left for about three hundred years instead of fifteen minutes. I am about to open the door when a wild, flailing paw lands on the lock. There is a whooshing, electrical-sounding multiple click and the car is locked with Rags inside it. And the keys.

An hour with Reggie from the garage ensues. Reggie has an unravelled coat-hanger and wiggles it about through the car window with the same expression of blissed-out concentration that he might wear for cleaning his ears with a Q-Tip. The morning is overcast and still, a pair of squirrels swarm and tumble around us, then vanish up the trunk of a vast horse chestnut tree, its branches still laden with pyramids of blossom. The Beauty and I purchase a packet of Rolos from the newsagent and loll on the grass watching Reggie. He has taken off the top half of his boilersuit, and its dangling arms fascinate The Beauty, who shuffles over for a closer inspection. It is clear to me that Reggie will never get into the car this way, and we will have to break the window. I am about to say this when he steps back in triumph, foiling The Beauty who is poised to grab a sleeve and tug the whole boiler suit down. 'We're in,' he says, and opens the door to remove the keys so that Rags the hysterical hell-hound cannot repeat her performance. There is now no obstacle to cake-making.

June 18th

The Beauty and I munch peanut butter sandwiches and join in with rippled applause as Giles and the rest of the Colts A cricket team zap their way to victory against Swinburn House. We find this a most civilised and pleasant way to spend the afternoon, and are cordially curious as to what is happening on the pitch. Giles is bowling now, but affects deafness when I wolf-whistle at him.

'Concentration is all-important to the bowler.' A pot-bellied father has sidled up to me, murmuring and sighing, his shirt straining warped blue checks over his paunch, his eyes narrowing to slits as he observes Giles. 'That boy is not bad for his age; not a bad little player at all.' Sudden spatter of clapping from the parents indicates that Giles has just made a successful move. 'Well played indeed,' says Papa Pot Belly, and I nod, affecting intelligence.

'Mm, yes, what exactly did he do, though?'

I am interrupted by a cheer from the parents. Something even better has happened, and Giles is part of it. Suddenly boys surround us, wolfing the sandwiches. Giles hovers over a silver ashet of cakes, and while he is hovering, The Beauty crawls over to him and wraps fat arms round his cricket whites. He picks her up to kiss her, and is suddenly, for an instant, the image of Charles, but the Charles I married, rather than the one I divorced. Am invaded by a million emotions and tears rush into my eyes. Furious blinking follows, while Giles stands in front of me holding The Beauty at arm's length.

'Mum, she's done a poo, I can smell it,' he hisses, frowning and dumping her in my arms before walking off with a friend towards the pavilion. More reminders of his father.

June 20th

Rose arrives at lunchtime with Theo, but without Tristan who has gone to Barcelona to an architects' conference. She has come for a midsummer night party, and is entirely in charge of it. We take the babies out to frolic in the garden and are mobbed by hens and chicks. The Beauty bats her eyelashes at them and pats the grass invitingly, hoping one will come and nestle next to her, while Theo ignores them utterly in his pursuit of a punctured football he has found. Rose has resuscitated her garden in London after eighteen months of its being a building site. Idle garden chat and glancing at my borders with dissatisfaction leads to the inevitable. Suddenly we are whizzing across Norfolk on our way to a rare-plants nursery, our car filled with music from the motion picture *Reservoir Dogs* to keep the babies quiet.

The outing is a big mistake. Rose and I are thwarted in our attempts to bankrupt ourselves by the pig-headedness of The Beauty and Theo. Both behave as if the rare-plants nursery is a nuclear testing ground, and will not be put down for a second, but clutch at us and assume terrified expressions if either of us tries to extract ourselves from their grip. Even when placed in a charming metal trolley together and wheeled round the walled garden, they sob unrestrainedly, reminding me of small eighteenth-century French aristocrats in a tumbril. The nursery owners are very kind, even when Theo pulls a peony flower the size of a hat off a plant and tears it to bits in front of them. Its crimson petals drip in gory echo of his cochineal experience.

'Do you think he'll make horror films when he grows up?' wonders Rose as we depart, the car pretty well laden under the circumstances. In fact, the inclusion of Theo's semi-double peony Arabian Prince, even without one of its flowers, gives our booty a much-needed glamour boost.

June 21st

The summer solstice is upon us with all its attendant pressures: why am I not staying up all night being at one with nature? Why have I yet again failed to take the children to an open-air production of *A Midsummer Night's Dream*? How can the days, and indeed the year, be diminishing again? How soon can I get to Norwich to buy fake tan for lovely summer-look limbs?

Such is the litany of soul-searching questions I am occupied with as I stroll into the village to attend the Village Show committee meeting. At home, Rose and Lila are creating a solstice feast. Rose, with her usual flamboyance, has provided whole lobsters, tiger prawns and pink champagne. Lila, ever the reformer, has soya milk, organic tofu and some sesame paste. As I depart to the meeting she is attempting to spread her weird pastes onto tiny crisps of fat-free wafer, and Rose is rolling her eyes. She mutters to me under her breath, 'There's more sustenance in bloody Communion bread than in that cardboard of Lila's.'

We have invited Simon and Vivienne to our feast, and also David, whom Rose bumped into on the village green this afternoon. Dazzled by the glamour of him in cricket whites and by being able to say hello to one of the team, once he was pointed out to her by Felix, she has become obsessed with him.

'He's so good-looking. Why aren't you having an affair with him?' she demands, ignoring Felix and Giles lying in the kitchen armchair, reading the *Beano* with their ears flapping.

The committee meeting is a shambles. Nothing is arranged, even though the show is in about six weeks. My only contribution, apart from agreeing to judge the Pet Most Like Its Owner class, is a suggestion that we have a teddy-bear parachute contest from the church tower. To my amazement, the committee is keen as mustard, and I am sent home to make posters forthwith.

As I approach the house it becomes clear that the feast is in full swing. Out on the grass, framed by a bank of thistles (sadly not the fashionable sort), is a bivouac with three tents, a high table and fairy lights twinkling from the trees. Simon, having provided a hog to roast, has built a spit, and clad in shorts and long thick socks like a game park warden, is busy doing his primitive man bit with the meat. Giles and Felix and Lila's children, Diptych and Calypso, have made the most of the dressing-up box and also my make-up bag, and are paid-up members of some Indian tribe. They have adorned the tents with my zebra skins and Felix is wearing the fur coat I bought in a charity shop for a fiver. They are splendidly non-PC: I am amazed Lila hasn't noticed and tried to ban them. All very elemental, and I look forward to Druid work and chanting taking place soon.

The rugged outdoor life stops there, however. In the kitchen, Rose, Lila, David and Vivienne offer a contrasting existence of hedonism. All the girls have plainly raided Rose's wardrobe, and are semi-clad in slivers of skirt and skimpy T-shirts in colours as vibrant as poppies. David is still wearing his cricket whites and is making tequila slammers. The table is awash with crushed ice and on the ice, little lemon-wedge boats are marooned here and there. My favourite musical medleys of the moment are movie soundtrack CDs, and one is blasting from the drawing room. Everyone is already flushed and half drunk, even Lila, who is so relaxed that she forgets to ask if the lemons are organic. I gulp my first tequila slammer and enter the fray.

June 22nd

Never. Ever. Again.

June 25th

The Beauty is one today. To make the most of the occasion, she rises at five-thirty a.m. beaming and beady of eye, and immensely pleased to have become the kind of person who can stand up in her cot when I go in to get her up. She has her bottle in my bed and I drink tea and stare half-wittedly out at the milky, misted morning. Sunrays which began palest lemon are now radiating jolly and vigorous beams at the mist, and by the time we go downstairs, the diaphanous veil has vanished and the garden sparkles with dewdrops, and is truly a paradise for The Beauty to enjoy. This she does with aplomb. It is still too early to wake her brothers, so I take her out and she stamps around holding my hands because it is too wet for her to crawl. She loves this new feely sensation, and lifts each small, fat foot high, pointing her toe before plunging forward with her next unsteady step. We pick a very gratifying bunch of pink and amber roses with which to adorn the birthday tea table this afternoon.

Present-giving is a huge success. The Beauty gets the hang of unwrapping straight away, and has no truck with the 'babies like the wrapping paper best' theory. Felix gives her a Teletubbies ball and Giles a drum. The Beauty is enchanted, and crows and slaps her thighs in a new swashbuckling way of indicating pleasure. Rose has triumphed and has sent, by courier, a doll-sized version of The Beauty's very old-fashioned pram. She straight-away sees the point of it and insists on being wedged in, becoming very Mabel Lucie Atwell with seraphic face appearing vast due to miniaturisation of her chariot. Charles arrives as Felix and Giles stage a pram race on the lawn with The Beauty in the toy pram against Rags in the real pram. The Beauty finds this huge fun and laughs like a squeaky toy as she is hurtled towards the pond by Felix. Rags, however, is terrified, and ruins Giles's chances of victory by leaping out of the pram and scuttling back to the house.

Charles parks and leans against his sleek bullet-like car wearing his usual smirk. He is dressed as an alien as far as we are concerned, in grey flannel trousers, polished slip-on shoes and a beige polo-neck sweater. No dog hairs or fluff balls have clung to him, and everything he is wearing is either brand-new or ironed so that it looks as though it has just been unfolded from its purchase pack. The boys abandon The Beauty and run towards their father. I am guilt-ridden and shocked by how much I mind that they are thrilled to see him. Giles reaches him first.

'Dad, come and have a race. Will you push me in the pram?' Charles sucks in his ribs and arches away backwards like a crab, raising his arms so that they at least are not caught in the chocolate- and grass-stained embrace of his sons. He pats their heads gingerly.

'I'd have thought you were rather old for that sort of nonsense now, Giles.'

Giles grins and retorts, 'Well I'm not,' and I turn away fast to hide my smile. Can't help being glad that Charles is a total bastard, as anyone less vile would cause me so much more misery every time the tireless, 'Did I do the right thing?' thought surfaces.

A rattling camper van creeps up the drive as the second pram race begins. This one is between Charles pushing Giles and Felix pushing Rags, as The Beauty has retired after her victory and is excavating the large box Charles has brought for her. Out of the camper van step my brother, Desmond, and a half-naked youth.

'I thought she'd like some entertainment for her

party,' says Desmond, and I stare at the stripagram as I assume he is, and wonder how old Desmond thinks The Beauty is.

'This is Oak, he's a mate of mine and he's going to do a bit of juggling.' Desmond squats next to The Beauty and hands her a red plastic rose. She bites the head off. Charles escapes from the pram race and moves in to help open the box he has brought. To complete the happy family scene, my mother arrives with The Gnome who has written a poem for The Beauty and wishes to recite it. He squats beside her and clears his throat. The Beauty is now surrounded by crouched men, none of whom she has any recollection of having met before. It is too much. She tries very hard to look pleased for a moment and then the bottom lip protrudes, wobbles and collapses and weeping commences. Her party is a disaster. She sobs and buries her face in my shoulder and I am attacked by the usual hysterical laughter, and so is my mother.

Charles has unwrapped his gift and is standing looking foolish next to a very done-up and *bijou* doll's house.

'Oh, Charles, how kind,' I say, 'you shouldn't have.' Am mentally computing price, and becoming red with fury that he can have forgotten the presence of my own doll's house, and so squandered a fortune on this soulless Bovis-style residence when he could have given her a musical box. The Beauty is becoming frenzied with misery and everyone else is standing about talking in groups as if at a garden party. Am saved from spiralling lunacy by Oak, who blows giant bubbles the size of footballs, and with them casts a spell of happiness over The Beauty and even her bored and cynical friends and relations.

Everything is looking up now: Charles says he has to go, and even the discovery of Sidney scooping cream off the top of the cake with his paw cannot diminish the new party spirit.

June 26th

The Beauty is still hung-over from her party and sleeps most of the day, enabling me to have two arguments with David over the bathroom and to plant a tray of *Verbena officinalis*.

Argument One: David wants to put gauzy fabric across the ceiling like a tent, and I think this will make the bathroom look like a Turkish Delight advertisement. We agree to try it and then decide.

Argument Two: The tent effect is in place, it looks wonderful and seductive and sensuous. I am enraged. Make a special trip to the village shop for a bar of Turkish Delight. I place it on the lavatory seat and stand back.

‘Look, David, I told you so.’ He removes the Turkish Delight without a smile.

‘Don’t be absurd,’ he says crisply. ‘Let’s leave it and see what you think tomorrow.’

Go into garden to avoid thinking about being defeated on this, and create a doughnut-shaped weed-free zone in which to plant the verbena. Move a few pink foxgloves to the centre of the doughnut, and a pot of slender agapanthus spears, and retire from the garden convinced that I have achieved a beautiful effect. The feathering green leaves and palest pink of the tiny-flowered verbena will look a treat surrounding raspberry Mivvi foxglove spikes, and then blue pompons of agapanthus. The design will be borrowed by many, just as if I were Vita, or Beth Chatto. Hooray.

June 29th

It is the last week of Giles’s term, and parents are expected to attend school as often as their offspring and for almost as long each day. This is maddening: the summer holidays always catch me unawares, and I can see life and work careering off into the gloaming like a runaway train. I had hoped to spend today and every other day this week filing, telephoning and writing, in a last-ditch attempt to save myself from hopeless inefficiency and brain death in the days to come. But Gawain, an old school friend of Charles's, indeed, the only friend of Charles's I ever liked, arrived yesterday. 'I've come for a week or so,' he announced gladly. He is a painter, nearly successful, and always neurotic. He plans to finish a series of canvases entitled 'Normal for Norfolk' while he is here. So far he has not even opened a tube of paint, but instead has spent the morning mowing the lawn. Or trying to.

'I think I'm more of a window-boxer than a gardener,' he explains the third time I am called out to help him push the mower out of the border into which he has driven it at high speed. I have noticed that the ride-on mower excites men when they first see it, but disappointment at the poor acceleration usually leads to boredom halfway through the grass cutting and it is left, like flotsam at low tide, marooned in the middle of the lawn. Gawain is no exception, and leaves the mower curtseying into the beech hedge.

Over lunch he shows me photographs of Normal for Norfolk I to IV, and I love III so passionately that I buy it there and then without really being able to imagine how big it is. Or how I am going to pay for it. I give a very small down payment and arrange to pay a monthly pittance for ever. Gawain is ecstatic. 'Man, this is groovy,' he yells, and rushes off to the larder to find the case of Red Stripe beers he brought as a house gift.

Halfway down the first can he is garrulous, and we cover such topics as the breasts of the girls on *Baywatch*, upon which subject he is lucid, the inspiration behind the Normal for Norfolk series, about which he is less clear, and whether it is worth driving five miles to Cromer to place a bet on the one-forty at Kempton Park. 'Yes, but will you take me, Venetia? I'm over the limit.'

By the end of the second Red Stripe he is dancing to *The Archers* theme tune on the radio and I am longing for him to become unconscious. Hours pass, and I make pea and mint soup because I can do nothing else; Gawain needs company. He unburdens his soul, gazing mistily at me, shaking his head sadly and murmuring, 'You're so understanding, Venetia, I love you, I love you.'

This is infuriating. He doesn't love me, he's getting me muddled with his manic depressive girlfriend. And I don't want to be understanding, I want to be in my study. When The Beauty goes for her rest, I try to leave the room but am foiled. Gawain follows me into the study and settles into the large armchair, pulling one side of the shutters to so as to protect his head from the sun, and continues a seamless narrative about a trip to Barcelona with the manic depressive girlfriend, whom he says has a good figure but is not as beautiful as me. I am underwhelmed by the compliment and am ticked off for gracelessness. In desperation I return to the kitchen and start to make bread, and Gawain is silenced at last. But still very present. He has decided to incor-porate me into Normal for Norfolk, and begins sketches for my portrait.

My mother arrives for tea and bonding with The Beauty prior to attending Giles's concert, and I leave her with her granddaughter and Gawain, under the guise of fetching something from the fridge, and charge back into my study.

When I come out three-quarters of an hour later, The Beauty is under the table with the remains of the sketch-book and a potato, there is a vodka bottle empty on the table, a large plate brimming with cigarette butts and my mother is singing her party piece, 'Three Craws Sat Upon The Wall'. I try to dissuade her and Gawain from coming to the concert, but she bridles, lights another cigarette and inhales deeply and with feeling. 'I am not missing Giles's moment of glory,' she insists. 'Neither am I,' says Gawain, swaying slightly in the background.

We are late. Giles scans the room anxiously, and his frown deepens when he sees my party. Gawain escapes and looms over to the row of chairs and looks around, his jaw squared as if for combat. Combat immediately turns up, in the form of the headmaster. Giles is hopping with alarm, but I decide that I can do nothing and affect ignorance. Mercifully the lights go down and the first squeaks and moans of the violin drown Gawain's inevitable ousting from the top row and his return to our party. He and my mother fall asleep with their mouths open for the rest of the concert. Gawain snores. Giles and I agree afterwards that this, although obvious and ill-mannered, had been a blessing.

June 30th

Gawain shows no sign of leaving, or of doing any work, but he is very keen to come to all the children's school events. Initially I am grateful, Charles having called yesterday evening, from a blipping and buzzing mobile telephone, to say that he and Helena are taking a much-needed break and will be in St Tropez for the week.

'I'll do a long weekend when I get back,' he says grandly, and is cut off before I can complain. Gawain overhears the conversation, and takes a dim view.

'The guy has become a total stiff. He's started to believe in his own product and has had his brain embalmed by that ridiculous pygmy. I can't believe we were ever friends.' He pours himself a large measure of vodka, adds tonic and swigs it before adding, 'You should have married me instead, Venetia.'

This is a favourite theme this week, brought on by a schism with the manic depressive girlfriend. It is well meant and very exhausting, as it involves him performing in character as perfect husband. He realises that the night of Giles's concert did not go well, but it has only put him on his mettle to do better at the many other school events there are. He thinks he looks like everyone else's husband, and takes much pride in this. However, he does not, and is a source of deep mortification to the boys. First, none of the fathers wears Birkenstock sandals, nor do they have their toenails painted purple and henna webs up to their ankles. Second, none of them addresses his wife loudly as 'babe', as in: 'Babe, you *said* I could be in the fathers' race, so I *had* to wear shorts.' Gawain starts stripping off his clothes at Felix's sports day to emerge in PE shorts and an oversized white T-shirt with 'Betty Ford Clinic' written on it in huge capitals. To my amazement, Felix is delighted.

'Mummy, look at Gawain, he's definitely going to win, he's got the right clothes. Daddy never wins, so it's really good that he couldn't come. Who's Betty Ford?'

Felix jumps about beside me, too excited to keep still, and Gawain jogs down to the start, hopping and side-stepping in the manner of a top athlete. Mrs Wilson, Felix's headmistress, puts him in the middle lane, and with much giggling fires the starting pistol. Gawain wins by miles, and once again looks nothing like a regulation father coming back from winning a race, as he is leaping about and catcalling in front of a small, puffing straggle of portly men with slacks and ties and cross, red faces.

Felix cheers loudly and unsportingly, and I forgive Gawain for the concert and buy a wine box as a treat for the evening.

July 3rd

Gawain receives a telephone call asking him to submit a portrait for a show in Cork Street in September. He has to send the picture within a week. He is disconsolate.

'I haven't got a portrait of anyone, not even a dog,' he complains to my mother at one of the daily drinking sessions they have ritualised in this fun-packed week. We are in my mother's garden having attended the very last school concert. The boys are fishing with The Gnome, and I am revelling in not having to care that their uniforms are torn and covered in mud. I don't even have to care that it is late, the summer sun is low over the wheat field behind us and the swaying green-gold is flooded orange in a path from the horizon almost to the yard. Our small yellow table slants gently towards the river, following the inclination of the lawn. To minimise any drunken sensation, we have plunged the legs of our kitchen chairs into the ground, and sit around with our chins at table height sipping Mateus Rosé and feeling light-headed. My mother has supplied straw hats for the whole party, and two for The Beauty, now sitting in her sombrero on the grass, ready to set sail. My mother has a bee-keeper's hat on and is busy smoking cigarettes behind the veil.

'The best way to keep the midges off,' she insists, then, suddenly inspired, flips back her veil and lurches forward on her chair. 'I know, why don't you paint Venetia?'

This appeals strongly to me, and I am just simpering and beginning to say, 'Oh, no, why would he want to—' when Gawain leaps up shrieking.

'Yes, yes, I'll do it. I've even got sketches of her. I can see it now. Let's start right away.'

The appeal is already dwindling for me; I was hoping for a glamorous pose with draped silken garments and so forth. My post-school look of tired hair and pink T-shirt generously coated in custard creams is not good. There is no stopping Gawain, though. He takes about twenty polaroids of me, mostly with a view of the inside of my nostrils as he is lying on the grass throughout the photo session. Then he vanishes into the house and orders a taxi.

'I've got to hit town and get my canvas sorted,' he explains. 'I'll be back to collect my stuff as soon as I can.'

Bemused, my mother and I wave him off just as Giles and Felix approach with two silver, sleek trout, sopping wet clothes and huge grins on their faces.

'The Gnome has lit a fire and we're going to cook them,' says Felix, and scooping up The Beauty and her hat, we remove to the meadow for supper.

July 7th

Egor the bull terrier is in residence as my mother has gone to Hadrian's Wall on a bus with The Gnome and his sculptor friends, the Foxtons. The sculptors are still keen to adorn my mother's garden, but have moved on from their wooden pig carcass idea and now want to install a series of boxes using sheep hurdles, in which they are going to place various cuts of meat and see what happens to them. My mother is looking forward to this installation as she will not have to buy Egor any dog food for a while. Neither she nor I can understand why Hadrian's Wall is relevant, but it's a nice place to go at this time of year, and my mother is always game.

Work and filth mount up in my house, as well as Egor's hairs and horrible trails of saliva which he spools about the place whenever he has a drink of water. It is all beginning to look very like Miss Havisham's, with no chance of improvement as I have no one to remove The Beauty while I scrub lavatories and so forth. This is my favourite kind of work avoidance, so I am desperate to find a Granny stand-in. Had not realised until now how mother-dependent I am. Perhaps I need to see a shrink? Actually, I'd rather spend the money on a sundress.

Desmond is still in residence at my mother's house, but is busy whittling a walking stick and says this will take him a week at least so he can't help. Inspiration strikes when stuffing yet more plastic rubbish into the bulging toy cupboard. I am able to create a dazzling sparkle on two lavatories and a bath upstairs while The Beauty bowls along the corridor inside a yellow nylon pop-up tent. It is a huge success. Even achieve a few minutes of paper-shuffling by pushing a couple of biscuits into the tent through a small slot in the zipped-up door.

July 8th

A big nit harvest this evening. Felix has forty-seven, Giles has twenty, I have probably at least a thousand but fail to evict them because Rags appears in the bathroom, apparently covered in young, podded broad beans. Closer inspection reveals the smooth purple-grey polyps to be ticks. *Gross*. Have to light matches and plunge red-hot match head onto each tick to dislodge. Giles is very keen on this, and watching his face lit with intent concentration and joy, I wonder if he had a past life as a professional torturer in the Spanish Inquisition. He says not, but maybe he has yet to unlock the memories. Repeated singeing of each tick only makes the little creeps waggle their legs harder. I give up, having burnt my fingers, used all the matches and singed Giles's eyelashes. Giles is as hard to remove from the terrier's side as one of the ticks, giggling and returning for 'Just one last go at them, please, Mum.'

He soon stops laughing, though, when I try to persuade him to wear mascara to cover up the damage.

'I am not wearing make-up. I'm going to Cambridge,' is all he can say.

I give up, but am nervous, as Charles is having him this weekend, and Helena the poison dwarf specialises in noticing my crimes and errors of motherhood.

July 9th

Charles rings the day before he is due to collect the boys and asks to have The Beauty as well. I am outraged. 'How on earth do you think you would manage a one-year-old? You've never changed a nappy—'

Such a relief that the telephones with TV screens are not yet invented, as in my fury I post myself through the hatch between kitchen and study where the telephone lives, and land, one arm flailing, the other clamped to phone, in the huge pile of photographs, faxes and pages torn from magazines which is my archive.

'Venetia, what are you doing?' Irritability raises the pitch of Charles's voice and makes him sound like Dame Edna but not Australian. 'Helena will be there to help me with the baby, and I understand from Felix and Giles that she is a very biddable child.'

I do not answer, as I am craning my neck to keep the biddable child within sight as she makes off down towards the wood, a carefully selected Rosa Mundi bloom in her hand and a pair of pants off the laundry pile slung rakishly around her neck. She stops by the steps down to the wood and turns back to look at the house before shredding the rose and stuffing a fistful of petals into her mouth. I must save her from the nettles ahead.

'All right, have her then!' I scream down the mouthpiece of the telephone and, slamming it down, run to scoop up The Beauty. She is enraged and bites me. I hope she does the same to Helena.

July 10th

Crunch of car tyres on gravel is terrible death-sentence drum roll in my present state of high anxiety and misery. It is Charles, early, coming to take the children for two nights. Can hardly bear to wave them off, and have to clamp teeth together in unnatural grimacing smile so as not to cry. Giles and Felix sense my pitiful state and hug me tightly. 'Don't worry, Mum, we'll look after her,' says Felix, robbing me of my last scraps of self-control. Things go badly from this moment. The Beauty's lower lip trembles and dissolves in sympathy, and Felix threatens to collapse too, but is bolstered by the appearance of Fabius Bile, the Chaos Commander he has been longing for, from Charles's pocket.

Charles struggles with the car seat while The Beauty and I skim about the house, weeping and gathering up suitcases and vital toys. Charles's ears are puce with frustration and he cannot fit The Beauty's seat. 'This is unspeakable,' he says through tight lips. Giles, who arranged himself in the front seat of the car hours ago, looks up from his *Warhammer* magazine.

'Oh, I'll do it for you, Dad,' he says, and puts the seat in the car and The Beauty in the seat in moments. The Beauty is much cheered by being in the car, and crows joyously and claps as all my precious children sweep down the drive with their father, Rags in hot pursuit as far as the gate.

July 12th

Am woken by plopping noise and murmuring from the gravel below my window. It is nine o'clock on Sunday morning, so it can't be a burglar. I leap bravely out of bed and open the curtains to a radiant morning and Giles, Felix and The Beauty sitting on the lawn with their possessions around them. Heave the window up and poke head out, bracing my shoulders so as not to be guillotined when the sash cord breaks.

'Where's your father?'

Three faces upturn and smile. I would be thrilled if not livid with Charles.

'Hello, Mummy, he dropped us off. He said we should wake you up, so we've been throwing stones at your window.'

'Have you had breakfast?'

'Yes, we went to the Happy Eater hours ago. Now we're hungry again.'

Bliss-of-motherhood sensation only lasts as I waft downstairs tying dressing gown and humming in time-honoured fashion. The Beauty bursts into tears when she sees me open the door. I pick her up and find a stigmata of eczema has appeared behind her ear, her nappy is dirty and green poo has squelched all over her pyjamas. Giles and Felix are similarly repulsive, both having Happy Eater ketchup and egg yolk around their mouths.

'Helena's mother had a heart attack, so they had to drop us off and go to see her.' Giles wriggles like a tick as I pin him down and wipe his mouth with the corner of my dressing gown. I am suspicious of this excuse.

'Why didn't he ring me?'

'You didn't hear the phone.'

'Did she have the heart attack at dawn this morning?'

'No, but I don't think Helena likes looking after The Beauty. The Beauty threw her supper on the floor last night and while Helena was clearing it up she pulled her hair.'

'And The Beauty bit her,' adds Felix with a broad smile. I am determined not to picture the scenes there must have been. Waves of exhaustion pour over me, and I trudge upstairs to change The Beauty, hugging her tightly despite wafts of nappy scent which wreathe her.

Have spent regressive sulking-teen-style weekend with terrible withdrawal symptoms from not having The Beauty issuing her mad gurgling commands from dawn until dusk. Insomnia both nights, followed by heavy morning sleep yesterday from seven a.m. until lunchtime. Could have done with the same today, and the early return of the children is therefore ghastly. Awful jet lag sensation pervades, and I can suddenly think of vast range of places I'd rather be this morning than in the kitchen breakfasting with offspring. Self-loathing kicks in when they are all sweetly munching peanut butter and jam on toast. This is what I have been monstrously missing while spooning down my sad meals of cold baked beans straight from tin for the past forty-eight hours. I am blessed and must not forget it. So busy despising myself that I forget to ring Charles's mobile phone and berate him for irresponsibility towards Little Miss Biddable and her brothers.

July 17th

The boys are neo-teenagers now and don't wake up until mid-morning. This gives me several hours in which to worship The Beauty and get round to dressing her and myself. We don't need to wear much; by nine o'clock sunbeams are everywhere and the morning dew has evaporated, leaving just a trace of damp warmth for bare feet on the grass. I am sure that The Beauty needs a hat for her matutinal stroll, but she knows better. No sooner is this confection (delightful sorbet-pink with a frill) clamped on her head than she removes it, saying 'Ha ha' in the manner of Tommy Cooper. We perambulate very slowly past the borders, with the hat propelled up onto her head by me, and back to the ground by her. She loves this game and lapses into her most guttural growl to emphasise her pleasure.

Inspired by the garden's high-summer loveliness, I plan a day of gracious living with a lunch party under the lime tree. The Beauty will wear a yellow gingham pinafore and we will have tortilla and salad with crimson nasturtiums. Of course, this is just fantasy. Felix and Giles appear, rubbing their eyes and demanding cereal, and take a dim view of gracious living.

'You said we could go swimming today and have a picnic. We want to go to the Sampsons and practise water-bombing.'

I compromise by putting nasturtiums in their ham sandwiches and we arrive at the Sampsons to find Sir Nicholas glowering as minions scuttle to and fro around and the pool, which is not quite full but very clean. Felix and Giles hurl themselves into the water, and my heart sinks as I contemplate a day of exchanging platitudes with Sir Nicholas as the toll for using his pool. Sir Nicholas nods a greeting, and I have to bite my lip to stop myself suggesting that he, like The Beauty, should be wearing a hat. The sun is bouncing shinily off his bald patch and his cheeks are mottled purple. It looks painful and wrong. He glides towards me, stopping at the knee-high box hedging and bending forward to kiss my cheek.

'Venetia, my dear, how lovely to see you all. Lucky you didn't come yesterday,' he says, picking up a springy twig and slashing at the lupin seed-heads in the border. 'That idiot daughter of mine left the gate open and the donkey fell in the pool in the middle of the night. Ripped the cover and nearly died. Had to call the fire brigade. Bloody teenagers. Pool still hasn't filled completely, so watch your heads, boys.'

Giles and Felix, hearing me exclaim, heave themselves out of the water and drip over to us. 'What happened to the donkey? Is it dead? How did you get it out?'

Sir Nicholas, soothed by all the attention, gives us a drink from a fridge in the pool hut and enlarges. The main thrust being that Phoebe is in big disgrace and has gone back to her mother in London. Sir Nicholas thinks her behaviour is craven and wet. She should be looking after her donkey. The poor donkey, as he coyly puts it, 'soiled the pool' in its terror, and was finally led up the steps and out by a fireman. Phoebe had apparently paid no attention to the donkey throughout the emergency, but had chosen this epic moment to begin a flirtation with one of the firemen. Sir Nicholas had found it necessary to threaten her with grounding. All this at dead of night and lit only by the moon, with the church tower looming above the fire engine. Giles and Felix are rapt.

'Cool,' says Felix, 'I bet the donkey's gone white and wrinkly from the chlorine now. Let's go and see her, but let's dive first and see if she left anything in the pool.' He makes a mad face, with googly eyes and tongue out, which enchants The Beauty, and cartwheels back into the water.

Giles races off with my camera to find the donkey, shouting back to Felix, 'Its coat may have shrunk by being washed. Maybe it could go in the *Guinness Book of Records*. Come and see.'

Sir Nicholas, who has been on gin and tonic while we were all sipping bitter lemon, is now beaming and small bubbles of perspiration are forming on his nose and upper lip. He graciously asks us to lunch in the house. I decline, but am forced, basic civility demanding, to offer him a share in our nasturtium sandwiches, knowing that the boys will be furious if he accepts and will quarrel over who gives up their Twiglets to him. He accepts, and making a few remarks about leaving a lady to sunbathe in privacy, takes himself off into the house, promising to return at twelve-thirty.

I settle down on a rug in the shade with The Beauty and *A la recherche du temps perdu*, which I always seem to have in the bottom of my bag, but never take out unless there is absolutely nothing else to read, not even a crisp packet. The Beauty coos and pats my shoulders and I begin to feel as languorous as Marcel himself, when my ear is invaded by a cold wet snout. It is Jack, Sir Nicholas's Labrador, and with him Leo, Sir Nicholas's eighteen-year-old son. Leo, blond, brawny and very California-beach-bum, lollops towards the pool, hurdling the box hedging. The enchanting, blonde cause of this athleticism follows wearing the merest hint of a bikini. Felix and

Giles return from their donkey-watch in time to see Leo execute an elaborate dive. We wait for him to surface, expressions of impressed awe at the ready, but disaster has struck. Leo rises from the pool with blood cascading down his face, his hand pressed against a wound in his forehead. He staggers out and collapses on the edge of the pool. The blonde rushes to his side, ministers for a second, then shudders and recoils, throwing something small and bloody onto the ground.

'Urgh! Gross. A bit of your head's come off,' she says.

Giles and Felix rush forward. 'Let's see, where is it? What bit?'

Leo groans. 'Quick, pick it up, *pick it up*.' But as if in a nightmare Jack the Labrador snuffles towards the small red dollop the blonde has chucked. Leo roars, 'That's mine,' and lurches, but too late – Jack's pink tongue scoops up the itinerant piece of flesh and it is gone. Slobbering goodwill, the Labrador moves over to Leo and affectionately licks his bloodstained face. Leo and the blonde sob unrestrainedly in one another's arms. Giles photographs the wet concrete where the bit of Leo's head had lain.

July 19th

At last, Giles and Felix have stopped kicking furniture and moaning 'I'm bored' every three minutes, and are building a tree house. The handbag crew are coming tomorrow to set up, and David will be here later today to prepare the ground for them, I am not sure why or how. Have not seen David since bacchantine feast and am apprehensive. How much can he remember? I have toe-curling memories of a nearly naked ping-pong tournament, a show-off session dancing on the dinner table and subsequent falling off, and, finally, singing 'Jolene' in a much too earnest voice. Oh, God.

David is early. The sight of him, carrying a ladder out of the barn with Felix, gives me a nasty fright as I trip across the yard in my dressing gown and duck-beak-yellow wellies. These are a vast improvement on the red ankle-length ones, and were sent by Rose with a gloomy note saying, 'The nearest we'll get to sunshine.'

Consider it best to ignore Felix and David until they speak, so set to work feeding the hens and staring at the sky. Hard to believe that sludge-grey clouds ever existed, and especially last week, as we are now immersed in sunshine and even the evenings are silk-warm and glowing with rose-stained sunsets. A puff of feathers and hot air greets me when I open the hen-house door in pursuit of eggs. No eggs, just a broody hen, clamped like a tea cosy over her clutch. I stretch my hand cautiously under her and count seven eggs. David, the ladder and Felix approach, David unnecessarily jaunty for this hour.

'Hi, Venetia, I love your boots. Can you come and give us a hand with this ladder?' He is not going to mention the party, his expression is preoccupied and distant. What a relief that men are so peculiar. We march in convoy with the ladder down to the wood, where Giles is perched high in an oak tree in his pyjamas. Peering down through rippling shade, he is green-skinned and ethereal in the underwater light. The wood is cool and dark, dew in exquisite droplets sparkles from the heart of curled leaves and the ends of grasses. David busies himself laying waste to a nettle wall with a scythe and I peer about me taking deep breaths of perfect air. Anxious to commune properly with nature, I raise my face and shut my eyes, still seeing bruise-blue shade in my mind's eye. Reverie hideously interrupted by a shaken-branch shower and the splat of dewdrops down my back and front. Giles sniggers.

'You look such an old hippy when you do that, Mum.'

Felix is frowning in deepest disapproval of me, and his eyes are swamped with sudden tears.

'Why can't we be a *proper* family? With Daddy here and you being normal, getting dressed before you come outside and stuff?'

If he had taken up the scythe and chopped off my

legs I could hardly have been more shocked or upset. Open and close my mouth a few times while battling with inner self. 'Poor Felix,' says Inner Self. 'That little swine,' says Outer Self. Mercifully, Inner Self takes over. Hug him, stroking his wild doormat hair. He begins to recover, wipes his nose on the back on his hand and in cajoling tones makes the most of an opportunity.

'Well, if you can't be normal, or married, Mummy, could you get us a PlayStation?'

'Come on, Felix, we need you up here.'

Before we can begin negotiations, David has picked him up and thrust him into the tree.

While he fumbles for a foothold, I scuttle back to the house and the solace of *The Grand Sophy* (nineteenth time of reading, I note from the tally I have marked up inside the back cover), and some cooing time with The Beauty.

July 20th

The silliness of the handbag crew knows no bounds. Most absurd is the photographer's assistant, a boy called Coll with a black quiff and orange velveteen Bermuda shorts. I overhear him asking Giles and Felix about the hens.

'Hi, guys, will you show me your mum's hens?' he says, crouching in front of them in a down-to-your-level manner which backfires as it makes his eyes level with their tummy buttons. 'I hear they wear trousers.'

There is an expectant pause. Felix grudgingly fills it.

'They wear flares, actually.'

Coll the Doll is not beaten yet.

'That's really great, guys, isn't it? Does your mum knit the trousers, or is there a shop around here where she buys them?'

The silence following this priceless comment is golden and laden with incredulity. I peer round the corner of the house, where I have been loitering to listen, in time to see Giles and Felix burst into peals of laughter. Felix's face is beetroot with mirth, and Coll is rooted where he squats, twiddling a pair of sunglasses which look like the plastic goggles that go with the strimmer, but apparently cost as much as a small pony. The children are merciless, sniggering and repeating, 'Does your mum knit the trousers?' over and over. Coll has assumed an expression of puzzled daftness, and I am considering rescuing him when the back door opens and Michelle the tiny stylist pops her head out.

'Coll, can you come please?' The hens, who live with an ear to the ground waiting for doors to open and food to be hurled into the yard, scuttle round from the garden, arriving at Coll's feet and fixing him with their beady yellow eyes. Coll stares in awe at their apricot bloomers. 'Wow, they are so cosmic,' he whispers, and is dragged into the house by Michelle.

I tag along, in search of The Beauty, who has been following photographic proceedings with interest. I find her ensconced in the bathroom surrounded by a sea of turquoise tulle, being a handbag prop. She has been given her own small reticule, apparently fashioned from a toy teddy bear, complete with pink sequin lips, matching ostrich-feather tutu and tiara. She is thrilled, loves the camera and bats her eyelashes and claps whenever it is pointed at her. The boys and I leave her at the centre of a ring of people all vying for her smile, and head off to pick strawberries. It is jam-making season, and having positively decided not to do any of this apron-string stuff now I am a single mother, was faintly appalled to find Felix in the larder this morning, matching jars to lids.

'What are you doing that for?'

'There isn't any jam left, so we'll have to make some today.'

I try to get him to see sense. 'But we're about to go away to Cornwall, to have our summer holiday; we don't need to bother with jam-making.'

Felix gazes at the larder wall.

'We should bother. We need jam,' he says firmly. Increasingly, Felix is taking over the running of the household. Am not quite sure who his role model is, but am determined that he shall be mine.

The strawberry field is empty of pickers but full of flamboyant scarecrows. The farmer is a big fan of

B-movies, and every strawberry season he adorns his field with mannequins in nylon bikinis and skimpy dresses from charity shops. Giles runs ahead, but stops short at the entrance.

'Look, Mum,' he yells, 'they've hung one.' The gate is guarded by a mannequin dangling on a rope from a vast oak tree, this one clad more in the style of a Brueghel peasant than Raquel Welch.

'I like the wedding one, she must have kept the birds away. I'm going to pick near her.' Giles grabs a punnet and makes his way towards the centre of the field where a fabulous blonde is positioned, with a vast confection of transparent polythene on her head and trailing down her back. Despite her green bikini, there is no question that she is a bride, and I make a mental note to tell the handbag gang to come down and photograph their wedding collection here instead of in my bathroom. Ten pounds of strawberries later we are home, and to my relief the recipe book says, 'Leave to steep in sugar for twenty-four hours.'

Miles the photographer is on a ladder outside the bathroom window, looking in at The Beauty in the bath with a handful of chicks he has scooped out of their run. There is no handbag visible in this shot, and when I mention this oversight, Miles rolls his eyes and says kindly, 'The product has a voice, you know, it kind of speaks through this sort of set-up.'

What a nonce, as Giles would say.

July 22nd

Jam-making commences at dawn. Utterly forgot the steeping strawberries yesterday, so have committed cardinal sin of leaving them lying around for two days. Kitchen quickly begins to resemble Willie Wonka's factory, with bubbling pink mess on the Aga and ruby droplets on small saucers and indeed the floor. Felix is not helping. He is lying in bed reading the *Beano* and is no longer my role model. Am scraping old labels off jars with my fingernails and listening to a practical pig-keeping report on *Farming Today*, when there is an ominous gushing sound followed by billowing black smoke. The Aga hotplate vanishes beneath a black mass, like sticky volcano lava, as more and more syrupy jam froths out of the pan.

'Bastard, bloody, sodding jam. God, I hate the Aga. Why is this happening? What do I do?' Wailing and weeping self-pitying tears, I wage war on my strawberry jam.

July 23rd

Ten jars, and it has set, and is delicious. Aga still thick with incinerated jam. David arrives for house-sitting instructions and is clearly impressed. Felix is not: 'Last year's was better,' he insists at teatime. No time to argue though, I must pack for the longed-for holiday.

July 25th

Have arrived in Cornwall after gruelling two-day journey in the car, including sleepless night at Welcome Break hotel on the M4. My mother, who refuses to sit in the front, has kept her eyes shut almost all the way and has been no help at all, so Giles has assumed role of navigator. Hurtle down the final winding roads, shoving the car into the bank as vast Jeeps and Mercedes cruise towards us full of families returning sandy and sun-kissed from the beach. Every village and indeed every house is called Tre-something, which confounds Giles, and we sweep up a rough track and arrive at Trefogey, a low white cottage in which a family of total strangers are having tea.

'No, Mummy, ours is called Trepanning, and the village is Tredition,' hisses Giles, ducking his face low as the family, all wearing pink polo shirts, converge by our car and stare at us with mild contempt.

'Sorry, you're the wrong people,' I shout out of my window, in what I hope is a hearty and jolly fashion, and we spin back down the track, a cloud of dust billowing in our wake.

Tredition is enchanting. A clutch of cottages clings to three criss-crossing lanes which plunge down to the cliffs between meadows and tiny golden cornfields. Where the lanes meet there is a village green with a mini shop on the corner, and a squat church whose delicate spire pierces the sky. Trepanning is at the end of a terrace with roses straggling up the walls and evening primrose nodding yellow beneath blue window frames. Lila has already arrived, and is standing on a chair in the garden fiddling with her mobile telephone.

'It doesn't work here, and Angelo was meant to ring to tell me his train times.' Heart sinks: Angelo is Lila's seventeen-year-old nephew by marriage, spoilt and disagreeable no doubt, like her children. My mother manages to extract The Beauty from her car seat where she has been embedded in biscuit crumbs, segments of orange and smeared raisins. We stand around for a few minutes while Lila teeters on the chair, waving her telephone above her head.

Felix and Giles rush round from the other side of the house.

'Can we go surfing after tea? Is the tide right? Can we buy some T-shirts at the beach and an ice cream afterwards?'

The tide is right, and I am amazed that they can remember the routine, as our last Cornish holiday was three years ago, with Charles at his most sergeant major-ish due to having invited his business partner, Henry Loden, and family to come with us.

My mother is worn to a shred by back-seat driving and elects to Beauty-sit. Leaving her in charge of a bumper bottle of gin and a few miniature tonics, we all squeeze into Lila's red convertible VW Beetle and roar up the road to Treboden and the beach.

Lose my head utterly in the surfing shop and find that I have purchased wetsuits for both the boys and am unable to resist a miniature one for The Beauty. 'It's all right, they're second-hand,' I whisper over and over to myself. Usual nasty moment behind the curtain in the hire hut, when I am convinced that I no longer fit into the size M wetsuit. Struggle to pull wet, sandy neoprene over thighs, while out of the corner of eye observe Lila sliding into a red short-legged version, which is dry and therefore much easier to get on. Final test is to thrust arms in and heave ever-tightening suit over shoulders. This is like peeling a banana in reverse. It is on, and, as always, have sudden conviction that I am a *Baywatch* star and have perfect figure and posture.

Felix and Giles are hopping excitedly on the steps to the beach, and I follow them down. We break into a perfect beach-bum canter as we hit the sand, dodging between every size and shape of wet-suited surfer to head for the surf. Can never get over how well neoprene suits everyone. Portly gentlemen in their sixties, liquorice-stick-limbed children and pear-shaped mummies are all glorious, fit and healthy: perfect cereal-packet people. In the sea, seal-like bodies are everywhere, rising gleaming wet and black on waves and tumbling from bright boards into the spray.

Immediately lose sight of children who hurl themselves onto waves and come riding in effortlessly every time, black shiny exclamation marks, perfectly upright on their boards. Flat on my own boogie board, in the beginners' area, I dither, hoping to catch the elusive big wave, but unsure how to. My face is full of sea; inhale it, trying not to think about number of people who have entered the water and found that they needed a pee. Perfect crested sea horse approaches; leap onto it and forget sanitation worries in a flash.

July 27th

The cottage has become little more than dormitory and wardrobe. Cushions pieced together like a jigsaw form Felix's bed in the sitting room, and Giles occupies the sofa. Diptych has been relegated to a small cot mattress and a few pillows under the window. Upstairs, Angelo sleeps in the top bunk of a room no bigger than a paper hanky, and Calypso and seven Barbies are in the bottom one. My mother and Lila have a twin-bed room, and The Beauty and I have the dubious pleasure of sleeping in a double bed together. Every inch of space not occupied by bedding is covered with clothes, and these garments are all sprinkled with sand and are mainly damp. There is nowhere to dry anything, as it has rained almost ceaselessly. The wetsuits have not been dry since we obtained them, and the path from the cars to the back door is strewn with every size of suit, thrown on the ground and left like deflated rubber dolls in a heap next to ice-lolly pink, blue and green slabs of surfboard.

Angelo has increased our street cred in Tredition no end, and a stream of long-limbed youths and exquisite girls with silver trainers and braids in their hair make their way to Trepanning each day to sit in the garden and smoke with him. His arrival, twenty-four hours later than expected, was greeted with shrill relief from Lila. 'Oh, Angelo, thank God you're here, I was dreading telephoning your mother to find you.' Angelo, king of cool in big-pocketed flapping trousers, shades and a camouflage Michelin-man jacket, was aghast.

'Never telephone my mother, she is the last person to know where I am. I have been down at the campsite with some friends.'

It transpires that Angelo has spent several holidays in this part of Cornwall, can surf standing up and has a large retinue of followers. He is indeed the King of Cool, and Giles and Felix are delighted to have him in the house. He treats me and Lila with the usual amused contempt that teenagers save for adults, but is so respectful to my mother that I begin to think he has confused her with a Mafia leader or a member of the royal family. My mother loves him. They even share nail polish. Angelo is very taken by my mother's poison-green, and in exchange offers her Party Time dark purple for her toes. My mother is blessed with an invitation to the Ploughman pub for local groovers. Am jealous and at the same time relieved not to be asked; too demoralising to be crushed by throng of lithe and lovely young, when all my clothes are crumpled and have something wrong with them, nose has somehow become sunburnt despite weather, and one shoe is missing after today's surfing.

July 28th

Weather gloomy, but we are not put off trip to rocky beach with magical green pools. Angelo leads the way, carrying The Beauty on his shoulders and followed by his friend Lowdown whom we found on the sofa next to Giles this morning, and who has not yet removed his wraparound sunglasses. Path to perfect beach meanders through wild flowers, about which flutter butterflies as small and vivid as confetti. My mother and I are beasts of burden behind Lila, who has managed not to carry any of the picnic, but is skipping ahead with the young, pausing to pat cows and sniff at flowers. Drag the wicker basket over a final mound, vowing in future to forfeit style in favour of comfort. Picnics shall come in plastic bags from now on.

Arms of rock reach out from either side of beach, embracing waves rolling and thundering in. Sun makes grand entrance and beams hotly, and The Beauty dons her exotic red bathing suit and yellow floral hat and sits happily in a rock pool, picking seaweed and catching transparent shrimps. My mother and I spread rugs, after much shuffling around the beach looking for the best spot, and lay food out. Rags hears the rustle of tin foil on sandwiches and bounces over, briny, sandy and wet from the sea. She puts her paw in a treacle tart and is hurled away back into the sea, but not before she has shaken herself briskly and wetly over the pile of towels. Egor is exemplary by contrast, his fear of the sea ensuring that he does not move from the boulder behind my mother.

'Why did we bring that little beast?' howls Lila, emerging from the sea. 'You should be able to control her, Venetia.' Am about to apologise, when Calypso, who has taken against The Beauty because she wants to be the youngest, runs up to her and jumps deliberately in the rock pool, startling The Beauty who is in a trance of pleasure making sand pies, and causing her to bellow.

'And you should be able to control your children,' I snarl back. This is the wrong thing to say. Lila sniffs and pulls herself up very tall.

'Come, Calypso,' she says with magnificent hauteur, 'come, Diptych, we shall find a more peaceful picnic spot for ourselves.'

Diptych is furious. 'No way, Mum, Giles and I are going to look for the conger eel; we've got fish fingers for it. Anyway, I hate those bean curd sandwiches you make us eat. I'm having a pasty.'

Lila stamps her foot and flares her nostrils like a small bull preparing to charge. My mother leaps up to create a diversion, clearly not having thought of what to say, but doing the haughty bit with great élan.

'Lila, Venetia, that will do!' She pauses and glares at us both. 'Now why don't we all go and look for the conger eel?'

The kindergarten approach is successful. When Calypso grabs The Beauty's cup and swigs her juice, her black eyes fixed defiantly on my face, I am able to rise above it with my own version of magnificent hauteur.

'Venetia, stop looking like a lemon,' whispers my mother, back on her rug, with no intention of looking for conger eels, and preparing to read the newspaper in the sun with the help of a pair of dark green plastic lenses attached lopsidedly to the front of her specs. Affect deafness and move away to seek out the children, clambering over steep, sleek rocks, shiny with sea spray, with The Beauty clinging like a marmoset to my shoulder. We find the boys perched like statues on individual ledges protruding from a deep, still pool, gazing at the water in silence. Felix has a packet of fish fingers on his rock, and, breaking one, he lowers a large lump into the water. We continue to stare at shadows, and after a while become bored. Just as I am about to return to the picnic spot, Felix gasps and points. At the back of the pool, where shadows meet cavernous rock behind, a streak of lapis blue flashes. The fish finger vanishes, there is a confusion of teeth and jaws and a vast eel glides away, as unstoppable and smooth as an express train, back to his cave.

'Cool,' whispers Giles with enormous satisfaction.

'Yesssss,' yells Felix, leaping up and stabbing the air as if he has scored a winning goal. Diptych grabs the fish-finger packet and tosses the rest into the pool, and waits again, his camera poised for the return of Jaws.

Calypso kick-starts a crescendo of complaint with the time-honoured whine, 'It's not fair. I didn't see it. Mummy, get it back. The boys wouldn't let me see, they said I couldn't.' She hiccups herself into full-blown sobs and kicks Lila while burying her face in her skirt. Lila's teeth clench.

'That is nonsense. I was with you and the boys did

nothing of the sort. They didn't even know you were there, in fact. Now stop behaving like this.'

'No, I hate the boys, they spoil everything. And that stupid baby.' More roaring and kicking.

I raise my eyebrows and carefully arrange my expression to one of sympathy and camaraderie. 'Dear little thing,' I say, ruffling Calypso's wire-wool hair as if I adore her, 'she's so passionate. Do send her to play with The Beauty when she calms down.'

Lila glares, and The Beauty, ever keen to enhance a situation, blows a kiss to the pair of them. The boys and my mother are well into the picnic when we return, wolfing Cornish pasties and recounting big game stories. Anything big appears to count.

'The French are building a giant stick as big as Mount Everest for New Year,' says Felix.

'It's not a stick, it's a French loaf and it's two miles high and they've already done it,' says Giles, condescension withering every syllable he utters.

'I saw a giant snail at a party once,' continues Felix, undaunted. 'It was the size of a hedgehog and it wee'd on my hand with a kind of squirt.'

Find the tone of conversation uninspiring, so sit down with The Beauty and my mother. My mother hands The Beauty a pasty.

'She's only eaten sand so far.' The Beauty says 'Ha ha,' and dabs it in the sand before tasting it, giving me a moment to wipe her forever running nose with my skirt.

A family adjacent to us have a tin foil barbecue and are cooking sausages on it, their well-mannered Labrador not even licking his lips, but sitting with an expression of resigned nobility at the edge of the rug. The Beauty loves Labradors, thinking they are all Digger, and approaches this one waving her pasty. He cannot resist, and it is a repeat of the conger eel show as a flash of pink jaw, white teeth and huge tongue precedes the disappearance of the pasty. The Beauty is delighted by this trick and sits back on her heels, clapping and cooing approval. Her nose is once again a disgrace, and absently I reach for a T-shirt of Felix's to wipe it on.

'Here, do have this, it's quite clean. You needn't bother returning it.'

The lady with the barbecue proffers a white handkerchief, small and fine, the sort that proper people keep tucked under their watch straps. She smiles understandingly.

'It's so difficult getting out of the house with everything, isn't it? I remember just how it is for you; I had four under five myself, although it seems years ago now.'

Four under five. And I can't even get a handkerchief organised for one baby, despite having ancient boys and an able-bodied assistant in the form of a mother on holiday with me.

Barbecue lady is arranging her picnic now. Out of a cool box and a hamper come Tupperware boxes in neat piles, each containing a clutch of different, delicious-looking sandwiches. Don't like to stare, but have seen enough to know that I wish I was at their picnic. The Beauty has had the same thought, but unlike me, is confident that they have invited her. She squats down and helps herself to a roast-beef-filled roll, stuffing as much as possible in her mouth and saying 'Mmmmm,' as if she has been starved for weeks. The woman shakes her salt and pepper hair out from a ponytail and smiles at The Beauty, who beams back and grabs another sandwich.

'Do you let her have beef? I brought a side down with me from our farm, so I can vouch for it completely.'

Hastily fling a towel over our supermarket pork pies and packet of plastic pre-sliced cheese.

'Oh, in that case I'm sure it's fine,' I say airily, and struggling to regain some sense of being adequate: 'Is it organic? We only eat organic meat now.'

'So sensible, you can be badly poisoned by those supermarket pies and one can't be too careful with a baby.' The woman smiles, speaking without a shred of malice, as she blows The Beauty's nose for the tenth time and gives her a pear.

How can I become more like her and less like my bag lady self?

July 29th

Ceaseless rain and no silver lining in the weather forecast. There is a farm open day inland, and we select it as our excursion for the day. Lila and my mother opt out and go to a supermarket and also a launderette to dry all our clothes. Angelo and I are in charge of the children. On the way have fond fantasies of clotted cream and 'How to Make Buttermilk' lessons. Can hardly wait to sample homely cakes and pies which must be for sale there.

Arrive, brimming with excitement, hunger and anticipation, at huddle of corrugated-iron barns surrounding cluster of Lego brick houses with vast carports. Mud clogs car park entrance and our wheels spin. Felix falls over in a cow-pat as soon as he gets out of the car, and is so covered in excrement and mud that he looks as if he has been dipped in brown paint. Farm open day is quickly exposed as a euphemism for selling show homes, and there is not a lamb or indeed a milk churn in sight. And no cakes. Angelo vanishes with Calypso on a quad ride, and moments later we see them hunched against the rain, creeping up a hill with Calypso locked into a cage on wheels and Angelo hanging on grimly to the bounding quad bike.

'Mummy, I'm frozen and there's mud in my eyes,' sobs Felix, who has not stopped crying since he fell over. In desperation he, The Beauty and I force an entry to a show home and find the bathroom. I run the bath and Felix begins to peel layers of mud and clothing.

'What do you think you're doing?' A beaky nose peers round the door, followed by a furious face, pearls and a blue rinse. 'This is disgraceful, you must leave at once.' The woman marches in and pulls the plug. 'Now come on, out of here.'

The Beauty dislikes her tone and gives a loud kung fu shout, 'Hah!' before hurling a pink soap brick at the woman.

'Ow, you little monster,' yells the woman. 'I shall call the police if you don't leave immediately.' The Beauty screws up her nose and growls like a fierce dragon. The woman holds the door open and we depart in deep disgrace, Felix still caked in the only evidence of animals we have found on the farm. No let-up with the rain, and Giles is throwing horseshoes at a pole with evident skill, as he has won two pink fur chimpanzees, each one bigger than The Beauty. Felix bursts into tears again because he wants a pink chimpanzee. I offer to buy him one, but he wants to win it. He throws a horseshoe and it hits a small boy in the back of the knee.

'Your children are a disgrace,' hisses the child's mother, deaf to sobbed apologies from Felix. The man who runs the stall says there are no monkeys left anyway, and gives Felix a consolation prize of a small Day-Glo-green alien dressed in a purple nylon robe. Felix yells more loudly and hurls it into the flames of the hog-roast fire. The Beauty, who had her eye on the dear little alien, opens her mouth and bawls too. Am ready to jump onto the pyre myself when Angelo and Calypso finally return from their ride. Calypso is weeping because she banged her head and no one would let her out of the cage.

We depart, having spent forty pounds. All the children crying except Giles, who is sulking because we had to leave before the welly-throwing contest.

July 30th

Last day, and we have organised a babysitter and are succumbing to Angelo's invitation to the pub and to a party on the caravan site. Try on three different dresses, and finally opt for the very dirty jeans I have hardly taken off all week. Children scarcely see us leaving, as they and their babysitter are building a camp in the garden. Babysitter is tiny, shorter than Giles and appears considerably younger. Can't face asking her age in case she is only seven, but am comforted by the fact that The Beauty is sound asleep and Giles and Felix are capable of looking after themselves. Just don't care what happens to Calypso and Diptych, as now loathe them unreservedly and Lila too, particularly when she comes out of the bathroom, having pinched all the hot water, wearing skimpy purple camisole top and a pair of my shorts, cast out of my wardrobe for being too small.

Angelo is already at the Ploughman, playing pool, and is clearly not going to acknowledge us at all. Thumping music of the sort Giles loves, and terrible Oxford Circus crush, except worse because all the bodies one is pushed against are limber and perfect reminders of own decrepitude. Have strong sensation of being the three ugly sisters as my mother, Lila and I settle ourselves at half a table and try not to notice that the youths at the other half have turned their backs to look out of the window at a row of overflowing dustbins. Angelo wins his pool game and is challenged to another. My mother drains her glass in moments.

'This is ghastly,' she says. 'Let's go.'

Stand around in car park wondering what to do next. Yearn for manly and capable escort to sweep me, in diamonds, to dinner.

'Shall we go to the Rock Top Retreat?' Suddenly remember genteel hotel, to which Charles's partner and wife took us for pregnant-pause-ridden dinner last time.

Very soon we are sipping martinis, feet snugly buried in lovely powder-blue shaggy carpet, listening to tinkling piano and watching seagulls swerve and bicker above the sea. Much more the thing. Covert observation of others in the hotel bar offers interesting view of proper family life. Mr and Mrs Perfect, in their forties, both suntanned, with big teeth and handsome faces, lounge and manage to look comfortable on the swing seat overlooking the tennis court. On court, their four big-toothed children play doubles without having tantrums or swearing, and the scene is truly an example to us all. Lila, my mother and I are impressed.

'Maybe they're aliens,' my mother whispers loudly, observing the eldest toothy as it holds out a hand to help its brother, who has tripped and fallen flat on his face but who is being brave and not crying. 'None of your children would do that without being bribed.'

Lila and I glare at her, but know it is useless to argue. Cannot pretend, either, that self and Charles plus offspring ever made such a pleasing and harmonious tableau as the toothy Perfects, who have now all jumped into a huge, very clean Mercedes and driven off smiling, probably to amusing dinner with other faultless folk. My mother, now on her third gin martini and in rollicking form, is quick to point this out.

'How I wish you and Desmond had turned out more like those people,' she sniffs sadly, acting up with every gulp of gin. 'What a joy it would have been to have a decent son-in-law who played tennis, not a creep with a crematorium.'

'Well I wish I'd done better and married someone I liked,' I snap back, goaded. Waving my glass towards the doorway I draw her attention to a spry sixty-year-old woman, sunglasses propped in her bouncy greying hair, immaculately clad in a navy and white striped sailor top and a white pleated skirt, escorted by a tall, courteous man with laughing blue eyes.

'And maybe if you and Dad had been a bit more like that we wouldn't be so dysfunctional.'

For a moment my mother inspects her role model, finding her glasses and propping them on her nose like a pince-nez as both the arms are now broken. But instead of looking stricken and gleaning a few fashion tips from this paragon she is unrepentant and speechless with laughter. Lila butts in.

'Look, we've got to get back, we said we'd give the kids fish and chips for the last supper, and it's half-past nine. We've still got to clean the cottage and pack and take all the surf stuff back.'

Holidays. Can't understand how anyone finds them a tonic. Am sure that marshalling an army across the steppes of Russia is more relaxing.

August 1st

Last day in Cornwall. Up at dawn scrubbing and hoovering. Children bicker and whine and ceaselessly remove items I have just packed from cases I have just forced shut. Lose car keys. Am so frazzled that immediately forget I have lost them until everyone is in the car and waiting to go.

'Where are the car keys?' Yell so loudly that The Beauty, asleep in her car seat like an angel, wakes and bursts into tears. Her wailing becomes louder and louder, and I crawl through the cottage on hands and knees looking under beds and chairs for goddamn keys. Sudden silence suggests that The Beauty has been released from the torture zone of the car. Felix rushes in to find me checking the Hoover bag.

'Here they are, Mum, I gave them to The Beauty to play with and then I forgot. Sorry.'

Count to ten, bite tongue to prevent filthy language and preserve appearance of dignity.

August 3rd

David has made everything much nicer than it normally is here. He is unusually tidy for a man. Even outside was improved by him, and we now have a dovecote for the fat pigeons Simon gave us for Easter.

'They'll probably nest,' said David as he gathered his things before going. 'You'll have a colony to look out at soon.'

Outside still lovely, and pigeons cooing from their palace, but inside has reverted to usual chaos. Am still excavating damp, fetid suitcases. Find that many clothes are mouldy. Gloomily scrubbing favourite antique lace camisole and failing to remove grey flecked fungus from it when huge van drives up, shiny and red and definitely not the organic veg round. Joyfully abandon the washing and scuttle to the front door to make friends with whoever it may be. Thrilling special deliveries courier waits in the porch, invisible behind man-sized bouquet. It is for The Beauty and is a forest of sunflowers in every colour the sun has ever been, from blackest crimson to bronze and citrus yellow.

'Thank you to our precious little Princess' reads the card, and I am split between delight at the flowers and nausea at the message until Giles puts the card in the bin. Moments later, while I am arranging The Beauty's gift in numerous pink plastic buckets as none of my vases do them justice, another van ticks up the drive. More signing for exciting parcels, and am delighted that this one is for me. Less delighted when parcel is ripped wide open to reveal a pair of high-heeled wellingtons the colour of aubergines, and a handbag designed to look like a watering can, or a watering can designed to look like a handbag. Cannot initially decide which, but dare not put water in to test. Have been speculating with Vivienne as to the nature of my thank-you present from the handbaggers, and had rather set my heart on a delicious icing-pink jewelled item with silk ribbons and much fragile glamour. Telephone Vivienne to deliver the bad news.

'God, how awful to think that that's how they see you.' She can hardly keep the glee out of her voice. Decide on the spot to donate the stupid bag to her, but will keep the wellies to add to my now considerable collection. Wrap the bag with some difficulty and post it to Vivienne forthwith, thus experiencing a rush of achievement for the day before returning to the mould battle in the scullery.

August 5th

A fine drizzle sets the tone for the village show today. Feeding the hens, pigeons and assorted wild birds now as tame as any of ours, my hair becomes cloudy with tiny raindrops and then properly wet as I scuttle around the garden pointlessly dragging already sodden prams and toys under cover. Bring The Beauty's pram mattress in and put it on the Aga where it creates a comforting Chinese laundry fug.

Felix has been up for hours completing his entries for the show. He has made a Christmas card of a jolly old Santa carrying two longed-for Warhammers called

Deathmaster Snikch and Nagash, and a Nintendo. The attention to detail is magnificent, but I fear that the message, which reads: 'Here you are, is this what you wanted? Ho ho ho,' will not please the fuddy-duddy judges. Having made two posters for the 'Teddy Jumps Off the Tower' contest, he is feeling very competitive about this class, and has dressed his bear as Deathmaster Snikch and is busy attaching yards of elastic to make him a bungee bear.

Giles has become unspeakable and refuses to do anything. In despair I put him in charge of fancy dress.

'You can go as anything you like as long as you aren't a Warhammer, and as long as you include Felix and The Beauty.' Have little hope of this ruse being successful, but he shuffles off, kicking the door as he goes, and is not seen again for hours.

Lila arrives, laden with produce she plans to show.

'I've grown this fantastic sea kale. Look, it's still got the bloom of ozone on it. I picked it up this morning, it was terrifying. Three huge chunks of cliff collapsed when I pulled the roots out of the ground, and I haven't even planted my sea kale close to the edge.'

Lila's tiny seaside holiday hut is inching its way towards the sea as the cliff below it crumbles. Lila is very calm about sleeping there herself, but insists that her children and their au pair stay at the guest house down the road. Am convinced that she does this to avoid cooking for them, but she is adamant that it is for their safety. This lavish way of life is paid for by what she calls the 'Poor Orphan Fund', a seemingly bottomless well of money she extracted from the Italian government when Roberto, her husband, was crushed by a ceiling he was renovating in a twelfth-century chapel outside Naples. The accident was six years ago, but Lila still wears black or grey almost every day and adopts a tragic, wizened pose when husbands are mentioned. Her ruthless quest to get the better of all lawyers is exhausting, but today litigation is far from her mind, and instead she overflows with competitive spirit.

'What have the boys done for the show? Gosh, is that all? Diptych has grown all these tomatoes. His grandmother sent the seeds from Italy. Look.'

I look. Irritatingly, the tomatoes are perfect, gleaming like a cluster of cabochon topaz and rubies in their festive harvest colours. Calypso has made a fairy garden out of an old vanity case of Lila's.

'I will win the prize,' she lisps unbecomingly when I admire it. Find myself hoping not and am ashamed.

Off they go to the village, a picture of organic wholesomeness and in extreme contrast with my own family. We are all in filthy moods, and apart from the Christmas card, have nothing to show. Suddenly I remember my jam, and rush to the larder, where I stand for some minutes debating which jar is most fetching. Plump for one with a gingham lid and return to the kitchen to find Giles coaxing Felix into my old spotty fake fur coat. He has turned The Beauty into a fat Dalmatian puppy by drawing black spots with an indelible pen on her vest and nappy. She has a black and white spotty ribbon in her hair and is dragging her own toy Dalmatian by the collar. Giles has borrowed a pair of white jeans from me and stuck blobs of black felt on with Sellotape. They all look wonderful. Am suddenly awash with love and admiration for my children. Noticing this weak moment, Giles hoists terrible silver mop and waves it at me.

'Mummy, please will you put this wig on and be Cruella? And can you wear this red dress and your velvet cloak?'

Love and admiration suffer a setback. I am to wear skintight, flame-red disco dress with slits up both sides. Clamber into ghastly nylon pod with much protest and regret at the impulse which stopped me chucking it after its heyday in the late seventies. Lashings of red lipstick and pallid foundation are applied, and Felix and Giles look on approvingly. The Beauty, though, is horrified, and refuses to let me pick her up, shaking her head and hiding behind Giles.

Fortunately, the fancy dress contest opens the show, so we are still unsmudged as we parade around the ring with our team leader Rags gagging on her leash and trying to look like a Dalmatian by wearing cotton wool pads glued to her sandy coat. The other entries comprise an enchanting bird of paradise – a little girl covered in glittery plastic feathers – and a bedraggled Humpty Dumpty on a pony. We look as if we have tried too hard, and as the only adult in the ring I am horribly conscious of my diminutive dress and vulgar fishnet tights.

Mortification is enhanced a thousandfold by the discovery that David is the judge. He winks when he catches my eye and I become scarlet in the face to match my dress. We win first prize of four magenta rosettes and David ties one onto each of our outfits. Shaking hands with me and presenting the cup, he is purity and loveliness meeting tarted-up depravity. Try to cringe away and am thus caught by local paper's photographer in hunched, wizened position for tomorrow's newspaper. The Beauty, in contrast, is very pleased to see David, and throws herself out of my arms and into his. This causes much clucking and clapping among the spectators. Hope the paper uses this picture if they have to use any.

Only just effect a change of outfit in time to shimmy up the church tower for Felix's teddy to make its jump. On the roof, we peer down at the churchyard below, an emerald handkerchief embroidered with scattered blobs of hurled bear. Giles is measuring the distance between each bear and the church door. The winner will be the one furthest away.

'Geronimo,' yells Felix, having paid his twenty pence

to the lady in charge, who is our Christian neighbour. He lobs the teddy with mighty force. It lands on the Spar shop's telephone wires. Felix starts to sob, and wails: 'Get him down, he's going to be electrocuted.'

I long to run away to a desert island where there are no village shows, no Spar shops and no children. Just apricot face cream, Pimms and Georgette Heyer.

August 6th

Weather still morose and Lila and her children are in residence, having stayed the night in order to celebrate their multiple victories at the show. Diptych's tomatoes won a huge cup, now towering on the kitchen window sill with our eggcup-sized fancy-dress trophy next to it. This is bad enough, but worse is Lila's small shield for the sea kale, to which she has attached my consolation certificate for failed jam.

Felix and Giles are malevolent this morning. They were forced by me not to watch *The Simpsons* video last night, but to cook sausages on a fire in the garden, in the rain. Much rudeness ensued, and just as they were becoming malleable, if morose, Diptych announced that he has become vegan and can only eat tofu. A sausage was slung and slid hotly down Diptych's shirt, after which there was a vile food fight. Hostilities have opened again this morning with Giles torturing Diptych by beating him hollow at croquet, despite having patronising self-inflicted handicap of one hand tied. Felix and Calypso, friends since yesterday due to them both having won a class, Felix for his Christmas card, Calypso for her garden, are operating on Action Man with a penknife and it is best not to notice. My mother telephones and temporarily diverts Lila from throwing away everything in my larder with preservatives in it.

'Desmond has chopped his finger off.' My mother's voice is shaky and I can hear the inhalation of a comfort cigarette.

'How did he do that? Was he drunk?' I am sickened and shocked by this news. Mind's eye dwells unhappily on finger lying useless on the kitchen floor like Felix's joke one with the nail through it.

My mother explains: 'The stupid fool slammed the door on it in a fit of rage. Luckily we had some frozen peas, so I put it in the bag with them and took it, and him, to the cottage hospital. They have sewn it back on now, and all I do is thank God for Captain Birds Eye.' Mind's eye positively reels at the thought of finger stump among the peas: will never be able to eat another frozen petit pois again. Add three packets to Lila's throwing-out pile, then return two to the freezer in case we need them for similar emergency.

My mother arrives half an hour later and saves me a lot of money by putting all my baked beans and tinned rice pudding back in the larder, stating firmly, 'This is expensive food. To waste it is criminal.'

Lila is furious, and huffs and puffs for about ten minutes before announcing, 'I shall go and see Desmond in hospital. He will need holistic help after the trauma of the National Health Service.' She chugs off in her Beetle, forgetting her children and her trophies.

August 7th

Desmond arrives in a taxi, having discharged himself from hospital. I am rather touched by his coming to me, and welcome him warmly.

'You poor thing, how is your finger? Get your things and come in.'

Desmond hesitates and looks sheepish.

'I can't, I'm on my way to Lila's. Do you know her address?'

Broad grin sweeps my face, and I cannot remove it. Am relishing the Desmond/Lila meeting about to take place on sea-sprayed cliff top. Desmond's leather jacket dangles from his shoulders, emitting a pungent aroma of old beer, McDonald's and cigarettes whenever he moves in it. His shirt is clean, but is a nylon Arsenal football one, and his biker boots are unashamedly leather and were therefore formerly alive. The bandage on his finger is ragged and stained. Relish the thought of Lila rushing out to greet the taxi in perfect harmony with nature, wearing flax and other earthy fabrics. She will be barefoot. Maybe he will tread on her toe.

Desmond still has one foot in the taxi, and has not asked the driver to turn the engine off. I give the address and ask casually, 'Does Lila know you are coming?'

'Oh, yes, she's going to cure my finger. She says all I have to do is lie flat with my hand resting on a marble slab for three weeks and it will heal. So I've had the stitches taken out and I'm going round to hers to use her marble slab.'

Cannot wait to tell my mother.

August 10th

Desmond is installed on the marble slab. My mother and I are fascinated by this notion and wish to see. Wonder if he looks like Frankenstein's monster and Lila has become a modern Mary Shelley. Do hope so. Set off on a surprise visit with The Beauty. Would very much like to harness The Beauty's energies into something useful such as making electricity or being a Girl Guide. Could she work on a wind farm? Or a treadmill? My morning bath was enlivened by her face rising over the side, radiant as the sun, blowing fat kisses at me. She diverted me with this sweetness, and while engaged in praising her, I failed to prevent her slinging into the bath a wet nappy, two toothbrushes and a pair of pants. Her lager-lout progress around the house is evident in the paths of debris linking all the cupboards, and ending up in the kitchen at the food cupboard. This is her favourite place. She climbs, like a limber little monkey, up the shelves to the tea bag zone, where she snatches a handful and tears them apart with her teeth. When tea is liberally scattered, she uses the papery remains of the bags to wipe a clean patch on the shelf surface and also to blow her nose. Such genius is naturally rewarded with laughter rather than discipline, with the result that she feels approved of as she tornadoes around the house. This may be good for her psyche, but her housekeeping methods are tipping the balance towards deepest squalor. It is becoming irreversible, and I can no longer face tidying up. A day at Lila's, or even just an hour, will be bliss. Lila has no cupboards and even if she had, there would be nothing in them. She stores her food in a humming fifties refrigerator with a vast handle and superb anti-baby suction keeping it shut. Everything edible is in there, even her beloved pulses, and Lila has never used a tea bag in her life.

The Beauty whisks into the house with her lips pursed

expectantly. Her cunning is remarkable. By the time I have greeted Lila and turned around to find her, she has spotted Lila's Achilles heel – a plethora of face creams and lotions, neatly stashed on a shelf beneath the huge sink-cum-hip bath.

'Get that child. Quickly!' Lila lunges, but is not quick enough. The Beauty grabs a wholemeal-looking tube and has the lid off in a split second. Orange gunge hits the floor in a jet. The Beauty licks a drip from her fingertip.

'Mmm, yummy,' she says. Desperate not to have to go home straight away, I grab her and bundle her outside, begging Lila to let me purchase her another dose of the cream, which appears to be puréed carrot.

'You can't. It comes from a Mexican apothecary and it has to be mixed in the presence of the user,' snarls Lila, adding unnecessarily: 'It was very expensive.'

A nasty silence ensues, cut at last by a male voice.

'Well it hasn't made you look any different. Venetia looks just as good as you and she's never been near a Mexican apothecary.' Oh, how I sometimes love my brother. Desmond is standing in the doorway, his usually slick black hair wild from the beach. The Beauty is in his arms, and they make a surreal pair, framed by the blue view of sea frilled with white waves.

'How come you aren't on your slab?' demands my mother, from outside the window where she has gone to smoke, but with the window open, so she can join in with the fun in the kitchen. 'I don't even believe there is a slab of marble here. There isn't room.' Cut off from the waist, and peeping between the red and white striped curtains, she is straight out of a Punch and Judy show. Lila gives her a dirty look, and I have to look at the ceiling not to snigger.

'Maybe it's under Lila's mattress,' I suggest. 'A kind of hard Lilo.'

'Aha,' says my mother, her expression becoming thoughtful. Desmond hands me The Beauty. She is tinted orange, as if with Man Tan, by the sandy damp of Lila's garden path. He confounds my love interest theory by pulling back a curtain and revealing a dank, larderish room, more like a cell as there is no food in it, just a marble shelf along one wall.

'Look what I have to endure,' he says. 'I've been on the goddam slab for an hour this morning. But then Lila needed some wood chopped, and she says that a bit of exertion is good for the circulation, so she let me get up for a few chores.'

Lila the canny slave-driver is innocently scraping her precious cream off the floor and into a glass. She wipes her hands on a dainty little towel.

'Let's go for a walk, or rather a scramble – the cliff is like brown sugar,' she says, keen to get us out of the house.

We tramp in single file down the cliff path, Desmond

nobly carrying Ten Ton Tessie, as my mother has christened The Beauty. Lila skips ahead, nimble as a goat, and turns to take a photograph.

'God, you look as though you are on day release from some institution,' she yells up to us, and I do see what she means. Desmond's arm is still in a sling, but he does not let this cramp his style, so is wearing bluebottle sunglasses and has perched The Beauty like a parrot on his good shoulder. She beams and points her fingers at his eyebrows, but doesn't dare touch the springy mass of them. My mother is wearing her usual uniform of thick black jacket, long wool skirt, black tights and large hat. I never got round to taking off my old-maid white cotton nightie this morning, but managed to add a pair of harlequin leggings for relaxed seaside wear. Thus clad, I look like a faded bag lady, with strange swirls and mini roundabouts on my ankles where I have failed to apply my fake tan properly. Fortunately, Lila is much cheered by this, and scrambles back to join us, amiably suggesting lunch in the café a mile along the beach.

Wish profoundly that Giles and Felix were with us, instead of in some shopping mall in Cambridge with their father, as we stroll along the shore. Sand scrunches and gives beneath my feet, dirty, streaky blond where the tide lapped it this morning. The sea is teal blue, heavy and still like oil, and inviting. I cannot resist. The first moments are hell, numb toes bump pebbles beneath the water and I stumble, holding my stomach in so that there is less of me to feel the frozen ring of water encircling my flesh. Shut my eyes, and, emboldened by piercing squawk commanding my presence from The Beauty, I launch into silken blue sea, so clear that the sand and stones at the bottom and my pale marble limbs are visible. Twenty strokes towards the glittering horizon and the water becomes a little colder, a little deeper. The others tire of watching me and walk on, leaving silence, the sea and me. Lovely. Nature's beauty treatments triumph once more. This must be better for me than a day with Mo Loam, and so much cheaper.

Idyll no sooner experienced than lost by cavorting splash twenty yards away. Terror-fuelled adrenalin has me racing for the shore at Olympic speed with *Jaws* music thudding in my head. Almost die from unusual amount of exertion, and have to lie, as if washed up, just beyond the tide on dry land. Coughing and wheezing, heart palpitating, I stand up to scan the horizon, hoping, now I am safe, to see a great white fin and know I have survived a dice with death. Instead, a smiling puppy-faced seal bobs in the shallows, rolling over to reveal sleek black barrel body and little fins. I half long to run back into the sea and cavort with dear cuddly creature in the manner of youths and maidens in Greek myths, but am too shaken. Wave, and am convinced that seal flaps a fin back at me. The others have vanished. I decide to catch up. Remember

Simon telling me that you can get anywhere if you run twenty paces then walk twenty paces. Arrive at the café almost as soon as the others, and hardly puffing. Excellent. This shall be my new gait. Bungaloid and cosy, the café has been a pit stop since Charles and I first came to Norfolk. As I walk through the door, the smell of walnut cake and Camp coffee fills me with indiscriminate nostalgia. Can still dimly remember the days when Charles had turned his back on his army training and was trying to be relaxed. He even liked my family at first, or pretended to. Mention this to Desmond, who looks blank but says 'Yes,' enthusiastically.

We all have crab sandwiches, and marvel at the seal story. My mother unearths a half-bottle of wine from the clear-fronted drinks refrigerator. She is thrilled.

'What luck. Someone must have left it here. It says Thistle Hotels on the label.'

'Stolen from a minibar and swapped for crab sandwiches,' Lila suggests. Half a bottle is just enough to make our table appear more civilised than it is, as The Beauty blows her chips out of her mouth and across the floral cloth, and the rest of us pay homage to the crab sandwiches by eating them in silence.

August 14th

Insane morning spent packing for three children, self and Rags, with The Beauty shadowing me and behaving as if at a jumble sale with all my piles. The whole summer is a disaster. Can't believe it is holiday time again. None of us wants to go anywhere, especially separately. Begin to weep while counting underpants in Giles's room. Giles and Felix are going to Club Med in Sicily with their father and the poison dwarf tomorrow, and The Beauty and I are going to Ireland with Rose and Tristan, who have taken a cottage somewhere remote. Rags has been farmed out to Smalls, and we take her there at lunchtime with her bed, bowl and one bone as luggage. Smalls's address is The House with Blue Windows, and we find it perched halfway up the one street of a tiny hamlet where all the cottages are built from uncut flint and are identical except for Smalls's window frames. Opening a wooden door, we troop into a garden occupied by three caravans and a number of ducks, basking as if moored, in the shade. Rags bounds towards a large white drake with a pompon on his head, but stops in her tracks when he rises, quacking, and waddles into a wall of hollyhocks. Smalls emerges from the largest caravan, his hands stained blue, his tiny green hat and leather jerkin, making him a convincing leprechaun. 'Woad,' he says.

If only I were not rendered idiotic with exhaustion,

would be able to ask him to explain ancient dyeing technique to the children. As it is, just manage to remember Rags's dietary requirements and areas of neurosis before Rags, like a heat-seeking missile, discovers an ancient, shivering lurcher tucked in a drawer by the kitchen door and wages war. Try to kick Rags, miss, stub big toe, and in great pain mutter to Giles, 'You sort everything out,' and retreat to the car, tears welling, to curse and suppress waves of nausea. A few minutes pass and the sound of snarling terrier diminishes. Smalls and the children come out.

'We've tied her up,' says Giles. Smalls opens my door and hands me a tiny brown bottle.

'*Basilicum*,' he says. 'Pour a drop into your palms and inhale the aroma.' A powerful Mediterranean odour fills the car, and I recognise it vaguely. 'It's basil, and it lifts you out of exhaustion and revitalises you after a hard day. People in offices should use it to get rid of sick office syndrome.' Smalls has never said so many words to me; this is evidently a ruling passion. Try not to look disparaging, but evidently fail.

'Just try it, you look as if you need a boost,' he urges.

'I will,' I promise, and drive off rolling my eyes and having negative thoughts. Afternoon of much labour, including stacking logs which were delivered in our absence at Smalls's, and block access to yard utterly. Why have they come? It's summer. Who ordered them? Cannot be bothered to discover answers to these questions.

Boys stay up late packing. Felix is taking twelve cuddly toys, two *Beanos* and half a packet of chocolate biscuits. Giles has tapes, Walkman, cricket magazine and bat. We watch the news and Sicily has a heatwave of monster proportions. More packing of sun cream, hats and water pistols follows. Wish and wish that I had followed my instincts and said no to Charles taking them away to ghastly caged oven of organised sports. Anxiety and exhaustion now making my legs ache; I fear that self-pity may be about to flood in. Suddenly remember *basilicum*. Sprinkle it about with vigour and inhale. Superb. Better than sex, as far as I can remember, and much easier to come by.

August 15th

Some strange impulse of masochism has placed me on the train with my three children and enough luggage to fill the *Titanic*. Car has gone for a rest cure with David, who promised to give it an MOT and fix the stereo. Hope he is to be trusted. The Beauty uses the opportunity, and the platform of the table, to perform a range of her finest kung fu noises and air chops before settling down to shred my newspaper. Felix, having mysteriously acquired batteries for his Gameboy, has become an automaton, and Giles wishes to spend all my money on the contents of the buffet trolley. Other passengers pretend not to look as The Beauty flicks the open end of a crisp packet around the carriage, and the contents whirl and settle like snowflakes on seats, briefcases, shoes and the floor. My longed-for plastic cup of coffee cools on the table across the aisle and I dare not even remove the lid in case of accident.

Suddenly a grey-haired woman bears down upon us, her eyebrows snapped together in dreadful rage: 'I can't bear this.'

I find this unreasonable. My children have made a mess, but they have not been fighting, swearing or even bickering. I bridle, but she brushes me aside.

'My dear girl, you simply must have a chance to have your coffee. Let me hold your baby and you sit there for five minutes.'

Thank God I didn't speak. This is an angel disguised as someone's mother-in-law. Tears of gratitude rush as she gestures to the seat across the aisle, and thrusts me towards it with the sports pages, all that is left of my paper. Plonking The Beauty next to the window with a toy, she takes my place, crunching her Liberty-print bottom onto the crisp-strewn seat, and says brightly, 'Now then boys, let's play I Spy.'

Astonished, Giles and Felix comply. All tension dissolves in me, and has vanished utterly by the time I reach the end of the report of England's tragic defeat in the Tour de France. The rest of the journey is accomplished in peace, The Beauty having fallen asleep on the table, clutching her kangaroo and surrounded by crisps and the little milk pots given out with tea and coffee.

Charles meets us at Liverpool Street and is elegance epitomised, tall, straight-backed and immaculate in a pale suit. The army taught him to stand quite still, and seeing him before he sees us as we walk towards the head of the platform, am struck by how unusual this is in the rush and pause that is a crowd in a station. Helena only becomes visible when we are almost upon her, hopping from one little foot to the other, trying to see us over people's heads. Like the angelic mother-in-law, she is wearing a Liberty-print dress.

'Hello, Charles, hello, Helena. Gosh, what a nice dress, did you make it?'

Why can I not manage to keep my mouth shut? And why, when I open it, does everything sound wrong? Fortunately the boys create a diversion by hugging Charles. He pats their heads feebly.

The moment of parting is immediate. I am left by the entrance to the underground watching their backs as they head out through the station to their car and the drive to Heathrow. Had planned brilliant self-defence against the boys going, of pretending I had decided to send them to Scout camp. Thought this would protect me from heartbreak of not going on holiday with them. But the back of Giles's head, hair gleaming and nit-free, as he looks up to say something to Charles, Helena's nod and Felix turning to wave at me are more than I can bear. They are a family. There they go, up the escalator in a family group. They are off on a family holiday. And I am not. Sit on my case sobbing into The Beauty's neck while she pats my head and says 'Aaaah.'

August 17th

In Belfast, in McDonald's. Not a good place to relax; have to change The Beauty's nappy by squatting on the floor of the ladies' loo and making my knees into the changing mat. She likes this and lolls her head back, looking up the skirts of those washing their hands. Rose, Theo, The Beauty and I have just eaten three McChicken sandwiches and two Egg McMuffins and we feel a bit sick. Soon forget this in Mensa-level intelligence test of attempting to put hired baby seats into hired car, followed by equally challenging map-reading moment. Eventually we are on our way, heading to Donegal and our cottage on the beach. Tristan will be there when we arrive, having flown direct to a landing strip on the sand, from his meeting in Denmark yesterday.

As soon as the babies fall asleep, Rose and I regress to teen-hood, with Joni Mitchell in the tape machine and much ground to cover in the fascinating parallel universe of film stars we have crushes on, make-up and clothes. Rose is driving, leaving me to guide us across to the west coast, which despite having no comprehension of left and right, I manage.

Very underwhelmed by landscape, which is scattered with DIY bungalows and dour grey villages, until we cross the border and climb an uninviting hill to find Donegal billowing ahead of us, wild, empty and romantic. Narrow streams, boulder-ridden and gushing white water rise and vanish again into the hills and still black lochs lie cradled in valleys. The Beauty wakes as we are descending towards the sea, and she and Theo become raucous.

'Ten minutes more,' pleads Rose. 'Do you think you can keep them happy?'

I sing a medley of nursery rhymes, but fail to keep their attention. The Beauty hurls her toy mobile telephone at me, clonking me on the temple. '*Ow*,' I shriek, and she bursts into tears. Theo tries to be brave, but as The Beauty reaches a crescendo, his lip crumples and he too wails. Mercifully, we spy a petrol station, and I leap out of the car and purchase many bribes and consolations. Rose shakes her head, watching in the mirror as Theo is corrupted with a square of chocolate.

'The Beauty is so depraved,' she sighs. 'I suppose it's having elder brothers. Theo's never had sweets.'

I try to rally her. 'Never mind, he probably won't like them much.' Fortunately her eyes are on the road, so she misses Theo thrusting a fistful of marshmallows into his mouth, batting his long eyelashes and grinning.

August 18th

Have adapted with ease to fashionable life in cottage with boat as sofa, chairs fashioned from tyres and driftwood, and pretty well everything else hanging from big ropes slung about the beams. Lila would be impressed by simplicity of first-night supper of lobster and scallops, although she might not have drunk three bottles of wine and gone cavorting in silk-warm sea at midnight. Routine-bound motherhood has been hurled out of the window, and The Beauty and Theo stayed up until they fell asleep, curled together in the cushioned boat hull like the Lost Boys in *Peter Pan*.

Tristan and Rose still not up although it is eleven, and the babies and I have examined a herd of cows, whose field ends in dilapidated hurdles a few yards from our back door. Boiling the kettle for The Beauty's dawn bottle, I was taken aback to find a vast bovine face sniffing the window frame, shooting out a long black tongue at the steam marks on the glass. The Beauty and Theo spent half the morning hurling unsuitable items, including The Beauty's bottle and Rose's delicious turquoise embroidered slipper, into the cows' field. Now they have moved round to the sea a few hundred yards in front of the house, and we have made two pilgrimages across the beach already. Theo squeals in delight, running naked into the waves, and The Beauty follows but sits down abruptly when the first breath of water covers her feet. This is baby paradise. Our cottage is just yards from the tide's highest point, and the sea rolls back over hard wet sand, the colour and texture of fudge. Shallow pools form in pockets by boulders and the waves are delicate as lace, lapping baby ankles. Have huge fun paddling with Theo and The Beauty and can believe again that the boys are at Scout camp.

August 21st

A seaside holiday without Giles and Felix is weird, and am riddled with the conviction that I should be enjoying it more than I am. Emphasis much more on eating, and food is laid out like fabulous colour supplement spread. Tristan sees each meal as a chance to flex his creativity, and Rose and I do nothing but play with the babies, plan excursions we cannot be bothered to go on and paint our toenails. Today lunch is to be a picnic with bonfire near a tiny harbour further up the coast. Tristan has brought everything, and sends us off while he sets it all up. He wields his wooden spoon, camp as a television chef in his navy silk scarf and dreadful PVC apron with bosoms on it.

'Go and look at the boats coming in for twenty minutes,' he urges.

Am very impressed; he gets full brownie points from me, despite his outfit.

'God, you're lucky, Rose, it must be amazing to have a husband who can do all this stuff.'

Rose lifts Theo onto the low wall above the harbour so he can see the boats.

'Well, it comes from his being power-crazed.' She sounds resigned. 'I sometimes wonder what I'm supposed to do. I'm not allowed to interfere with the cooking at all, or even buy the food for it. He does everything. He even picks flowers for the table. And he thinks doing it all on holiday and at weekends gives him the right to behave like a total slob the rest of the time. And as for that apron, he wears it because it annoys me. No other reason. Ask him.'

Gaze out at knife-edge horizon, beneath which the sea is crisp navy blue and above which palest clouds scud about, and try to imagine being annoyed by a husband who does everything but who wears PVC bosoms, when view is eclipsed by hands over my eyes.

'Well hi there, gorgeous girls. What's grooving?' Gawain is standing behind me. Rose jumps up to welcome him.

'Gawain, you're here. How was your journey? That little plane is terrifying, isn't it?'

She is not a bit surprised to see him, even though she doesn't know him as well as I do, and I wonder if I have forgotten that I knew he was coming.

'What on earth are you doing here, Gawain?' Gawain has expression of joy writ large at the sensation his arrival has caused.

'I ran into Tristan rollerblading in the park, and he said that you lot would be here for a week, so I arranged with him to come and surprise you, Venetia.'

'Well you have.' Rose is glaring at me; I realise that I sound rude and graceless. Relax lemon face by hugging The Beauty tightly as we walk back to the picnic.

Gawain is an exotic addition to our party, and I covet his clothes: his shirt is lobster pink and crinkly like cheesecloth and his trousers are purple velvet. He is on excitable form, and dashes to the pub for beers to add to the picnic. We expect him to return in moments saying the bar fell silent when he entered. He does not return.

Am sent to fetch him, and find him playing darts with

two old fishermen whom he has just bought pints of Guinness. In Norfolk his appearance would stop traffic, but in Donegal he is accepted and enjoyed. He finishes a rollerblading anecdote, and, gathering a box of beer cans from behind the door, returns with me to Rose and Tristan.

The picnic is prawns, shoals of pink curls matching Gawain's shirt. The Beauty enjoys them hugely, especially when she learns to pull the prawn from its shell, and she eats eleven of them. We return to the house and The Beauty and I collapse in the swinging boat and sleep all afternoon.

Wake up refreshed and discover Gawain pretending to be domesticated and podding peas on the doorstep. He passes me an envelope. 'This came yesterday, and I wanted to tell you.'

Snatch it and tear it open, heart banging because for no reason, am convinced it is bad news about the boys. It is from New York, so can relax, but am too traumatised to be able to read the whole page of close typing.

'I can't face reading it, Gawain, what does it say?'

He returns the letter to his pocket and grins saying, 'We won the portrait prize for the show next month.'

Much clapping and jumping up and down pleases him, but I can tell I am still not reacting properly. Must show more interest.

'Who is the portrait of? Have you got a photograph

of it? Will it make Normal for Norfolk more valuable? Speaking of which, where is my painting, Gawain?'

Gawain groans dramatically. 'Christ, you're a halfwit, Venetia. Have you really forgotten? It's you. Remember, I took some photographs of you in Norfolk for it, but I haven't got a snap of it here, I'm afraid.'

Amazing, delightful news. Surely this must be how Miss World feels, but better, as I did not have to wear high heels and a swimming costume. Rose appears from the beach like a mermaid, wrapped in a silver-green sarong, hair dripping down her back, skin glowing from sun and the sea. She looks exactly as I should like to look when emerging from the waves. I beckon her over to share the glad tidings about the portrait, and we caper about screeching, 'Hooray!' until Tristan brings champagne and olives to the doorstep. Am becoming increasingly at ease with this grown-up and civilised way of life. Wonder if I can recreate it at home without Tristan. Doubt it.

Second glass of champagne and Tristan is becoming ever more my ideal man. He has persuaded The Beauty and Theo to lie down in the boat sofa and is singing Bob Marley to them. About to suggest to Rose that we share him when notice his long yellow toenails for the first time. And he burps at the table to annoy Rose. And, of course, there is the apron. Gawain is crawling around in the sea singing a shanty and resembling a Labrador. It is hard to imagine a holiday romance with him, let alone a life. Why am I even bothering to think pointless thoughts about putting a man back into my life?

August 24th

Home again. House seems vast after Donegal cottage, but garden a minuscule doll's house version of a jungle, now that I am used to having the serene sea as my lawn. Make shepherd's pie in triumphant non-fashion statement. Shaking Worcester sauce into it and enjoying nursery-kitchen aroma, I know that I am a pedestrian housewife at heart rather than chic free spirit with a need for everything perfect about me. The Beauty is overjoyed to be home, and dashes from room to room shouting, 'Ha ha,' and patting cushions. Rags returns in the sidecar of Smalls's motorbike, and The Beauty squats on the doorstep and hugs her. Have terrible anticipatory butterflies by the time Felix and Giles are dropped off.

'Mummy, we're back.'

'Hello-oo, where are you?'

They burst through the front door ahead of Charles and are so different. Brown and freckled faces which have cheekbones I had never noticed before are smiling at me. Felix nearly as tall as Giles, and both surely six inches taller than a week ago. The Beauty jumps up and down wrinkling her nose and shouting, ''Allo, 'allo,' at anyone listening. Charles is international man of mystery in appearance, with suntan and his usual smirk. Practically push him out of the door before the boys can say thank you, so desperate am I to have them to myself again.

August 25th

Club Med was not a success. 'It was like a prison with a huge fence and we never saw Mount Etna,' is Felix's verdict on the holiday, and, in mitigation: 'There were loads of really cool lizards, and I saw a snake in the swimming pool.'

Giles is hardly less surreal. 'They had a thing called the Black and White Minstrel Show at night, and we did circus stunts every morning and it was so hot that one boy passed out and fell off the trapeze and had to go to hospital in a helicopter.' He pauses, looks at me measuringly and adds, 'Helena liked the entertainment. She wanted to do belly dancing, but Dad wouldn't let her.'

Mind boggles. Cannot wait to see holiday snaps.

August 26th

Mistakenly saw garden as jungle on my return from Ireland. Closer inspection reveals it to be arid parched zone with yellowing bindweed, vast sunflowers and strident fuchsias. Must do something about it. Good intentions are set back when putting on wellingtons. Sidney has been using them as a game larder. Unearth a dried shrew in one red ankle-length boot, and the tail feathers of a blackbird in the high-heeled aubergines. Discouraged, I opt for my oldest pair, green with holes in heels and soles, and stomp out leaving Felix, The Beauty and Giles watching *Dirty Dancing*, our latest bargain from the Spar shop, and at £2.99 for two hours, cheaper than a babysitter.

Satisfying session with wheelbarrow and spade getting rid of all but the sunflowers in readiness for autumn planting. Am wiping brow and enjoying dark chocolate brownie texture of the soil I have turned, when gravel-crunching and vehicle-groaning interrupts. A small blue van with Heath Robinson trailer is inching up the drive, terrible squeals suggesting a need for oil. Waving from the front seat and beaming are Vivienne and Simon. I chuck my tools down and rush to bang on the playroom window, interrupting Patrick Swayze at a particularly suggestive moment.

'Quick, boys, the piglets are here.'

This visit was arranged months ago when Simon's sow, Portia, gave birth to fourteen piglets, some spotty like fruitcake, some ginger and some plain pink. All very clean and reminiscent of old-fashioned sweetshops and Sam Pig stories. Had powerful desire to knot red spotted handkerchiefs around their necks. Simon offered us six of them. 'You can have them to stay and they'll clear some of your rough ground,' he said, flicking cigarette ash into his jacket pocket, his face smothered in generous smiles at the thought of his clever plan for getting someone else to bring them up for him.

Six piglets in June, when they fitted into the palm of a hand or the crown of a hat, had seemed scarcely adequate for the rough ground, but now six large snouts sniff the air. Hairy faces and guttural grunts greet the boys, reaching towards the bars of the trailer to stroke them. They are warned off by Simon.

'No, wait. Let them get used to you. Their teeth are very sharp. Come on, let's put up the fence,' he says, and wreathing the boys in electric fencing tape, marches off with them to the wood.

Vivienne is still sitting in the car, with The Beauty beside her, standing at the wheel as if she is Boadicea, making vrooming noises and waggling all the levers. Keen to sit down after my digging, I climb into the back seat for a rest. Next to me is the watering-can handbag, no longer an object for derision, but somehow amusing and chic, and coordinating with Vivienne's sea-green cashmere cardigan and little lavender skirt. Am amazed at her choice of outfit for pig husbandry.

'How can you keep clean?' I ask in wonder, glancing down at my formerly white jeans, now skewbald with mud patches and speckled like an egg where I spilt tea on myself at breakfast time.

Vivienne strokes The Beauty's hair. 'I'm not clean, these clothes are filthy, that's why I'm wearing them.'

Evidently, we have different standards of hygiene.

Felix runs up from the wood.

'Simon says can you bring them down now, and he says you'd better drive across the lawn.' He gives Vivienne his most pleading look.

'Vivienne, please, please could I drive?'

She is no match for him.

'All right then, at least you can see over the steering wheel, unlike your sister.'

The Beauty is passed back to me, rigid with fury, howling into my ear. I elect to walk with her, and we stand well back as Felix crunches the gears and bounces van, Vivienne and piglets across the lawn. Simon and Giles are putting the finishing touches to the corral, and with an old door propped up on bales for a house, and a big sink as a water trough, it is very inviting and Three Little Pigs-ish. Blood-curdling screams and trumpetings herald the piglets as the ramp of the trailer comes down, but no movement follows. Two fruitcake ones are prone across the doorway, the rest milling about behind them unable to work out the route. Simon shakes a bucket of food and the fruitcakes leap to attention, trotting out and into their field like veterans. Vivienne has reclaimed The Beauty, and takes her into the corral to sit on the largest piglet. An early morning oversight prevented The Beauty from dressing today, and sitting on the rusty brown piglet in her white embroidered nightie she looks like a painting, maybe 'Baby Circe and the Swine'. Must ask my mother if Circe knew any pigs as a baby.

'They love having their backs rubbed with a stick,' says Vivienne, and Giles and Felix set to work at once, scrubbing away.

'Mummy, look,' Felix shrieks, and his piglet succumbs and collapses, front legs buckling first, until it is flat on its side and grunting blissfully, Felix still scratching away at the back of its neck.

August 28th

We love the piglets so much that Giles and Felix are moving in with them. They have cooked supper, sausages unfortunately, on a little fire just outside the electric fence, and are now snuggled down in a row with the ginger piglet and two pinks in the pig shack. Giles and Felix have sleeping bags, but are sprawled on top of them, sound asleep. Dusk is giving way to a hot, still night, and I hover with Rags between the house where The Beauty slumbers and the pig shack, unsure as to whether I should sleep out with the boys. Golden harvest moonlight glimmers on the pond, and, inhaling deep calm, I smell the nicotianas I planted rather late on and hear distant squawk of a tawny owl. Wonder if I might be nervous with just a few pigs and a tiny terrier to protect me and my children from spooks and worse. Distant squawk comes closer and up the drive, apparently preceded by Salvation Army tambourine. Out of the shadows cast by trees at the gate steps David, rattling a biscuit tin and followed closely by three piglets.

'I found this lot on the green, and I thought I'd better get them back to you before anyone saw them. They aren't allowed to go anywhere without a licence, you know.'

The three piglets are grinding their teeth and salivating expectantly at our feet. I chuck the biscuits into their corral and they spring over the fence in pursuit. This must be how they escaped, but cannot imagine how I failed to notice their absence; anyway, am delighted to see David.

'Thank God you saw them. Would you like to stay the night now you're here?'

David's face is black and white like an old movie in the moonlight; he laughs.

'Why?'

I point to snoring boys and piglets.

'I wondered if you might sleep out here with them because I can't make up my mind whether I should be here or inside with The Beauty.' As the words leave me I realise that the request is ambiguous and that I may have propositioned him. Blush scarlet, but probably appear grey in moonlit night. David does not seem enthusiastic or eager. I make it all worse.

'If you stayed, I wouldn't have to sleep outside.'

'No, you wouldn't.' He glowers through the dusk at me, then capitulates. 'Oh, all right then. Have you got another sleeping bag and a tent, or do I have to go in the pigsty as well?'

Fall over biscuit tin in hopping excitement and grovel happily. 'No, no, I'll get you some stuff. Would you like a camp bed and a pillow as well?'

Withering glare, and David mutters, 'Don't push it, Venetia, just give me the pillow and forget the bloody camp bed.' I run to the scullery to unearth the tent, congratulating myself on my good fortune. Now that I do not have to do it, can acknowledge sensation of utter terror at prospect of spending night outside and in charge. Pimple tent is erected in moments and I crawl around inside making it cosy by laying out a pillow and lime-green sleeping bag in which David will look like a glow-worm.

'What would you have done if I hadn't come?' David is sitting on the steps by the pond smoking a cigarette. Sit down next to him and am instantly bitten by three midges, so start scratching.

'I don't know, I think I'd have had to drag the boys back inside, or else spend the whole night patrolling between here and the house.'

'Don't, you'll make it worse.' His hand is warm over mine on my leg, stopping my absent-minded scratching. My heart is hammering away and we look at each other for half a second which feels like several hundred years. Leap up, unable to cope with suspense and anything more significant, and scuttle off to the house shouting, 'Ni-ight, sleep well,' very casually over shoulder.

August 29th

Breadcrumb-head and peeled-eye sensation caused by night listening to the hall clock ticking and wondering how to face David in the morning. Needn't have bothered as he is not here. The Beauty makes straight for the pig zone before I can even get her bottle from the kitchen, and peeps into the tent in the hope of action. Finding none, she crawls into the sleeping bag to make sure, but all is empty. The boys crawl out from their shack, shaking off straw and yawning. The Beauty is diverted and heads off to be a piglet in a dust-bath just vacated by one of the fruitcakes. Giles clambers carefully over the electric fence.

'Did you see David, Mum? He's gone to look for a frying pan. What's he doing here anyway?'

David arrives back brandishing the pan and crouches to light the fire.

'I rounded up your pigs in the village last night and when I got here and saw you two looking so comfortable, I decided to join in.' He turns to me.

'Good morning, house dweller, will you join us for breakfast?'

No time for embarrassment as we try to consume bacon and marshmallows without the piglets finding out and becoming cannibals.

August 31st

Truly hideous day spent buying trainers, pants and socks for Giles and Felix in Norwich. Purchasing the stuff is bad enough, worse is the fact that I will have to sew name tapes onto it all. Must remember to write to school governors with my brilliant idea. Have long believed that all school uniform should be pooled. Each parent could pay a set amount at the beginning of their child's school career and that amount could pay for another set of clothes to go in the pool. With no name tapes and no ownership of items, there would be no lost property and no ghastly clothing list to upset mothers at the end of each holiday. It is all part of Utopian dream, like free bicycles in Cambridge, and just needs setting up to become a huge success.

Dawdle in the Games Workshop, mystic temple to Warhammer, and am forced to sit in corner while Giles is given a demonstration in painting the Blood Thirster by the whey-faced, black-clad shop assistant. Felix, a box of Dwarves in one hand and another of Boar Men in the other, is in a trance of indecision at the counter. Hope he chooses the cheapest ones, as his Warhammer collection spends much time scattered across his bedroom carpet and then in the Hoover bag waiting to be rescued, and so is not good value for him. Giles on the other hand has gone bigtime with his. The Blood Thirster is a hefty purchase. He has been saving up for it since the beginning of the holidays. Curious to see this object of desire, I get him to show me one in the shop. It does not look, as I had imagined, like an orange squeezer, but is a lump of moulded metal in the shape of the ghoul in Munch's *Scream* but with skeletons and sundry corpses dangling.

Wish my children would spend their pocket money on

something more wholesome, but am comforted a little by the thought that it could be worse. Charles is bringing out a line called Heavenly Pets, a range of plastic toys inspired by too many visits to McDonald's with his children. Preying upon susceptibility of small, grief-stricken owners, he plans to sell tiny take-home wind-up coffins with pet of your choice within, ready to pop out when wound up. Only discovered this atrocity when Felix finally unpacked his bag this morning. Charles had given him a prototype hamster coffin.

'Look, Daddy's going to sell these and I helped him decide what colour they should be.' The purple coffin, playing 'Merrily merrily merrily, life is but a dream' opens slowly to reveal an orange nylon blob, presumably the hamster, reclining on cushion-effect plastic bed. As the tune finishes, the blob levitates, hovers and flops back and the coffin closes again. Utterly repulsive and tasteless. Felix loves it. I send a postcard in complaint, and only notice as I am posting it that I have used the one of the mummified cat from the British Museum.

AUTUM

September 1st

Greatly looking forward to term-time and also to wearing jerseys again and lighting fires. Summer still lingers, though, and combine harvesters bumble through the last cornfields creating herringbone tweed patterns as they cut. Out for the evening and the road is a neat centre parting between smooth golden stubble. Dust and heat follow me down it on my way to have dinner, or rather 'kitchen supper', at the Sampsons. Zoom along with windows down, hair flying and the plangent twang of Deborah Allen on the tape machine. She gets to my current favourite song and up goes the volume. I sing along with gusto, especially when we reach the chorus to which I have learnt all the words and all the instrumental flurries. Tap the steering wheel and shriek 'Yeehah' a few times. Excellent stuff.

Vast copper beach trees around the Sampsons' lawn increase autumnal mood, their shadows long and inky across springy grass. Getting out of the car, am covered in goose pimples within seconds, having chosen to wear tiny lime-green and lemon-yellow sundress, purchased today from a market stall on impulse because it was so cheap.

It is made of nylon and causes me to leap with static whenever I touch anything. It is most unsuitable, and, worst of all, I am convinced it would look better on a fourteen-year-old.

Sir Nicholas is passionate about his lawns and employs a man full-time to roll them, mow them, pull dandelions out of them and water them. Passing the pool, I glimpse a hunched figure on all fours behind a wiggle of box hedging: it is Sir Nicholas, sent out by Hilary to find mint, and overcome by a desire to be at one with his sward. I wave and call a greeting.

'The grass here is wonderful, Sir Nicholas, mine has become a tundra now, so it's lovely to remember what grass is supposed to look like.'

He bounces up, 'Venetia, come through, my dear, how splendid to see you.'

He leads me in through a French window to the drawing room, where a handful of people are sipping tiny drinks from eggcup-sized glasses and trying to look relaxed. Hilary introduces me to the others, but not one of the names sinks into my head as I am crackling with static and embarrassment, both caused by my unsuitable dress. On top of the dress is fashionable boiled-wool shrunken cardigan. As an advance treat to myself for doing the name tapes, I persuaded Jenny the babysitter to sew puce ribbon around the edge of this cardigan last week and have been longing to try it out on an audience ever since. This audience is not appreciative.

'Dear me, it is so irritating when the daily shrinks one's clothes,' says a well-meaning middle-aged woman in a piecrust frill and pleated skirt, watching me fumble to do up a button on my cardigan in an attempt to hide as much of the silly dress as I can. She has a daughter at Giles's school, and she shows off about having bought and name-taped all her uniform at the beginning of the holidays.

Can think of nothing at all to say except, 'Oh.'

Kitchen supper is pretty fancy, and delicious. I dispose of my goat's cheese log in two mouthfuls and eat three pieces of bread while my neighbour prods his first course unenthusiastically. Having not listened to any introductions, I plunge in.

'Which is your wife?'

He looks baffled. 'Oh, I'm not married,' and then, as if it follows, 'I'm in the army.'

Of course, this is why I have been asked. Remember my mother telling me that Sir Nicholas was taking an interest in my single status and thought something should be done about it. Particularly thoughtful of him to provide an army man for me, like Charles but newer model. On my right, Sir Nicholas is busy with his other neighbour, the piecrust, and is not talking to me. The army man gives up pretending to eat the goat's cheese, and concentrates on the large amount of my thigh visible despite my primly spread napkin.

'What was your husband's rank and regiment?' he asks.

'I can't remember,' I reply, graceless but truthful. Am immediately ashamed. Of gracelessness. Now I will have to ask him about his rank and regiment to make up. He drones away and I fiddle with my ribbon and listen to Hilary's conversation with the splendid husband of piecrust. His hair is almost blue with snowiness, and he sports a beautiful tweed jacket and shoes polished until they gleam like walnut wood. He is judging the cattle classes at the local agricultural show. I would love to know about this, and cannot bear to miss the conversation, so apologise to army man.

'I hope you don't mind, I just need to know about cows.' He is very understanding.

'Of course, I do see. Why don't we swap places?'

Soon I am leaning in my plate, topping up my wine-glass and learning how to tell if a cow has championship potential or not. Arrive home late, determined to purchase a small bovine as soon as possible, preferably at the show tomorrow, and to keep it in the orchard and milk it in the manner of Marie Antoinette. Small green dress will become milkmaid outfit and will therefore be useful.

September 2nd

Almost negligible hangover in no way diminishes my enthusiasm for bovine purchase. Giles and Felix groan about it being the end of their holidays and wanting just to be at home, a line which I used to fall for but now recognise as euphemism for playing on the Gameboy and watching advertisements on television. It is raining as we depart for the agricultural show, and The Beauty is wild-eyed and dangerous with new teeth causing trouble. She throws all toys on the floor of the car and shouts fiercely all the way there, shattering my nerves. At the show, cannot bear the queue to enter, so deviously convince car-parking youths that we are members and drive straight to the main ring. Just as well, as downpour commences, to coincide with the Belgian Blue class. We watch from the warmth and comfort of the car, with the windscreen wipers on, as a slow procession of white cows with big blue ink spots and terrible shaven buttocks shuffle past us. Many of the bovines are creating cowpats as they go, and many others are walking through them, cloven hoofs squelching. Suddenly do not wish to own a cow.

'Mummy, look, his balls are massive.'

Felix is standing with his head out of the sunroof and is waving a large pink umbrella with 'Voo Doo Dolls' written on it. One of the Belgian Blues shies as he trudges past us.

'Felix, put it away,' I hiss, shamefaced to be found with such an accessory among the countless weather-proofed oilskins in assorted puddle and mud colours. The umbrella and Felix hurtle to the ground beside the car.

'It doesn't work as a parachute, Mum,' he tells me.

'So I see.' Two passing ponies shy and the judge in the ring breaks off from his inspection of a bulging blue backside to glare at us. 'Let's go and look around,' I suggest, and am deaf to pleas for ice cream as we stagger to the dog ring, The Beauty's pushchair becoming a snowplough in effect as it gathers clods of mud and straw in its wheels. These no longer turn, and I am eventually forced to drag the buggy, with The Beauty moaning piteously and struggling to escape. In the dog ring, a low-slung collie is whisking and skulking around a small herd of white ducks shaped like folded umbrellas. A jovial commentator booms away and the crowd titters and claps. The Beauty pulls her socks off and hurls them over the rope and into the ring, in the manner of a medieval damsel bestowing her colours on a favoured knight. The ducks waddle up some steps and down a slide. Ice cream beckons.

September 3rd

Haircuts. Jenny the babysitter's mother Enid is a travelling hairdresser. She zooms up to the house in a convertible Morris Minor with pulsing music issuing from her car stereo, and impresses Giles and Felix hugely. Sensing a kindred spirit, Giles brings his radio into the kitchen where the haircuts are to take place.

'Do you like this?' The volume is increased and I abandon the kitchen, leaving The Beauty standing on the table bobbing up and down in time to the music and holding hands with Felix, while Giles and Enid sing along to a very fast rap song. Spend very enjoyable half-hour with hose, using high pressure to zap the wheels of The Beauty's pushchair and remove the huge cakes of mud, straw and cowpats collected at the show. Scrub away, employing toothbrush for awkward bits, and experience great calm and happiness in completing the task and in having lovely shining pushchair to hurl back into the car with all the spilt earth, inexplicable gravel, sacks of hen food and crunched crisps that live there. Return to the kitchen to find two sons with terrible shorn patches of felt like Action Man instead of hair.

'We've had number twos,' Felix shouts, 'and The Beauty's going to have hers done now.'

Enid, clearly a fanatic, has strapped The Beauty into the high chair and wrapped her in a red towel. Only her head is visible. She pats her hair and beams at Enid, ready to lose her jaunty topknot, which is bound by a scarlet velvet bow and is especially fetching today. Enid's broad pink rear sways rhythmically behind the high chair, keeping rapid time with the music as she combs and dances, her scissors snapping and chattering in anticipation about The Beauty's head.

'No, don't!' I scream above the music, and The Beauty bursts into sobs. 'Turn that bloody noise off.'

Cannot believe that Giles and Felix can look this ghastly, and scarcely recognise them. The Beauty is furious to miss out, and writhes in my arms, as, shaking with rage, I pay Enid ten pounds for having turned my sons into aliens. She leaves, and I return to the kitchen from seeing her off, preparing to counsel the boys gently and supportively through the first glimpse of themselves in the mirror. No need. They have turned up the music even louder, and have got the mirror out of my make-up bag and are taking it in turns to stare admiringly at themselves in the tiny glass.

'This is the coolest haircut we've had in ages,' says Giles, reaching to run his palm over Felix's scalp. I clutch The Beauty tightly and swallow to stop myself weeping. They are thrilled; I must be supportive. I must be positive. It will be easy to deal with nits. Thank God there is no need to photograph them for some time.

September 5th

The Beauty and I are making the most of a balmy, late summer evening by cleaning out the greenhouse, and Giles and Felix have gone to the final cricket session in the village. Have found plangent country song on Radio Two and am singing along loudly and inaccurately as it is not one I know, but one I wish I knew. The Beauty is dressed for gardening in her first pair of wellingtons, green and glittery and found by my mother at a jumble sale last week. She is also wearing a crocheted cyclamen-pink and royal-blue dress sent by Lila who purchased it on a trip to the West Indies, and looks utterly eccentric. I must encourage self-expression, though, and let her look like a mini bag lady if she chooses to. Have given her some potting compost and a trowel, and she is making mud pies and eating them. I assume that Fisons peat compost is perfectly healthy and leave her to it, while I repot an exhausted pelargonium and take cuttings. Musk and lemon scent from the leaves create a feel-good aroma and the sky blazes pink and orange as the sun sets. Am at one with serenity and joy. Neil Diamond's song 'I Am' is next on the radio and I join in. Suddenly, though, pleasure evaporates as Digger trots past the greenhouse with a chicken in his mouth. Not a feathered one, an oven-ready one. The chicken I had defrosted for supper.

Erupt from the greenhouse screeching, 'Why is that bastard dog here? Rags must be on heat. She's always on heat. Sodding hell! Where is David?' Digger has vanished, leaving the chicken upside down and very naked in the newly turned border. Pick it up muttering and march round house to the front where I can hear Giles and Felix, and, I hope, David. There they all are, playing cricket and laughing, enjoying their own reverie without interruptions from scavenging bastard dogs.

'Why do you have to bring that creep with you?'

David, Giles and Felix all assume expressions of hurt astonishment, and glance at one another wondering which of them is the creep in question.

'Mum, David can stay to supper, can't he?' Giles ignores my stamping fury and tosses me the ball in his hands. Of course I miss it, even though I instinctively drop the chicken to be prepared to catch it.

'Yes, and he can bloody well cook it.' Pick up the chicken and hurl it at David, irritation rising even higher when he catches it easily. Giles is rolling on the grass giggling. Felix frowns.

'Mum, why have you brought the chicken outside?'

I retreat, slamming the door into the house, and take The Beauty up for a soothing bath.

September 6th

Last dregs of the holidays arrive not a moment too soon. After ten weeks Felix and Giles are as delighted as I am by the prospect of school, both having been supplied with huge quantities of new clothing and gumshields, and being keen to replace a nagging mother with enthusiastic and understanding friends. The gumshields are a particular triumph, and have been worn non-stop since we collected them from the dentist, making my formerly attractive children look like a pair of Neanderthals, particularly when combined with the new felt-head haircuts. I hate the gumshields especially because they represent a total outlay of almost one hundred pounds, which is three-quarters of a cashmere cardigan. The Beauty loves them, and has made one of her own with a wedge of apple, which she clamps between pursed lips, before grimacing fiercely and blowing the fruit hard across the room. Her manners are becoming atrocious, and she has learnt a lot from watching *The Simpsons* with her brothers. This she does with gusto, plumping herself on the armchair next to the television, biscuit in one hand, beaker in the other, sitting up straight and bouncing excitedly as the credits roll. Whenever Bart Simpson farts or does anything remotely ill-mannered, she cackles and claps, making sure that the boys are sharing the joke too. In the kitchen, or indeed a supermarket or other shop, she shouts a crescendo of 'Oh! OH! OHH!' when she wants something, and grabs my skin in a pinch-and-twist torture movement if thwarted. Am covered in scabs and gouges from my dealings with her, and wish she could go to school with her brothers on Tuesday, too.

September 7th

The last day features a medley of favourite treats, with a brief and painless moment at the dentist for The Beauty thrown in. This happens straight after breakfast and is her first time in the chair. She takes to it well, hurling herself back several times before taking up a relaxed position perched on the arm. She bops Mr Jensen on the nose with her purple plastic sunglasses and stands up to caper about as piped music fills the surgery. Mr Jensen hovers over her head for about thirty seconds, making tentative dabs with his lollipop mirror and wooden ice-cream stick.

'Lovely teeth,' he says, tugging at the stick which she has clamped between them. 'Don't be in too much of a hurry to bring her back. A year is fine.'

We troop out. Felix manages not to say, 'Can we have some sweets?' until we are on the pavement outside.

Crab-fishing is next on our list, time-honoured

end-of-summer ritual and another first for The Beauty. She is not an asset, and has to be trapped in her pushchair, where she roars in red-faced rage. Turn her to face the sea lavender and the clanking wind-chime masts of moored boats, and she instantly falls asleep.

'Mum, Mum, there's no bacon. Where's the bacon? Did you bring it?' Of course I didn't. We are four miles from any shop, with the sea on three sides of us and a silver-veined grid of creeks and mud on the other. Very soon our crab dyke will vanish with the tide. Felix bursts into tears and I curse my constant fallibility as a mother, and general hopelessness as a human being. Saved by Giles, who produces bacon from his pocket in repulsive, slimy plastic bag.

'I thought I'd better be in charge of this; Mum always forgets to bring the bacon,' he says with a smirk. Must stop comparing him to Charles, although I suppose it's not harmful so long as the comparison remains in Giles's favour. Sit on the bank of the creek untangling orange-handled crab lines and cheering as the boys fill their bucket with snapping, glaucous crustaceans. By the time the tide turns, there are enough crabs for a Grand National race. Giles draws the starting line, scoring the black mud with the handle of his net, and Felix follows him, dropping the runners well back so they can set off at speed. The Beauty wakes just in time and her throne is turned to face the track. In an instant they are off, sixteen crabs and one inert anemone scuttling sideways back towards the creek.

'How come they always go the right way?' asks Felix. 'Can they see the sea or do they smell it?'

'It's primeval because crabs are really old,' Giles explains kindly, and I nod enthusiastically, delighted not to be taxing my brain.

Le Moon in Cromer for eating Chinese food with chopsticks is next, and requires a complete change of clothing for all of us. This is effected on the street outside the hideous breeze-block edifice which houses the boys' favourite restaurant. Felix presses his nose to the steamed-up window, savouring the prospect of being inside.

'Hooray, there's no one else there. Look at the aquariums, Mum, I wish our house could be more like Le Moon. I want silver and red wallpaper like that in my room.'

He has a point; it would be great to have a room like Le Moon, with vast paper lanterns and gold and red tasselled lamps and huge clean aquariums with bubbling water and frisky fish, rather than our tiny, miserable tank where Pesce the fairground fish gapes at a bare wall through murky brown water. Make mental note to track wallpaper down, from God knows where.

We enter and are straight away seated beneath a three-dimensional gold-framed painting of a swan on water, and automatically begin cramming prawn crackers into our mouths where they stick to our tongues. The Beauty becomes high on monosodium glutamate and creates a fun game piling pancakes on her head. Have noticed that she has recently taken to Hair Protests. Anything wet or sticky, crumby or flaky is rubbed into her scalp, accompanied by a manic smile. Chastisement, or even the most gentle suggestion, is met with a defiant lift of the chin and increased dollopings onto the hair. Muse about The Beauty's problem-child behaviour for a while and resolve nothing. Hair protest is better than dirty protest and, anyway, I am powerless to stop her. I have no control.

September 10th

Joy. Peace. Calm. A whole afternoon of silence. My mother has taken The Beauty as her companion to a wine and sausage-roll party she has been forced to attend by The Gnome.

'It's to raise money for a hostel for artists,' she groans. 'I'm only going because I hope it will be built soon so that The Gnome can go and live there instead of in my garden.'

Her new autumn look is formidable, and includes a cone-shaped fur hat given to her by a Russian sculptor who came to stay with her and with whom she consumed two bottles of vodka in one fourteen-hour session. She had to wear dark glasses for a week afterwards, and has only just removed them today. The Beauty and she swoop away like a pair of Tsarinas in their chariot, both now wearing hats, The Beauty having donned a damson velvet beret with turquoise beadwork. I wave them off, and struggle to stop myself curtseying and throwing rose petals.

The hours loom drearily. A corporate hospitality brochure awaits, my brief being to turn it into readable English. I can't bring myself to read it, and instead plunge into my file of autumn plant catalogues. Order a dozen roses, including one called Spanking Prudence, a hideous cake-pink standard tea which I shall give to Gawain because his last girlfriend was called Prudence. The new postman turns up, four hours late and swerving much too fast up the drive. Can't see what the rush is for, as all he has brought are two *Reader's Digest* envelopes emblazoned with lies about vast sums of money I have almost won.

Work crawls, brain is like a very stale loaf of bread, crumbling, bone-dry and non-receptive. Finally decide to relax officially for a few moments, and lie down under my desk, with no pillow or rug so I don't give an impression of slacking. Extreme discomfort does not prevent me from nodding off, and am woken by crunching of gravel and the arrival of the organic vegetable delivery. A further, and legitimate, respite from work, hooray. Dash out to assist in carrying box of goodies to larder and am drawn into conversation with Mrs Veg about gassing bananas. Am aghast when she shows me picture of piteous bananas suffocating in poisonous blue polythene and limply dangling from trees. Tomatoes also apparently wretchedly treated. Offer to join support group, but am secretly relieved when Mrs Veg says there isn't one. Wave her off and return to house, reflecting on ghastly banana situation and also on own increasing dependence on people who arrive in vans to deliver things. Even quite fancied the new postman when he finally arrived. Return to work, and try to muster enthusiasm and extended vocabulary to describe the Van Den Plas suite of Organza Delaney's conference centre.

Must have nodded off again, as am suddenly jolted awake by plaintive gulping noise of my computer asking me if I want to save what I have done. Have only written four words, but save them all the same. Searching brain's hidden depths for a fifth word to add to my total when I notice a tiny Silvanian-style mouse gliding about on my zebra-skin rug. Teetering on mini-twig legs, it heads off towards the hall. Follow it, heart palpitating, convinced that if I lose sight of it for a second it will instantly conceive and bring forth a multitude of baby mice. Or, more likely, Sidney will get it.

Stalk it, and effect brilliant mouse coup outside the

downstairs loo. Am tiptoeing speedily towards the back door with the poor, sweetie-pie mouse cupped in my palm when needle-sharp pain jabs my hand. Shriek 'Ow,' and drop vile little brute on hall floor. It has drawn blood. Dare not lick it off in case wound is contaminated with mouse spit. Have probably been poisoned. Do mice have rabies? Can't remember having read about it, but have read about them having hepatitis; or was that monkeys? In an instant, a sensation of warm lunacy is coursing through my body. The mouse uses the opportunity to vanish into the kitchen where it will doubtless meet and marry its dream lover at any moment. Can't worry about that, though, as am convinced that I have Weil's disease and will die in a few seconds. Remain rooted in hall, observing minutest changes in mind and body. Feel as if tripping, and experience faintness, dizziness and heavy breathing. Limbs now leaden. Have to harness every ounce of courage to take my socks off and look to see if my feet are beginning to go black. Impossible to tell due to Blackcurrant Dream polish on each toenail. Hyperventilation averted by David's arrival.

'What are you doing?'

Tears spring to my eyes and trickle down face. Am not sure why, but cannot stop crying. David leads me into the kitchen, guides me to a chair and sits holding my uninjured hand.

'What's happened, Venetia? Are you all right?'

Weeping now unbridled, and nose begins to drip as well. Have to get a hanky, and find that standing up improves the situation enough for a tragic utterance.

'The mouse bit me.'

'What mouse?'

I point quavering finger towards the corner of the room most likely to be a rodent hideout: 'That one.'

On cue, mini-mouse totters out from under the sink and pauses by a chair to take stock. It is roughly the size of a sugar lump. David calmly places a jam jar over it and a postcard beneath it and removes my arch-enemy without fuss or violence. Having found a bottle of rescue remedy in the cupboard, I am using the drop dispenser as a kind of straw, and am swallowing every last hint of delicious brandy-flavoured flower juice when he comes back in.

'How about a proper drink?' he says, surveying my red nose and wobbling lip. A splendid idea. I nod eagerly and am poised for a marathon drinking session to start when I suddenly notice the clock.

'Oh, bugger, I can't. It's time to go and collect the boys. Some other time, David, thanks.'

Must still be suffering from slight mouse shock, as when he says, 'Are you all right to drive, or would you like me to take you?' I jump at the chance of being a passenger for once.

Felix is waiting by the gate, socks collapsing around

his ankles, knees grass-stained and decorated with several plasters. He waves and jumps about when David's clattering old Land Rover ambulance grunts into the school car park, and races to greet us.

'Hi, Mum, why did David come? Can I sit in the front?'

There is in fact nowhere but the front to sit, as the back half of the ambulance does not even have its canvas hood on today, but is heaped with wooden planks and evil-looking saws. Giles is less pleased when we roar through the gates to his part of the school. Hands in pockets, face expressionless, he slowly extracts himself from a group of boys kicking a mini rugby ball and lunges over to us.

'Where's our car, Mum?' He ignores David's cheerful greeting, and Felix's, and slumps back next to me, closing his eyes and muttering, 'And I bet you haven't brought anything for us to eat, have you?'

Am mortified by his behaviour, and furious.

'Giles, how can you be so graceless? You're jolly lucky to be collected from school at all. Maybe we'll just leave you there tomorrow—'

Pulled up short by glancing down at him to find that he is rubbing his knuckles in his eyes and holding back tears. Am transported to the agonies of my own schooldays, the wrongness of my parents' car, the wrongness of the parents themselves, and the knockout hunger and exhaustion experienced at the end of a long day. Hand him a packet of biscuits Providence has placed on the dashboard, and put my arm around him.

September 11th

I have a vile cold, and it is spoiling what should be a carefree day with The Beauty now that the corporate brochure is safely faxed to the publisher. Throat red and prickly, eyes ditto and am experiencing non-specific pain, gloom and self-pity. Hope it is not delayed Weil's disease. Have consumed three Lemsips, two hot toddies, each with at least two inches of whisky, and six spoonfuls of cough mixture and it is still not lunchtime. The Beauty rises from her morning sleep much refreshed, and I follow her around the house for a while, blowing my nose every thirty seconds and putting on another jersey each time we pass one of the piles of clothing which are dotted about the hall and landing.

'Bouffe,' squeals The Beauty, body-surfing through a heap of vests and socks at the top of the stairs. Felix was her dresser this morning, and his choice of flouncy skirt, hairgrip and his own old Aertex shirt give her a very adorable St Trinian's look. The Beauty is on riotous form, and pays scant heed to me, coughing and sneezing on the top stair. She has engineered that her pram shall be upstairs, and is a tank commander, driving it through every obstacle, crashing against walls and door frames as she pursues her aim of world domination, starting with my bedroom. I lie on my bed groaning and overflowing with self-pity until a slender-heeled and mud-caked shoe hits me in the midriff.

'Oooh,' The Beauty cries, poised with its pair for another grenade attack.

'Ow, you little monster.' Rage hardens me against her instant sobs and I march out of the room with her under my arm, determined at last to put the washing away. Trap her in the empty bath, where she immediately cheers up and starts pretending to wash her hair.

I trudge about, becoming increasingly bowed beneath vast piles of clean laundry, and wishing my life was less pedestrian and more like Rose's, when inspiration suddenly strikes. What I need is a laundry room, of the sort generally found in the nether regions of stately homes. Start hurling washing onto the spare-room bed and quickly use up my piles. Make a dash through all the upstairs rooms looking for more clothes to add. The spare-room bed will act as a giant clothes holding station for all of us. No more boring folding and putting away of garments; I shall simply chuck them onto the heap and send Felix, Giles and The Beauty in to select their outfits when necessary. We will all dress and undress in the holding station, and dirty laundry will vanish into the bedroom's en suite loo until I can be bothered to take it down to the washing machine.

September 14th

Spend the morning harvesting lavender with The Beauty hovering at a distance with her wheelbarrow and some sand. She has found a pair of gardening gloves, and has huge fun dipping them in a puddle and then cuddling them. God knows what she thinks they are, amphibious dolls, perhaps? Bees drone about nearby, the sun shines and the heady, feel-good scent of lavender fills the air and I am sure begins to work its magic on my cold. Leave lavender in a heap in the hall until can think of something to do with it. Lavender bread, perhaps? Or lavender bags. Could become upstanding member of the WI with schemes such as these. Linger outside, admiring nature. Someone has lit a bonfire nearby, and gusts of smoke scent puff across the garden and through the lavender, until even the lawn and the trees are grey and softened.

September 17th

Am proud of our pig husbandry. We have had the piglets almost a month now, and they are a credit to us. They simply get on with life, rootling and grunting, scratching or snoozing under their garage-door roof. One of the fruitcakes has made a good wallow next to the water trough and is lying in it, a neat tidemark making him look as if he has been dipped in dirty cream.

Leave them and saunter up to the orchard with The Beauty to pick some windfalls. We count the apples into the bucket and The Beauty throws them out again, guffawing and seeking applause. The garden is suffused with a rich, damp earth smell, and the golden afternoon light sparkles through wet leaves and petals until the borders are wreathed in precious jewels. One or two horse mushrooms gleam in the grass, and squatting over them in admiration The Beauty is a Teletubby lookalike in her purple dungarees with her paintbrush topknot. All is blissful.

I take a deep breath and begin to panic. Am suddenly assailed by dreadful cabin fever. I have not spoken to a human being over five feet tall and ten years old for four days. My cultural references are down to one toddler's TV programme, I haven't read a book or seen a film for months. I can only cook fish fingers and macaroni cheese and have forgotten what grown-ups eat, let alone how you cook it. All my clothes have holes in them, all my shoes are covered in mud and many are no longer pairs, having been requisitioned by The Beauty for dressing up in. A glance at the mirror in the downstairs loo reveals terrible wire-wool hair in need of much expensive attention. Remember that I have not dared open the sunroof in the car for weeks now in case I accidentally catch sight of my grizzled locks. I must go to London and improve myself. Immediately.

Fate has placed a glossy magazine next to the telephone. I open it at the beauty pages, among which I remember seeing an article about a new hairdresser in a very expensive shopping street. Moments later I have booked myself into the Concept Salon, where my hair will be serviced and I will also be massaged and generally mollycoddled. What heaven. I ring Rose to share the great news and she is delighted.

'I've been longing to go there. You are clever to have organised it. I'll come and meet you afterwards, then we can go and buy things.'

Can't wait for this day of girlie hedonism.

September, 19th

Any residual guilt feelings at the amounts of money I hope to spend on my outing with Rose vanish when I receive a telephone call from Mo Loam's Temple of

Beauty, where I have had an appointment for an overhaul since practically the dawn of time. The High Priestess has apparently fallen off her pedestal and broken her collarbone, so no beauty magic will be dispensed until after Christmas.

'Don't say that horrible word,' I shriek at the assistant priestess who rings, 'I can't think about Christmas now.'

Although I had utterly forgotten my assignation with La Loam and would have missed the appointment anyway, as I have not written it down anywhere, I am still furious not to have it to look forward to.

'We'll book you in for February 12th then,' purrs sub-priestess, ignoring my whingeing with regal serenity. 'Do please now give me your credit card number so I can take a deposit. It's thirty-five pounds, and is redeemable against Loam products.'

Am so gobsmacked that I do exactly as she tells me, and afterwards find a tiny crumb of satisfaction in having accidentally paid for it from Charles's account in my confusion.

September 23rd

Have cleverly timed trip to London to coincide with Gawain's preview party. Cleverness is accidental, as I had most unfortunately used my invitation to the show to splatter a superwasp on the kitchen window sill and was forced to throw it away weeks ago, but Rose has the date etched on her soul and is determined to take me there in new clothes.

Read the beginning of *Frederica* by G. Heyer, and the whole of *Hello!* on the train, revelling in the atmosphere of serenity in my carriage, where there are only five passengers, all reading, all drinking coffee. Escaping to London during term-time, leaving my mother and Egor holding the fort, is a rest cure in itself, and hysteria ebbs as the train thunders away from home and the school run towards shops, hairdressers and cinemas. Am, of course, very keen to do culture as well as retail therapy, and have even made a plan to meet Lila at the Royal Academy tomorrow. Make a list of everything I want to buy as the train pulls into London and realise that I will have to marry a millionaire or win the lottery in the next twenty minutes if I am to achieve even a fifth of the desired purchases.

The Concept Salon is terrifying. I enter through a mirrored door, deliberately not looking at myself, and am suddenly in a vast white room like a photographic studio or an operating theatre. Everything is white: the floor, the chairs, the frames round the huge mirrors, even the brooms wielded by the juniors. My dress, forties floral crêpe, with a tiny hole under one arm, which looked utterly chic and bohemian when I left home, now feels like an item from a jumble sale. Which, of course, it is. Jude, my hair technician, approaches, as if from the future, his white-blond hair sleeked back to touch the collar of his silver neoprene bodysuit. He is chillingly beautiful. I wish I had worn my wetsuit, and succumb to his ministrations.

Rose does not recognise me when she enters the café we have arranged to meet in. I watch her scan the room, missing me because I am the eiptome of blissed-out cool after a head massage, a manicure and a complete hair overhaul. Have purchased a red wool jacket to hide my bag-lady dress, and with new highlighted, sleek fair hair I feel as groomed as a Hitchcock blonde. Raise a sultry eyebrow at Rose and she shrieks and rushes over.

'My God, you look amazing. How did they do that? It's fantastic. I can't believe it.'

Am torn between delight at how impressed she is and irritation at how surprised she is.

'I asked him to make me look like him, and he said he couldn't but he'd do the next best thing. I don't think he even realised how vain he sounded.' Rose and I giggle hysterically, and are too overexcited to drink our cinnamon-flavoured coffee. We depart and plunge into a wild afternoon of extravagance. Am astonished at how quickly I adapt from rustic hayseed to town-bronzed sophisti-cat; wielding my credit card like a machete in the urban jungle, I am soon forging ahead in the smart-bag count. The final purchase is the most fraught and the most rewarding, in a shop where the assistant looks at me as if I am Sidney the cat walking in with a decapitated rabbit in my jaws. She stalks up and sticks her nose in my ear as I examine a rail of clothes.

'Can I help you?'

Determined not to be intimidated, I turn on my heel and walk across to the changing room, grabbing the nearest garment.

'I'll try this,' I say languidly, and shut myself in the cubicle.

I have brought in a fluid, strappy ink-blue dress. Size ten. Completely unsuitable for me, being the wrong size and totally impractical. It also costs more than a washing machine. There is no way I can have it. What the hell, I may as well try it on. It slides onto my body and hangs from my shoulders, a vision of chic slenderness, a caress of wondrous fabric. I love it with all my heart, mostly because it is size ten, but also because it is truly heaven. I must have it. I must. In a fever of adrenalin I dress myself and rush to the cash till brandishing my credit card. The girl slides the card through the machine and stands surveying her perfect nails while the machine grunts and sighs. Affecting disdain, I too survey my nails and try to control my panting breaths. Am sure something will prevent me from having this scrap of pleasure, this tiny size-ten indulgence. Sure enough, Perfect Nails is calling for assistance.

'Your card has been declined. Do you have any other means of paying?' The paper bag with my dress inside it is on the counter between us. She taps her fingers on it possessively. I try to look nonchalant again.

'Oh dear, what a bore, I can't think why that's happened. There's plenty of money in my account. Masses, in fact,' I lie, beginning to perspire in my red wool jacket. 'Can I write a cheque?'

The girl arches her perfect brows. 'Not if this is your cheque card,' she says softly, her tone especially designed to make me feel like a Category A criminal. Am now close to tears and cannot think what to do. Fumble for a tissue as my nose begins to drip. Can't find one. Use the back of my hand.

'What's the matter, Venetia? Why are you taking so long?' Had utterly forgotten Rose's existence from the moment she popped out to the chemist until now, when she has popped back in looking alarmed. Salvation. Explain my crimes to her and stand at her elbow watching with ill-suppressed delight as she flings her card at the assistant.

'Here, I'll do it. You can write me a cheque, Venetia.' Could swear that Perfect Nails is disappointed; she would rather lose her commission than see me walk out with the dress.

'Let's go and drink cocktails and look at everything,' says Rose, and I hurry after her through the streets and into a bar, rejoicing that it is six in the evening and I have no childcare ahead of me. No bathtime, no de-nitting, no evening of ironing. I can drink Americanos in smart hotels until dawn if I like. I do like; so does Rose.

September 24th

Thumping hangover not improved by the arrival of Theo at my bedside at seven in the morning. He is clutching a book, a pair of red wellingtons and a plastic train.

'Thomas the Tanker. You read it and take me for a walk,' he urges. 'Come on. I say you read it.'

Groan and turn over. 'Go and find Daddy, Theo, he'll read it, he didn't get drunk last night.'

'You're a silly old lush,' says the tiny tormentor before departing. Am rather impressed by his vocabulary and repeat his words to Rose when we meet some time later in the kitchen. She rolls her eyes.

'He copies everything. He heard Tristan saying it to me because I couldn't get up this morning.'

A morning at the Royal Academy with Lila prancing about in ballet pumps and a black polo neck as if she is Audrey Hepburn does nothing for the hangover, but an afternoon at Rose's health club sees it off. Am able to approach Gawain's party with poise and courage thanks to the hour spent sweating out poisons in a seaweed wrap. New dress and new hair give the final boost, and I arrive at the gallery with Rose and Tristan, my heart thumping in excited anticipation at the thought of the ravishing, prizewinning portrait of me.

The show is in a room much less intimidating than the Concept hairdressers', more like a big sitting room and painted the colour of wet sand. I see Gawain at the other side and begin to thread confidently between throngs of guests to greet him. Feel as if I do this all the time, and, more importantly, am sure I look as if I was born to go to cocktail parties. Hooray, am ready for a top-notch evening, and will flirt with everyone. Huge fun. A shadow looms, quite literally, and Charles appears in my path, blocking my view of everything except his ghastly sidekick. Helena bobs and titters like a small tugboat at his elbow.

'Charles. How weird to see you here.'

'Not as weird as seeing yourself will be,' he smirks, 'look at this.'

He takes my arm and steps to one side. And I am met, face to face, by myself. Experience shivering breathlessness, as if iced water has been poured down my back. Cannot stop staring at the haunted, horrible version of myself. Me as I do not like to think of me, with bags under the eyes and a too-small shirt with buttons missing gaping pinkly over my stomach. Me with sadness in my eyes and a sunburnt nose. Me with lank strands of hair hanging around a tired, lonely face.

'It's a marvellous piece of *veritas*,' says Helena, her beady eyes fixed on me, drinking in my horrified reaction.

'God, it's depressing,' is all I can say. I grab a glass of wine from a passing tray and gulp it in one.

'Darling, beautiful Venetia. I'm so glad you came.' Warm hands are on my back replacing iced water sensation, and I am engulfed by Gawain hugging me, kissing my shoulder and grinning delightedly. 'There's a photographer here who wants to take a picture of you with your portrait for the *Standard*. Come and meet Vernon, the gallery owner, and the sponsors. In fact, come and meet everyone. You look gorgeous. It's great to see you.'

And Gawain sweeps me off, away from Charles and hateful Helena, and over to an important-looking table where there is champagne instead of the usual gallery white wine, and flashbulbs are popping like balloons at a children's party. Immediately become overexcited. All this attention is astonishing, and compares favourably with an evening at home doing the ironing. I try this line on one or two people who look at me with mild distaste as though I have mentioned haemorrhoids or boils or some other defect. Decide to pretend from now on that I lead an exotic life and am usually sinning on tiger skins in the manner of Elinor Glyn and wearing silk camiknickers. Try out this version on a Young British Artist friend of Gawain's; he scuttles away in terror. It is perhaps best not to admit to any form of existence beyond the here and now.

Events speed up. People, compliments and glasses of champagne whirl like a carousel until it is late, the lights are low and I am dancing in a nightclub with Gawain. Don McLean is singing 'American Pie'. Rose and Tristan are arguing by the bar. I have no husband to argue with and therefore not a care in the world. I lean on Gawain and close my eyes. Surely there can be no better sensation than that of having someone's arms around you? Particularly someone as handsome as Gawain. Can't believe that I've never noticed this before. Handsome and talented. Why did I never take him up on all those propositions he has put to me through the years? 'Gawain Temple is a genius, and this is the picture which shows it', was the headline in today's newspaper preview. Lucky I didn't see it before the show or I would never have come. Loved the party, though, after Charles and the poison dwarf had gone, and spent much of it nodding and trying to appear artistically worthy. All very intoxicating. Just as well I am catching the nine-thirty train tomorrow morning and can't join Gawain and his friends for a party on a houseboat at lunchtime.

Drift off to sleep in the indigo darkness of Rose's super-minimalist study-cum-spare room, conjuring an image of myself as a Tess of the D'Urbervilles type, tending the fruitcakes and their piglet siblings with my rosy-cheeked children all wearing cheesecloth blouses and breeches. Gawain can be Angel. Can't remember his role, so have to change the plot to Georgette Heyer. Fall asleep while deciding which Regency hero he could possibly resemble.

September 28th

Back in the school run rut, a million miles from my life as a glamorous artist's model, I seem to be no closer to Tess or Georgette Heyer either. Terribly stormy weather means we are all wearing cagoules and wellingtons rather than cheesecloth, and the piglets have become malevolent; a pink bit me yesterday morning when I attempted to give it an apple. The Beauty and Felix are both festering with my vile cold and are now at the streaming-snot and raised-temperature stage. Giles has no symptoms, so he and I rise at dawn to prepare for school. Rather wish he was ill too so that I wouldn't have to bother. I have the light-headed, carefree sense of not having been to bed, which I know will later turn into wrung-out-rag fatigue, caused by a night of pouring Calpol and cough mixture into alternate children, with a few minutes of sleep between each pharmaceutical call. The bathroom mirror confirms that all the benefits of two nights in London and the squandering of a fortune on my appearance are now as dust, and I have developed a tic in my left eye which I fear is permanent. Irritation rises while in the bathroom because David has still not mended the dripping cold tap and I know nothing of washers. Will ask Giles to find out how at school. In Home Economics. Bundle the ill people into the car in their pyjamas, and pass Giles a small surgical mask.

'Here, put this on so you don't inhale the germs from those two.'

Giles stares at me in horror. 'No way, Mum, I hate masks. I won't catch their germs, I'm in the front. Why do you keep winking like that? It makes you look evil.'

Cannot believe his intransigence. He should be deeply impressed at my foresight and top-class parenting. He should not mention my tic.

'Please wear it, Giles. I've got one too, I'll wear mine if you wear yours.' I put it on and mumble, 'See, it's fine.'

He is flattening himself against his door now, cringing away from me, only partly as a joke.

'Mum, you're crazy. You can't drive around with a mask on. And your eye winking. You'll be arrested.'

Felix interrupts from the back seat.

'Mum, Mum, you've got to wipe The Beauty's nose. It's like toffee, it's really gross.'

Turn around to look with the mask on and both The Beauty and Felix burst into tears.

A day for the gas oven, but I do not have one. Instead put my head in the Aga to retrieve a baked potato at lunchtime, and manage to burn my forehead on the door. Leap away immediately but ghastly scrunching, singeing noise suggests that damage has been done. Back to the mirror, where worst fears are confirmed. I now have a sore like a streak of strawberry jam across my temple, too big to hide with hair. The baked potatoes are also burnt. No lunch. The ill ones choose this moment to trail into the kitchen in their pyjamas, both clutching teddies, both with white faces and purple smudges beneath their eyes. They range themselves in front of the Aga and deliver a monstrous array of coughs, one after the other. Sidney, perhaps in sympathy, goes into a paroxysm himself under the kitchen table and regurgitates a skinless shrew at my feet. I need help. I send an SOS message to my mother forthwith.

September 29th

She arrives, twenty-four hours later, in her wellingtons and appears to have become twice her usual size due to her costume of yellow rubber fisherman's jacket. Felix and The Beauty are still coughing and corridor-creeping at night, and I am a zombie, beyond gas ovens.

'I've been bailing out the pub,' she announces. 'They lent me this coat.'

Scrutinise her closely, but can detect no signs of red wine or other beverages. Mystifying.

'Why aren't you drunk, then?'

She draws herself up to express innocence outraged, and looks down her nose at me.

'That is not my way,' she says piously. 'The pub was flooded and we had to form a human chain with buckets to empty it and then pile sandbags in the doorways. I'm worn out, and when I got home, I found that that fool Desmond had left the bath running while he went to answer the telephone, so the ceiling below has fallen in. I left him dealing with it, and I've come to stay until he has mended it.'

Divested of her coat, she is back to her usual proportions except that she has a hot-water bottle tucked into her skirt. Decide not to mention it, as she may feel I am being critical.

Felix is delighted to see her. 'Hooray, Granny's here,'

he shouts, and The Beauty runs and buries her face in her skirt, murmuring, 'Granneee, Granneee.'

Granny is astonished by the strength of their feeling. 'Have you been torturing them or something?' She looks more closely at me. 'Goodness, perhaps you're the one being tortured. What happened to your head?'

Depart to collect Giles, early for once to avoid explaining, and purchase two bottles of red wine as bribes to prevent her changing her mind and going home. Listen to Willie Nelson on the way to school and brood on my inability to lead a grown-up life without prop of mother to keep me going. Should I by now be standing on my own two feet, or does divorced status confer special privileges usually reserved for the sick?

Catapulted into grown-up level of hysteria upon reaching home again. Charles has telephoned in my absence to say I am needed at a very urgent meeting of the directors and shareholders of Heavenly Petting on Thursday, and can he please cancel having the children next weekend as Helena is worn out so they're going to Barcelona. My mother prowls back and forth in front of the Aga, and delivers this message with a snarl. We put the children in the playroom with a video of *Some Like It Hot* in order to have a therapeutic anti-Charles session in peace. Both bottles of red wine are consumed as we rant and fantasise. Charles will be humiliated, his constant dipping into capital for holidays, new golf clubs and cars will be revealed and he will be made to apologise. I wish.

September 30th

Have evicted three superwasps from Giles's bedroom this evening and have painted my toenails water-lily-leaf green. Fire lit, hair washed, mother returned to her own home, Aga burn healing. Have borrowed Giles's school briefcase for the meeting, but have not yet thought of anything proper to put in it. Giles suggested tuck, so it contains a Penguin biscuit and a carrot so far. Might put my book in as well, as I'm sure I won't finish *Frederica* tonight, and am immersed. It is an especially fine example of Georgette Heyer's ease with the mayhem of Regency family life. I am poised and businesslike and ready for Heavenly Petting tomorrow.

October 1st

Leave for Cambridge after dropping The Beauty at Jenny's house and Felix and Giles at school. Had to shove breakfast into them all at arm's length while keeping elegant but no longer fashionable suit unsullied, and found experience acutely stressful. This is the lot of working mothers. How do they do it? How do they stay clean? How do they put the children in the car without laddering their tights? Do they have special boiler suits for cross-over moments between kitchen and office?

Offer prayers of guilt-ridden gratitude to Heavenly Petting for providing for my children and allowing me to pursue my so-called career from home, as I drive towards its offices through the fog-bound fens. Impossible not to be astonished at the scale of Charles's business now. Pause at gate to be met by courteous, uniformed security.

'Can I help you, madam? Are you attending a service, or do you need counselling in planning one?'

Am unreasonably irritated that he does not know Who I Am.

'Neither, I'm here for a meeting,' I snap, and am further infuriated by the double take he is unable to disguise as he steps closer to my dented, muddy, litter-strewn car.

'You'd better park with the contractors, I think.' He waves me past the director's car park where I can see Charles's car hobnobbing with other sleek and expensive beasts, and sends me round to a space in between a Clean-Your-Crem van and a pick-up truck full of plastic dahlias on plinths. The front doors of Heavenly Petting open automatically as I step onto a doormat with a pair of hands clasped in prayer woven into it. In the foyer, a high desk dominates, and behind it a Dolly Parton type perches, her smile a well-balanced combination of welcome and sympathy. Am pleased to note that this changes to fear and deference when I tell her my name. I am ushered into the boardroom and away from the hideous loop of piped music, now metamorphosing from the Black Beauty theme tune to 'Seasons in the Sun' by Terry Jacks.

'Venetia, how good of you to come.' Charles swoops over and shakes hands, which for some reason seems very odd to me and I have to bite my bottom lip hard to keep a wide grin at bay. Reflect that Charles's manner has always been more boardroom than bedroom as he leads me around the table reintroducing me to the five directors. Knees become unreliable as we tour; have not seen any of them except Henry Loden, Charles's business partner, for a year, and am convinced that they are all comparing me to Helena, who is junior embalmer here now. Wish I had brought The Beauty to protect me. As usual pay no attention to what Charles is saying as he opens the meeting. Am still mulling silently over my clever boardroom/bedroom pun and wondering whether Jenny will remember that Felix has trampolining this afternoon as the meeting begins.

'. . . Trading has been extremely healthy, sales are up and the company is showing good margins on paper, increasingly good margins. . . although of course. . . still room for improvement.'

Doodle on the paper provided and make mental note to ask Charles why I am not receiving a bigger dividend if figures are so rosy. Henry Loden is speaking now, running his palm across thinning, side-parted hair as he bulldozes through civilities and motors on to the point of the meeting. Heavenly Petting is extending into the gifts market and the company is starting production of plastic mourning rings to be sold at Pet City, Toys R Us and also at the chain's own crematoria.

Henry has stopped rubbing his pate and is greasing his hands, palm to palm, as his speech climaxes. He is so excited by what he is saying that little bubbles of spit have formed a pearly foam on his lower lip.

'We hope also to reach the supermarkets to coincide with Valentine's Day next year. We feel that a "Love and Loss" promotion would be a great start for us in this market.' He pauses, slaps his calculator on the table and steps back, hands on hips, ready for admiration. 'Any questions?'

Am astonished to find that I have leapt to my feet, and am shaking my fist and heckling.

'Have any of you stopped to think about what you are suggesting? I think it's grotesque. A mourning ring indeed. Next you'll be pretending that the hair in it – if you aren't too cheapskate to put hair in it at all – belongs to a real animal. Maybe you'll even say it belongs to their own pet. You could do a tailor-made range, a couture version for clients.'

Am on full throttle now, and although furious at the slimy, seamy nature of Charles's latest venture, am really enjoying the effect of my rage. Continue to list details for ever more tasteless rings until Charles hauls himself to his feet and raises a hand to quiet me.

'Thank you, Venetia, shall we continue this conversation in my office? There are a couple of matters pertaining to the children that we need to go over.' He shepherds me out, pushing me ahead, and then darts back in to say to Henry and the others, 'Get to work on Venetia's hair and couture ideas right away. I think she's got something.'

I sit down in his office with my shoulder abutting a shelf full of sample coffins for mice, budgerigars and other size A (which means tiny) pets. Charles leans against the door with his arms folded and looks at me levelly.

'You may complain about the way I make money, but you seem to have no trouble spending it,' he says coldly. I take a deep breath and maintain my cool.

'And neither do you. Or is yet another holiday for you and Helena a research trip?'

And then he drops his bombshell.

'Helena is pregnant. She is expecting twins at Christmas and she needs a break. This is her last chance to fly. When we return, we are moving house, so I can't have the boys until November.'

Extraordinary that I didn't notice at Gawain's exhibition. It just illustrates the terrible truth: I am self-absorbed and unobservant to the point of stupidity. Come to think of it, she was wearing a smock, but I took that to be her interpretation of fashion, and thought nothing of it. Except that it was horrid.

It is not until I am in the car, driving away from Cambridge with the sun like a blood orange streaming in through the back window, warmly caressing my head and my hair, that the shock thaws and I remember that Charles has had a vasectomy. Such was his fury when I announced that I was pregnant with The Beauty that he went to the BUPA hospital that week and made the arrangements, and by the time the bump that was to be The Beauty showed, Charles had done the deed.

'He's got no lead in his pencil now,' was Henry Loden's revolting, leering remark to me when we met in the hospital lift as I arrived to collect Charles and he was leaving, having visited him.

October 3rd

A freak hot autumn day. The Beauty and I spend the morning picking blackberries on the old railway line before driving to meet Vivienne for lunch in order to discuss Helena's immaculate conception. Mist has draped fairy cobwebs in the shade beneath great oaks, and the hedgerows are busy with colour and bustling invisible creatures, all intent on gathering what they can before winter. The Beauty trundles ahead, her own choice of spotted handkerchief as headscarf and red woollen jersey giving her a timeless, story-book quality. Beyond the green seam of former railway, with its springing borders of hawthorn and elder, the newly ploughed fields are rich brown and herringbone-striped. A church tower drifts blue on the horizon, its backdrop the last square of golden stubble, shrinking every moment as a tiny toy tractor drags a gleam of plough along it.

By lunchtime we have two baskets of blackberries, black crescents beneath our nails and deep purple lips. The stubble square behind the church is down to one shining stripe and the rest of the gilded world has turned over and taken on the rich chocolate hue of high autumn. Have been weeping and cursing into the blackberries intermittently, and am not sure why.

If Helena chooses to have children, what business is it of mine? Can never get far with this thought before being sidetracked by how she managed it. Perhaps Charles had his operation reversed. Painful, but devoted. Cannot imagine inspiring such a gesture in anyone. Cannot imagine the poison dwarf inspiring it either.

On the way to Vivienne's, am immeasurably cheered and lifted by my first view of the sea, a crisp navy-blue triangle glimpsed through a cut in the headland. 'Sea saw, sea saw,' says The Beauty, thrilled with her ever broadening vocabulary.

Simon has evidently been alerted to the drama, and his sympathy has manifested itself in a brace of partridge and an invitation for Giles to come beating. A bowl of soup and a bottle of white wine and Vivienne's unruffleable presence are great healers. Gradually, Charles and Helena recede until, by teatime, their significance is the size of Mrs Pepperpot and we are giggling over Simon's latest business venture: wormeries.

October 5th

Have become housewifely and apron-wearing in the extreme since The News. Begin to make blackberry and apple jelly, hypnotising Giles and Felix with the sinister sight in the kitchen of an oozing cloth hanging by strings and Rags's lead from the beam while wine-dark drips of juice splash into a bowl on the table beneath it.

'Cool. Has it got a severed head in it?' whispers Felix, walking around it, almost brushing it with his nose. Giles cuffs him across the shoulder. He shrieks melodramatically and falls over, and Giles puts one foot on his chest and grins down at him.

'It looks berry heavy, though, doesn't it?' he says.

Felix rolls under the table, screeching with laughter and repeating, 'Berry heavy. Berry heavy.'

What a pair of halfwits. Sudden tears spring, causing frantic washing-up, as reality of my role as provider and protector overpowers. Will Charles cease to love them now? How could he?

Am making quince jelly as well as blackberry, and by mid-afternoon it is plain that I have taken on Too Much. Pans of melted sugar everywhere, furry, fragrant quinces rolling about the floor, until retrieved by Giles who takes three outside to juggle with. Finally pour the blackberry and apple goo into pots. All my efforts have amounted to a paltry one and a half tiny pots of the jelly. Gaze disgusted at the results of my labours in scabby-looking jars with half their old labels still unbudging. Total waste of time, sugar and fruit. Would be cheaper to buy gold-leaf jelly (if it exists) from Fortnum's, and more enjoyable.

October 6th

Rose telephones late to discuss Charles and Helena. Am still mad on housewifery, and battling with EU-sized quince mountain. Still hundreds of them lying, as if part of a Renaissance painting, on a vast red ashet, glowing yellow and amber and softly sensual. I love them, and don't care that they are filthy to eat and useless for anything but jelly. And sponge pudding. Mmmmm. Better not, the children will hate it; I will have to eat it all. Not slimming.

'I have news for you,' says Rose, 'big news. Are you sitting down?'

Have come to my own conclusions, and try them out on Rose. 'Do you think the poison dwarf had an affair?'

'No, you idiot. Haven't you worked it out? She's done IVF.'

The quince jelly chooses this moment to burst out of its pan and slurp across the Aga. More like a B-movie than a Renaissance painting now, it creeps down the Aga and onto the floor, dragging the usual acrid billows of smoke and stench with it. Yank the telephone across to find a cloth, knocking a chair over, unable to leave Rose for a second.

'How do you know? Are you sure? Whose babies are they, then?'

'They belong to her and a sperm bank, I suppose. I don't know, but it's definitely true. Henry Loden told Tristan that she and Charles are over the moon. Apparently she's been trying for ages.'

In the inferno of my kitchen, on hands and knees with a wet cloth, a sticky telephone and surrounded by amber jelly, I reach my lowest moment.

October 7th

Three autumn-flowering cyclamen are peeping through fallen leaves beneath the beech tree and a pot of candy-pink *Nerine* have been left on the front doorstep with no card. Or maybe there was one and it blew away. The American hurricane, which was booked for an appearance two weeks ago, has arrived in East Anglia, late but forceful. The hens are most upset and fed up with having their feathers ruffled, so they have stopped laying any eggs and are sulking beneath the yew chicken, making random food runs to the back door whenever it is opened.

October 8th

The Beauty and I take a flask and sandwiches and drive onto the edge of the rugby pitch at Giles's school in order to watch him in the first match of the season. A terrible mistake.

'Rugby isn't really a game for mothers,' comments

Giles's games master, as a boy from the opposing school is taken off the pitch on a stretcher, teeth clenched, tears spilling down dappled purple cheeks, bravely hiding the pain of a twisted knee and a thigh trampled over by metal-studded boots. Giles has the ball and is thundering towards the touchline for a few glorious seconds before a giant beefcake, supposedly also under eleven years old, but weighing at least nine stone, knocks him flying. I scream inadvertently and leap out of the car, longing to run onto the pitch. In a moment, though, Giles has crawled out from a pile of vast boys and is himself grabbing someone around the waist and hurling them to the ground.

'They've scored three tries and made two conversions. They're doing really well.' Mr Jensen the dentist materialises at my side; his son is also playing.

'What's a conversion?' I ask without wishing to know, and drift off as he explains. Am greatly comforted by the professional presence at the match: among the parents watching today there is a doctor, two lawyers and Mr Jensen. All we need now is an ambulance driver and every eventuality is covered. The Beauty has turned on the car stereo and is dancing on the driver's seat, taking a hostess's role when parents pass her.

'Helloo, helloo,' she warbles to them, waving her hand to communicate that she would like them to pass on to the other end of the pitch while she finishes her telephone call. She has a calculator, picked up from the floor of the car, clamped like a telephone to her ear, 'Byeee,' she shrieks, slamming it down on the dashboard before rushing after her guests on the field.

The final whistle blows and the boys line up to shake hands. Giles approaches, grinning and mud-spattered, as if he is auditioning for a soap-powder commercial.

'Mum, we won twenty-nine to ten and I scored a try. James Lascelles scored one too, and Tom Jensen got a conversion.'

He is inured to my ignorance now, and always gives me a quick debriefing on the game on the way back to tea so I don't embarrass him when chatting to masters and other parents about it. Wish they didn't change the game every term; just as I think I have got the hang of one – cricket, for example – they have all switched to hockey or rugby and I have no hope of knowing what's going on. This term's mystery item is studs. Giles needs some safety studs. How does one come by such things, and how does one know that they are needed in the first place? And anyway, what are they?

'Oh, I've got a bag of studs for Tom and he doesn't need them all,' says Mrs Jensen. 'Giles can have some if he comes to the car to fetch them.' Thus my ignorance is left intact and Giles achieves his studs. Maybe I will learn when Felix needs them.

October 12th

Gawain is coming to stay. He rings to deliver his verdict on Charles.

'Must have cost him a bit to sort Helena out. Those Petri dish babies are a few grand. You'd better watch out that he doesn't start defrauding Heavenly Petting and cutting down on alimony.'

'Oh, he isn't that bad, Gawain. He's a good father.'

Very odd to be protecting Charles. It seems to help maintain my new relaxed Just Don't Care attitude, which is becoming more authentic every day. Off to the spare room to make it fit for a guest. This is always a fine work-avoidance scheme, and unlike washing-up or folding clothes, has novelty value. Open the door and discover it to be stuffed with numerous garments which were until now missing presumed lost. Had utterly forgotten that this was to be laundry room, and after initial enthusiasm for dumping piles of washing in here, have not been in for weeks. Tempted to throw all the clothes into the bin forthwith, as we have managed fine without them, but miserly instinct prevents me. Instead, put them back in piles dotted about the landing.

Make bed, plumping pillows and so forth, trying to achieve magazine-like appearance of comfort and elegance in the room. All going well until I notice the chair. Or rather, what is on the chair. A most antique cat poo in the shape of a question mark. There can be no doubt about whose it is. Sidney specialises in lavatorial humour in the spare room.

'Bastard filthy cat, Sidney. God, how I loathe and despise you.'

Rant around the room, venting spleen for a bit, then fetch rubber gloves and paper to clear it up. No need for either. The fossil comes away easily and is a worthy exhibit for the boys' museum. Have usual guilt pangs at the thought of the museum: it is drastically underfunded, and so far has only a cigarette butt belonging to George Harrison (courtesy of Rose and Tristan who met him and snatched it from the floor where he dropped it) and a piece of cake with a bite out of it. The missing mouthful went down the Prince of Wales's throat when he came to open a local old folks' home. Felix, having watched His Royal Highness closely for signs of regality, whispered, 'How do you know he's real if he isn't wearing a crown?' but was convinced enough to put the cake in his napkin and smuggle it home.

In the barn, which houses the museum, a house martin's nest has been added to the exhibits. Remember David promising a glass case to the boys last time he was here. He has not been around for ages. Must ring him.

October 13th

Ring him. He has been in London, making furniture for film sets. Why is everyone else's life more glamorous than mine? Even Digger went to London, where he enjoyed the dustbins hugely.

'What have you been up to, Venetia?' Some men's voices are neither here nor there on the telephone; others achieve a richness and depth of timbre which brings out flirtation. David's is one such voice. Find I am standing on one leg, winding the other around it and giggling.

'Oh, nothing much.' Cannot in fact think of anything at all I have done, except clear up cat shit. Catch sight of The Beauty on tiptoe, reaching for a flowerpot in the garden, and have to cut short the conversation.

'Oh, come over any time, we'd love to see you. I must go. Bye, David.'

'Bye, Venetia. I'll fix up the glass case and bring it over at the weekend.'

October 14th

Purchase two hundred wallflower plants, rust and crimson according to the bundles they are in. Plant them along the front of the house. It takes all morning. Spend the afternoon worrying that it will look like a municipal roundabout when they all flower in the spring. But at least I remembered them this year. A sign of success for sure. Although I did forget to sow the seeds I bought in February. Oh well, there's always next year.

October 15th

Power cut at teatime reminds me of the three-day week in the seventies. We still have the Aga, but Giles and Felix elect to make supper on the open fire anyway. We toast teacakes and wrap potatoes in foil and throw them in. Start gathering candles in the hall as night falls, and torches too. Hugely enjoy this, as Georgette Heyer often has meaningful interludes when the spirited heroine is handed her candle by a gorgeous Corinthian with whom she is involved in tempestuous dispute over something. Give an impromptu living history lesson by explaining to the boys that hundreds of years ago the family living here would all have met in the hall to be given their candle by the man of the house.

'We haven't got a man in our house,' wails Felix, for whom the excitement is wearing off.

'Oh, yes we have. Two, in fact,' says Giles, who has run to the window on hearing a car. 'David's here and so is Gawain. Gawain's getting out of David's car. I didn't know they were friends.'

Our cosy firelit evening is abruptly invaded, and the peaceful pre-bath, post-tea house erupts in a chaos of stamping boots and voices and two tall, broad figures with the evening chill rising from their coats. David drops two of Gawain's bags at the bottom of the stairs, and addresses me coldly.

'Would you prefer me to make another date to do the museum? I imagine you would like to spend this weekend in peace with your guest.' He appraises Gawain. 'I saw him at the station, and he asked me how to get here, so I offered him a lift.'

'Thank you,' I reply. 'Presumably you've introduced yourselves to one another. Gawain is Felix's godfather.' Why should David be interested? Oh, well.

Gawain wraps me in a bear-hug. 'Good to see you, gorgeous. How's the gang?' He has brought Felix a longed-for PlayStation, and is as desperate as Felix is to get it up and running. Try to tell him about the electricity, but he ignores me, and despite having to take a candle, remains touchingly oblivious as he heads up to Felix's room with a huge box of computer leads under his arm. 'We'll be going places with this any moment now. Let's hit the controls, Felix.'

Such is Felix's excitement at this longed-for moment that he too has forgotten about the power. Giles and I roll our eyes to heaven and sit down again by the fire.

'I'll leave you to it.' David extracts himself from The

Beauty, and her game on the rocking horse with him, and stands up to go.

'Oh, not yet,' pleads Giles. 'Come and see how we've got on with the tree house since you were last here. It's brilliant.'

David's protests are brushed aside and Giles drags him into the dusk. A moment of quiet, then Felix and Gawain erupt into the drawing room through another door, Gawain hopping with excitement and reminding me of Tigger in *Winnie-the-Pooh*.

'God, Venetia, this is so primitive. There's no electricity. How long has it been like this? It's great.' Gawain throws himself down on the sofa and opens a can of Red Stripe which he pulls from his pocket. 'Where's that guy gone? I asked him in for a beer to say thanks for bringing me, but he said he knew you anyway and was on his way here.'

'He's with Giles, outside.'

Firelight and candles suffuse the room with rosy, cosy glow. David and Giles finally come in again. Gawain leaps up to shake David's hand.

'Listen, I've twisted Venetia's arm. We want you to stay and have supper.'

David's brows swoop up. He looks at me, hardly smiling.

'How cosy, but I'm afraid—'

'Oh, please stay. Please, David. It won't be fun

without you.' Giles and Felix drag him onto the sofa, and laughing, he takes off his coat and agrees.

'I wish we never had electricity, it's much more fun,' says Felix when he is finally dragged up to bed, adding, with glorious inconsistency, 'Can David and Gawain stay so we can do the PlayStation tomorrow?'

Seems to me that David and Gawain are unlikely to go anywhere. An hour with Gawain at his most bombastic has thawed David utterly, and exhausted me. They are playing poker, two candles in Wallace and Gromit candleholders illuminate the cards for them and the scene is deliciously rakish. David wins the first hand, and they are dealing again within seconds, scarcely aware of me as I begin to gather up plates, glasses and the ketchup bottle from the gloom beyond the firelight. Am light-headed with tiredness and with relief that David is here and I do not have to shoulder the burden of Gawain's machine-gun energy. I slink off to bed as the first candle gutters and is replaced with another.

October 16th

Set off on a mushroom-picking expedition with my mother. Gawain carries The Beauty on his shoulders, earning himself thousands of brownie points with me because I can saunter along with a spring in my step as if I am seventeen, untrammelled by the pushchair or worse, the backpack. However, Gawain loses all the brownie points again as soon as we get into the woods. Forgetting The Beauty, he forges through hanging foliage. A terrible roar alerts me, and I turn to see The Beauty, peering red-faced from a frond of chestnut tree, her arms wrapped around it while her feet drum in frustration and fury on Gawain's collarbone.

'Ow, stop it. You can't do that to me, I'm carrying you, for Christ's sake.'

'Don't be such an idiot, Gawain, you'll drop her.'

I reach the sobbing Beauty as she is wrenched from her branch, and snatch her from Gawain. Scowling, he marches off into curling golden bracken where my mother is inspecting a fairy ring of fungus. Fury blasts my cheeks. I crouch to let The Beauty climb onto my back. She cannot. Making the most of a dramatic opportunity, she continues to sob woefully into my shoulder. We follow the others slowly, and her spirits lift with every sighting of Giles and Felix, now way ahead, dark blurs racing through the copper leaves, weaving between smooth grey beech trunks and moss-covered heaps of piled logs.

October 21st

It is Wednesday and Gawain is finally departing. He has not had a restful sojourn, but has survived. His relationship with The Beauty has deteriorated still further, and she will not now be in a room with him without bursting into tears. Am glad he is not her godfather, and that he lives miles away and will not be dropping in too often. He is a pitiful sight, leaning out of the train window to wave. Half of his face is hidden by reflecting sunglasses, but the bits above and below the shades are pale green and damp and spasms of trembling occupy him every few minutes. The doctor said this was to be expected, and that Gawain would be better within a week.

It is all my mother's fault. She administered a highly toxic mushroom in an omelette on Saturday night and poisoned him. For three days his life hung in the balance, or so it seemed from the fuss he made; the doctor said there was no danger at all.

'I'm so glad you aren't dead,' were my mother's bracing words when she came to view him in his sickbed. 'You could be. I thought they were wood mushrooms, but I've looked them up and they're yellow staining agarics, which are very similar but horribly toxic.' Her smile was sepulchral. 'I'm amazed it hasn't happened before, actually.'

Moderately contrite, she salved her conscience with a

packet of orange and lemon cupcakes, presented, along with a half-bottle of vodka, to the invalid. Still too enfeebled and sensitive to look at them, he cringed away, shuddering. My mother ate all except the final orange-flavoured cake. This was given to The Beauty who was peering round the door, anxious that Granny might be in danger from the dreadful creature. My mother sipped briefly from the vodka bottle, then rose to leave.

'I'll leave the rest of the vodka. I've just had one small shot myself, but you don't really need visitors, do you? You just need a big bowl by the bed.'

'Why don't you send him back to London in an ambulance?' she demanded downstairs. 'You've got enough to do looking after the children without sick artists as well.'

Shocked by her lack of sympathy, although secretly agreed, but felt I must be hospitable for as long as Gawain required a bed. His image as Corinthian superhero was a little tarnished by the sick bowl, and I discovered that Florence Nightingale will never be a role model.

* * *

Return from dropping Gawain at the station and on the way decide that autumn is the perfect time to reread *Anna Karenina*. The thought of lovely wicked Vronsky speeds my path through the puddles and mud to home. Yum yum. Can't wait.

October 23rd

Must go on a date or similar excursion for fun and frivolity, with or without member of the opposite sex. Am becoming set in lemon-faced, lone-parent ways and need to get out. Have not been out for the evening since London trip. This cannot be healthy. Who can I go with and where can I go? Vivienne and Simon are on holiday, David is not answering his telephone, my mother is having her hair dyed in Cromer. I have no one to play with. Cabin fever takes possession of my brain and makes me choose a class with Fabrice Wrath's Seven Rhythms Ecstatic Dance Group as my outing. Must not admit the depths to which I am sinking to my mother, so ask Jenny to babysit and make her swear to secrecy and to tell anyone who rings that I am at the cinema.

Jenny arrives with a large bag of washing and two small tubs of dye.

'Is it OK if I use your washing machine to dye my clothes?' she asks. 'I thought I could do some tie-dyeing with the boys too.'

'What a wonderful idea, they'll love it.' Am jealous.

Why do I never think of creative and stimulating things such as tie-dyeing to do with the boys? Could I join in and learn new skill from Jenny rather than having to drive ten miles in the dark?

Dress in boring black and grey clothes as usual, but a different configuration of them. Hopes that I resemble a nubile extra in *Flashdance* are dashed when I go in to say goodbye to Giles and Felix. They are immersed in the vile PlayStation and can scarcely bear to look up.

'Go away,' growls Felix from between gritted teeth.

Giles finishes his go, so has a small window of time for me before his next turn. He hugs me and I am engulfed in a huge, loving smile too.

'Mum, you're so silly, you've forgotten to take your trousers off. You've got a skirt on as well. It looks totally sad.'

Why did I bring them up to believe in freedom of speech?

The ecstatic dancing takes place in a village hall, and is led by a man with a straggle of long green hair and cringe-making white ballet tights. He looks like a spring onion. The participants are two wan, middle-aged women wearing bedroom slippers and macintoshes, and a skinhead in boxer shorts and a singlet. I take my place among them, clammy with embarrassment and very conscious of my yellowed toenails. Should have made time to apply nail polish before leaving home. A strip light falters into action, washing the hall and the five people in it in harsh white light. No one is at all ecstatic. Silence is heavy between us. Onion Head puts on his music. Horrible rasping wails fill the hall, backed by spooky pipes of some sort and a fast drumbeat. I begin to feel nauseous.

'Let the music seize you from inside,' urges Onion Head, and shutting his eyes, he bends his knees outwards like a Cossack and begins to bounce from side to side. The strand of tired green hair flaps across his forehead, and his legs are stringy and knotted with veins. No one else even attempts the squatting bounce. One of the ladies sheds her mac to reveal a clinging mauve tracksuit. Her lips are a ruby slash in between dumpling-fat cheeks. She starts marching on the spot, her eyes fixed above the bouncing form of Onion Head, her hands moving, twirling an imaginary baton. She may not be wearing a pleated miniskirt or bunches, but she is clearly an American cheerleader, a bobby-soxer. The skinhead has also been seized by an inner ecstasy. He teeters on the tips of his trainers, every leg muscle taut and forcing him taller and straighter. His arms shoot in and out from his shoulders, faster and faster, and this impulsion soon has him bouncing, while his face turns puce and scarlet like Zebedee in *The Magic Roundabout.* The non-cheerleading middle-aged lady and I are spellbound. Zebedee, Onion Head and the Cheerleader are bopping away at full speed, while the two of us shift uneasily from foot to foot. I catch her eye just as Onion Head changes gear and begins hurtling around the hall in a kind of squatting solo waltz. The cheerleader has developed a more elaborate routine too, now, involving head-tossing and pouting, while Zebedee is a veritable dervish. We both explode laughing, and cannot stop. Soon we are leaning against the stage, legs crossed, dying for the loo but still wrapped in mirth.

October 24th

The excitement of the ecstatic dancing causes me to wake today renewed. Sides and stomach ache from unusual exertion of non-stop laughing, but no other ill effects. Will not, however, be returning to Fabrice, as he announced at the end of the class that he is going to India for the winter, and has to be there before the clocks change. Am not sure if this is valid, as time zones make clock-changing meaningless anyway. Or do they? Am, as usual, confounded, caught out and depressed by the end of British Summer Time. And by the vast heap of manure which has been deposited in the yard by Mr Loins.

'You ordered it last year, and said I wasn't to forget

you, I had the cheque and everything. You said you were getting ahead with the garden.' He cackles in triumph when I object to the fulsome trailer load.

All very well for the garden, but have no volunteers for shit-shovelling save self. Wallow for a bit in self-pity as I recall the optimistic day last year when I ordered the manure from Mr Loins. Remember saying to him, 'Oh, I'm sure there will be someone around to help me,' when warned that there would be an awful lot of it.

October 26th

Half-term enables me to enlist Giles and Felix as helpers. Both are keen to earn money, so I offer them fifty pence a barrow load. Perhaps too lavish. I have been appointed barrow-pusher, and the morning passes slowly for me. Giles stands at the muck heap with a fork and tosses treacle-brown dollops into the barrow. When it is full, I trundle it to Felix, who waits, leaning on another fork by the flowerbed. He then flings feathering sprays of manure out of the barrow and somewhere near the bed and I trundle the empty barrow back to Giles. By elevenses, I have become a Russian peasant from Kitty and Levin's farm, and am almost enjoying the wrung-out, strung-out exhaustion. My red wellingtons are heavy and bristling with muck so I am forced to shuffle, and Giles and Felix have earned five pounds each.

'That's practically plutocrat rate,' I inform them.

They are sitting on the back doorstep, sipping scalding hot chocolate and watching The Beauty climb over me. She is refreshed from her rest and is a land girl in khaki trousers which I found in the dressing-up box. Recognise them as Felix's from toddler days, and suspect that they have been inside out in the dressing-up box since he took them off five years ago to put on his cowboy suit. I cannot move. Am collapsed on the grass beside the boys. My back is in a spasm of protest against the ten barrow loads of muck I have moved, and is building up a painful resistance to doing any more. Am otherwise keen to continue and get rid of the Mount Rushmore muck heap; it is black, ugly and it smells. Rather like Digger, who appears, jangling his collar as he pauses to scratch and then lift his leg on the newly planted wallflowers under the kitchen window. Refrain from yelling obscenities at him or throwing anything, as Digger equals David, and David equals assistance. Hooray, shall not now have permanently crooked back or long-term muck monolith.

David is on his way to London and wants to leave Digger here.

'I wonder if you would have him, Venetia; he hates the traffic and I can never get him out of the dustbins, so it takes hours even to cross a road with him. He's brought you a present to try and bribe his way in.' He thrusts a bottle of red wine at me and turns to greet The Beauty. Nod absently, as am transfixed by the snappiness of David's outfit. The glamour of a white shirt should never be underestimated. The black corduroy suit is the kind of thing I used to try to get Charles to wear, without success, and only the silver trainers are recognisable as David's wardrobe. He does not look eligible for shit-shovelling. And I have not got the nerve to ask him; he is dazzling in his splendour. Am unfortunately dazzled enough to agree to Digger.

'Oh yes, of course we'll have him. It'll be fine. When are you back?'

'On Saturday, in time for Hallowe'en,' says David. 'I'll see you then.'

He puts The Beauty down and saunters out of the yard. We resume our labours.

October 28th

Am turning over a new leaf. Recent phase of gloom and shit-shovelling is to be replaced by spirit of optimism, some new shoes and many treats. Am throwing an impromptu Hallowe'en party, spurred on by competitiveness with Charles, who is having the boys for Guy Fawkes Night. He says he does not want The Beauty, and has not had her overnight since the early summer. She will be supplanted in his affections by the Saucer Babies. How can I protect her from this? Have been ghastly, whingeing lemon-face mother for weeks now, and have not told the boys why. Am convinced that it is Charles's job to break baby news to them, not mine, although wish that they could be spared. Futile half-hour of 'if only' thoughts follows, staring out of the kitchen window at shivering trees desperate to keep hold of leaves now past their prime and yellowed. Am only distracted from my torpor by Rags, who is whimpering and turning circles in a crescendo of excitement because I am standing near the back door. Capitulate and take her out.

Tramp along the edge of the newly ploughed back field, with Rags zigzagging at a distance, nose to the ground and hopelessly excited. The Beauty rides high on my shoulders in her rambler-baby backpack, and we swing up to the brow of the hill, out of breath and yearning for the view.

October 31st

Is there time for fudge or jelly to set before the party? Where are The Beauty's black velvet bloomers? When will I be allowed out? Am zipped into the yellow pop-up tent with the tiny tyrant. She is wearing a silver plastic knight's helmet with the visor up; I am wearing a kind of wimple made from a roll of kitchen towel. My Knight in Shining Armour keeps blowing her nose on the wimple, and is engaged in sucking apricot face cream from a tube she refuses to surrender. She has a will as tough as any armour, and the voice to assert it. I may be here for hours. The Beauty hands me a pink thimble.

'Tea,' she says, breathily. In fact, I could be here for days.

Rescue appears in the form of Desmond and my mother and a vast pumpkin from The Gnome's vegetable plot. My mother also has three red plastic tridents. She adores parties and is already very excited. She engulfs the kitchen in a puff of smoke from her special black Hallowe'en cigarettes and arranges her wares on the table. It takes the united effort of me and Desmond to get the pumpkin into position.

'This is bigger than the piglets. We could put one of them inside and cook it,' I suggest.

'We thought it would make a good carriage for The Beauty,' says my mother, settling down in the tent with the delighted Beauty. 'You chop the top off and scoop it out like an egg. Desmond is going to dress up as Dracula and hide in the coal shed. We must make some cocktails, I've brought black food colouring for them, and some should be green.'

Am tying a string across the kitchen and suspending sticky willy buns from it when Lila rattles up the drive in her Beetle.

'Ah, the witches are convening,' says Desmond, watching her leap from the car and begin frantically to wipe its seats clean of journey crumbs while yelling at her children.

'Either you tidy yourselves up or we go straight back to London. I have had enough of you two and your lippiness, so don't bother answering back. . .' Her haranguing head vanishes into the boot space in the bonnet of the Beetle. Desmond whistles under his breath and opens a can of lager.

'She's going to be one to avoid this weekend,' he whispers to me as Diptych bursts into the kitchen in a warty monster mask.

The relationship between Desmond and Lila broke down irretrievably when Desmond's decapitated finger went septic after his third night on the marble slab. Despite Lila's fevered application of much organic, pre-packed mud, pond weed and other oozing lotions, Desmond insisted on going to hospital. Antibiotics and twenty-four hours of potential amputation were the final passion killers. The finger survived, but Desmond left to go to Reading in August, vowing never to get mixed up with anything New Age again. His band, Hung Like Elvis, were the success story of the festival, and at other venues throughout the summer. Now, at last, after seven years as a joke, they are considered a happening band, and Desmond has shaved his sideburns, groomed his eyebrows and found a Dolly Parton lookalike girlfriend called Minna whom he met at a gig. Minna loves Tupperware and having her nails done, and believes in supermarket prefab food. Wish Minna could have joined us for Hallowe'en, as I long to meet her. Have to make do with grumpy Lila instead.

The kitchen is becoming a cauldron. The windows have steamed up, something foul is bubbling on the Aga and The Beauty stands on the table with a wooden spoon, stirring the hollow in a gap-toothed turnip lantern. She and my mother have excavated three turnips, two swedes and are about to start on the giant pumpkin. Felix has found a bottle of white foundation and is slapping it onto his face to complement the gruesome red felt-tip line he has drawn around his throat. He is freakish in the extreme to look at, with just his eyes and his school uniform indicating that he is human. He removes the school uniform in favour of a black cloak and a pair of flashing devil horns, and hurtles into the garden with

Diptych and Calypso to play at being Undead. Giles has taken it upon himself to blow up twenty orange and black balloons, and is lying in the kitchen armchair panting. No amount of coercion or pleading will persuade him to dress up this evening.

'It's too babyish,' he says dismissively, and as if to prove his point, the leering, disguised faces of the other three crystallise for a second at the back door before they vanish again screaming and shouting into the steel-cold dusk.

'Try this and tell me if it needs more nutmeg.' My mother thrusts a steaming cup at me, and another at Lila, and stands back, as if observing an experiment. Glance uneasily at the potion, which is the colour of old blood and has black bits floating beneath a foam of bubbles. My mother looks even more unnerving than her concoction, having run her hands through her hair several times without realising that pumpkin seeds have attached themselves to her. Her hair now stands completely on end and is adorned with the seeds, while her mascara has smudged around her eyes. Her Hallowe'en costume, however, is immaculate, if overpowering, in its suggestion of an endless sweep of viridian-green satin under festoons of black lace.

'It's mulled wine, but I added some cherry brandy and a few other new ingredients. Do you like it?'

Suppress sissy urge not even to try it, and imbibe.

Molten alcohol bursts down my throat; I choke and spout teardrops from swimming eyes. Croak, 'It's great,' and gulp the rest as if it is a frozen vodka.

Lila is being a real wet blanket: 'I'm sorry, I can't drink it; I read that heating cheap wine literally turns it into battery acid and I'm not prepared to run that risk with my metabolism.'

She turns her back to find a clean glass for the wholesome life elixir she has brought with her, and my mother sticks her tongue out. In contrast to grumpy Lila, I am now feeling very much more cheerful than I have for ages. Another swig of the potion creates a woosh of energy and power reminiscent of Asterix, and I dash into the garden to call the children for the games to start.

'We can't be bothered to wait for the others,' I shout. 'They can join in later. Let's start with apple-bobbing.'

'What others? Who else have you asked?'

I turn to answer Desmond and am jolted into a scream. He has changed into vulpine, glistening Count Dracula. The Beauty has had enough, and clutches my hand in terror, hiding her head in her skirt, only emerging to wave her hand and shout, 'Taxi, taxi,' in a bid for escape when car headlights flare out of the darkness towards us. The car pauses halfway up the drive, and although I cannot see anything save headlights, I can hear the driver laughing at the scene on the lawn. Five buckets filled with water and bobbing apples are illuminated by the various lanterns, and kneeling at each bucket is a child, his or her head sleek and wet like a seal from immersion in the apple-filled water. My mother, followed by Lila, who has been forced by Calypso to wear a Victorian child's sprigged bonnet, marches between the contestants with her torch, counting apples and administering towels. Beyond the grinning, glowing light of the lanterns, Desmond is dimly visible in the woods, flitting to and fro with torch spectacles on, very spectral with his whited-out face, but also reminiscent of the barn owl.

'I have never seen such an insane bunch of people, or rather, not since that midsummer party you had, Venetia. How's Digger?' David climbs out of the car leaving the lights on, and saunters over to kiss my cheek. Am taken aback. He doesn't usually kiss me. Perhaps he's drunk. I turn to call Digger out from the kitchen where he has been guarding the sticky buns, but he has already shimmied silently to David's side. So has my mother, proffering a beaker of mulled wine and almost as pleased to see him as Digger.

'I've been meaning to get in touch with you about those friends of yours with the handbags. Would they like to use my house? I read somewhere that location work is hugely lucrative, and I'm told that—'

'It's the drink talking,' I whisper, lemon-like, in David's other ear, annoyed because I wanted to hear about his trip to London, and now he will probably leave while I am putting The Beauty to bed.

He affects deafness towards me and I march upstairs, feeling both martyred and ashamed of myself, to bath The Beauty. But he is still there when I come down. Mayhem has muted now, and the children are eating cheese on toast by the fire David has built, and are listening wide-eyed to my mother reading M. R. James's 'Oh, Whistle, and I'll Come to You, My Lad'. David throws more logs onto the fire and comes over to my side by the door.

'Desmond has challenged Lila to a darts match, so they've gone to the pub. I think it's to the death. Do you want to go as well? Your mother can look after the kids.'

The sitting room is cosy and smells of autumn leaves and the chestnuts David is roasting. The children are agog at my mother's knees, hardly breathing as the suspense mounts. Contentment wraps around me.

'No, I'd much rather stay here. Let's have a drink, I want to hear about your trip.'

November 2nd

Rose telephones at length to complain about Tristan, who has gone on the Hay Diet and is making her do it too, and Theo. He won't let her have any breakfast except a fig.

'We're not allowed pasta with Parmesan cheese or even bread and butter,' she complains. 'Theo hates it; I have to sneak him sandwiches when Tristan's out, but I have to hide the bread because we're only supposed to have rye bread now. It's frightful. Theo has started jumping out of his cot at night. I'm sure it's because he's hungry. He bit me three times yesterday. Do you think that's a sign of hunger as well?'

I reassure her and suggest she buys another fridge and puts it somewhere Tristan never goes. 'Then you can fill it with things you and Theo can eat.'

'What a brilliant idea. A small one will be easy to hide, behind the coats or somewhere like that. Thanks, Venetia, that's so underhand. I love it. Anyway, tell me what you've been up to. How are you coping with the Miracle of the Immaculate Conception? I think it's time you found a new man, you know. It's been ages. I'm going to come down and plan a strategy with you.'

This is a favourite theme of Rose's, and I meet it with my usual response.

'There aren't any men around.'

Anyway, I don't want one except for wood-chopping and taking the rubbish down the drive. Explain this to Rose.

'I've had enough of all that emotional angst and

having to look after them. It's as much as I can manage to look after the children. And I couldn't bear not to be allowed pasta and Parmesan.'

Change the subject and tell her about our Hallowe'en party. She is petulant to have missed it.

'Typical Lila, to get down there for the party. I wish I'd come. Theo would have loved it. We could have covered him in cochineal again. Is David that bloke who came to the midsummer madness night? With grey eyes and great legs? God, why don't you go for him, Venetia? He's delicious, and he must fancy you, he's always hanging around.'

Rose is unshakeably convinced that lust lies behind any male–female friendship.

'You read too many women's magazines,' I tell her before hanging up.

November 3rd

Spend hours dragging branches and heaping leaves to make a bonfire. Not wishing to leave anything to chance, and remembering Charles telling me that enormous skill and intellect are needed to structure a bonfire, I pour a quantity of petrol over it before attempting to light it. Terrible muffled *woomph* noise, flames leap around me and am convinced I have been engulfed by them. Hurl myself on the ground and roll back and forth like Rags when she has found a nice old corpse and wishes to be wreathed in its scent. Dare not stop until my clothes are damp and my skin is grainy with earth and crushed twigs. Try opening and shutting eyes and mouth to test whether the top layer of skin is still there. Seem to have miraculously escaped being burnt to a crisp, and the bonfire has already gone out. Resort to firelighters, and slowly a core of orange flame begins to lick the outer branches and I can prod the crackling structure, releasing a puff of blue smoke and a roar as the fire cranks up hotter and hotter.

Much later, putting Felix to bed, I close his bedroom curtains and see the pink glow of my fire still burning. A triumph over unlikeliness.

November 4th

Drive the children to Cambridge through umber-tinted afternoon to take them to Charles. All are sweetly excited, even The Beauty, who has only been allowed to stay with him once before. On the telephone last night he capitulated towards her finally, saying, 'If she can walk, she can come.' Not only can she walk, she can run, and is a very fine limbo dancer too. She is a total music-head and is happy on any journey as long as the volume on the tape machine is high and some lovely rap and disco music is thudding out. Her dancing is sublime, wiggling of shoulders like Madonna and shaking of head like Karen Carpenter. She is not at all interested in children's tapes, quite rightly in my view as the singers always have such awful patronising voices. Maybe she does her head-shaking to satirise them. Hope so. We listen to louche rock music by Hole and also to Kris Kristofferson and arrive at Heavenly Petting on radiant form.

The fluffy receptionist is dressed in marshmallow pink, and is markedly more friendly than she was when I came on my own to the meeting. This time she slides out from behind her desk to greet us, her wonderful cleavage gleaming in a nest of softest mohair, and her whole being hourglass-perfect and tiny.

'Hello, I'm Minna. Welcome, all of you. I've been asked to entertain you for half an hour while Mr Denny finishes his meeting. Would you all like to come into the Reflection Room and have a drink?'

We follow obediently and are led into a thickly carpeted room decorated to look like a bruise or perhaps a sunset. The walls are marbled mauve and lilac, grey and pink, and the sofas are upholstered in yellow fabric. Minna busies herself with glasses and packets of crisps, her long frosted-blue nails clicking on the cans of Coke as she pours them.

Giles has been watching her intently and suddenly comments, 'You've got such tiny feet. I didn't know grown-up feet could be that small.'

I automatically shove my great boats back under my chair so no one can see them. Minna tosses her silver-blonde curls and throws him a saucy look.

'Well, not much grows in the shade, does it?'

Her bosom hovers some distance in front of her as she pirouettes. Giles turns scarlet and suddenly I am enlightened – she is Desmond's Dolly Parton.

'Minna – of course. You're Desmond's girlfriend, you must be. Desmond is my brother. He came to our Hallowe'en party and told us all about you.'

I babble on, half astonished at the coincidence of finding her here of all places, half to help Giles recover from his embarrassment. The Beauty takes to her immediately, and throws herself at Minna's mini feet, even lying down with her kangaroo on the perfect Barbie blue high-heeled shoes. Minna alights on the arm of a sofa; The Beauty watches her beadily, and sensing a moment when she is preoccupied, displays astonishing deftness in removing Minna's right shoe and placing it on her own small foot. The left follows, and the triumphant Beauty hobbles between the sofas, shouting 'ha ha' and pointing at her cerulean footwear.

Reluctantly tear myself away from Minna's life story, but not before I have learnt that she is a form of saint. She has thirty-seven cats and fourteen dogs at home, and her mission is to save animals from owners who have succumbed to Charles's rhetoric and to his advertising and have decided to end their little pets' lives, 'On a Good Note, On a Good Day,' as Charles always puts it.

'I go along to places like puppy obedience classes, or maybe local pet shows,' she explains, 'and I talk to the owners about their twilight plans for their older pets. Lots of them are so relieved to have the decision lifted from their shoulders.'

Although Minna's secret mission is at odds with the success of Charles's business and therefore my children's allowance, I am utterly beguiled by her. Finally depart to drive home, leaving her playing monsters with Felix and The Beauty, while Giles, still shy, is referee.

November 5th

In no frame of mind to enjoy the evening I have ahead of me. Vivienne and Simon are taking me with them to a friend's farm for a fireworks party and barbecue. I must go out because it is too dispiriting to sit at home on Guy

Fawkes Night when the beloved children are whooping it up in Cambridge at a vast party on the Backs with carousels and hot dogs and glorious fireworks bursting over water and medieval spires.

They telephone as I am debating whether to wear wellingtons and my filthy waterproof, or to freeze. We have an awful, textbook divorced-children conversation. I may have to ban them from ringing me when they go away in future.

'Hi, Mum, it's Giles.'

'Hi, Giles, how are you all?'

'Fine thanks.'

'I'm missing you hugely and thinking about you all having sparklers and toffee apples.'

Long pause.

'Is everything all right, darling?'

'Yup.'

'Are you having fun?'

'Yup.'

Long pause. Then Giles speaks.

'D'you want to speak to Felix and The Beauty?'

'Yup.' Oh, God, now I'm doing it. 'I mean, yes please, darling, have a lovely fireworks party, won't you, and do be careful with sparklers and everything. . .' He has gone. Conversation with Felix identically awful and stilted. My usually garrulous children have become polite, pretend people with cardboard manners. I also dry up.

After a relatively short silence, Felix says, 'I'll get The Beauty now.'

Now we have a very lengthy pause, followed by clunking and heavy breathing. I try speaking, by this time torn between hysterical laughter and sobs. The Beauty howls as soon as she hears my voice and is whisked away from the phone. Someone hangs up.

* * *

The firework party and barbecue takes place in, on and very close to a large Range Rover. We arrive to find four or five people milling about in the dark with sticks and torches, and a very small, sulky bonfire. Simon immediately takes over as chef and party planner, and discarding the hosts' many Tupperware boxes of food, he starts cooking some steaks he has brought which are oozing blood in Vivienne's basket along with a bottle of sloe vodka, three vast Chinese rockets and a slab of chocolate. The hosts scuttle to do Simon's bidding, and Vivienne and I clamber into the car with brimming glasses of sloe vodka and turn on the heating in preparation for engrossing conversation and gossip. Steadied and cheered from earlier telephone hysteria, I sip the sloe vodka and find its smooth sweetness comforting and medicinal.

Simon's bossing is effective. The display begins with

three delicate bouquets of lacy vivid green and pink Roman candles, followed by a great golden rocket. Even more lovely with a second sloe vodka. And a third. On the way home, having exchanged effusive farewells with co-guests whose names I still have not discovered, am thrilled to find I have hardly thought about the children all evening, and haven't missed them in the slightest. A marked improvement from last time they all went to Charles's.

November 7th

How can I help them? Charles drops the children back late. Felix trudges upstairs, his favourite cuddly toy in one hand, the other plunged into his pocket. He does not look up at me, nor does Giles. Both have crescent shadows of exhaustion beneath their eyes and chalk-white skin. The Beauty is asleep with her mouth open, small, plump fingers clamped around a Smarties tube.

Charles hangs around while I put them all to bed. He doesn't come in, but hovers at the front of the house in the dark, unloading the luggage, brushing the seats, removing The Beauty's throne. By the time the children are tucked up, his car has reverted to its customary state of luxury, and there is no trace of squalor, or of the children.

‘They are not talking to Helena,’ he says. ‘She is very upset.’

We are on the doorstep, having a conversation I hate already. My throat is tight with anger, and adrenalin courses through my veins as if on the Cresta Run.

‘They’re upset too. Your news was bound to be difficult for them. They’ll be fine when the babies are born.’

‘Oh, do you think so? I’ll tell Helena; it’ll cheer her up.’ He shuffles his feet and looks wretched.

‘I think you should make some plans for your time with them that are separate from Helena and the babies. Just for a while.’

He nods, his brow clearing as though he has confessed and been absolved, and salutes my cheek before driving off. There are not many people these days who still salute a cheek. Charles does it with the driest brush. It is painless to receive, and about as thrilling as a roll of kitchen towel.

November 10th

The only flower in my garden is a white chrysanthemum, given to me last year by a school friend of Giles’s as a thank you for having him to stay. Not being a big chrysanthemum fan, I let it hang around in the porch until it had finished flowering, then planted it without thinking, on the edge of the drive. Now, when the rest of the garden slumbers beneath a thick carpet of manure, and leaf interest is everything, it has burst into soggy flamboyance. Keep catching sight of it when arriving or leaving the house, thinking it is a collection of discarded tissues or other litter, and having mini-apoplexy. Similar temper caused daily by Rags, who is loving the easy access to well-rotted pig shit and rolls in the flowerbeds before coming in to lie on the sofa every morning. No matter how many tuberose joss sticks I burn, the house remains sty-like in ambience. Odd how a bad smell can affect appearance also. House is becoming trailer-park and tawdry. Shall not be discouraged or dragged down myself, but will improve everything. First, the chrysanthemum must go.

November 14th

Desmond's birthday. Fortunately he is in Sri Lanka, washing elephants, so don't have to give him a present.

November 15th

My mother's birthday. The children give her a Glamorous Granny mug with transfer of Dolly Parton/Minna type on one side, and, mysteriously, a large dog on the other. I give her a purple inflatable chair and a pair of yellow ankle-length gardening boots like my red ones. We make a cake in the shape of a Teletubby and take it to her house for lovely family tea. She is out. We telephone the pub. She and The Gnome are there. Their words are slurring. Return home in giant lemon mode.

November 16th

Poison pygmy Helena's birthday. Send her a pair of outsize knickers from Woolworths.

November 17th

Travel many miles under cover of darkness to procure bargain of the century – a proper snooker table for fifty pounds. Find this covetable item in the free paper and have to bribe Jenny the babysitter with double time to get her away from her seed germination trays in order that I can be first on the vendor's doorstep with the cash in my hand. It is to be Giles's birthday present, and must therefore be erected tonight. More bribing of Jenny, and the presence of Smalls, are the only way to get the vast slab into the house. It takes hours, during which there are many moments of tight-lipped silence, and bursts of strong language. Comforting to think that the rows are nothing to what they would have been if we had all been married to one another. At last it is up. The glossy balls beckon in a neat squad on acres of smooth green. A quick game is called for to celebrate, and a few beers to relax us. Totter to bed at three in the morning, with muscles seizing up after unnatural exertion of becoming a removals woman, and crone-like curved spine setting in. Sleep is scarcely achieved when The Beauty begins her matutinal calls at six o'clock in the morning.

November 18th

Giles's birthday. He tears downstairs to open his cards, and tries to look grave and don't care-ish that his present pile consists only of Silly Putty, a pair of Superman socks and a book token from a great-aunt.

'Oh, it's great,' he says of the Silly Putty, 'I've always wanted some.'

The rest of us, having festooned the snooker table in ribbons while Giles was getting dressed, cannot bear the suspense. Before he can finish his bacon, Felix has blindfolded him and he is being propelled by The Beauty, through rather than around furniture, to the playroom.

'Surprise. Happy Birthday!' Felix and I shout, and Giles opens his eyes. The hugest grin splits his face.

'Wow, wow, wow,' he gasps. And then hugs me and Felix, patting The Beauty's head, trying to thank all of us at once. 'Thank you, Mummy.'

Weep mawkishly into a tea towel as he and Felix purr and exclaim at the top-notch present. Charles has supplied cues, a triangle, many blocks of blue chalk, one of which The Beauty is keenly sucking, and some bar towels. Why bar towels? Instantly find a use for them, though, and ambush The Beauty with a towelling rectangle saying 'Carlsberg', before she can leave the room to smear blue slug trails from her fingers and face onto everything.

Six boys come back from school to stay the night. None of them sleeps, preferring to play snooker and watch videos of *The Full Monty*, *The Simpsons* and *Fawlty Towers* all night. Following Giles's instructions to the letter, I feed them marshmallows, Coke, Twiglets and slices of processed cheese. I am banned from going into the attic, which they have made their lair, but have to communicate via walkie-talkie.

November 19th

The tallest of Giles's friends thanks me for a lovely time and for being 'a totally chilled mother'. My day is made.

November 23rd

My birthday. As usually, totally birthdayed-out by this point and have reached a point far beyond civility or even partying. Elect to go to the cinema with my mother and Simon and Vivienne in the evening. Giles and Felix are adorable and make me breakfast in bed. Scrambled eggs, toast, strawberry Nesquik and Toblerone arrive on a tray with three home-made cards. Felix's has a zebra on it wearing sunglasses. It has a cartoon balloon wafting above its mouth announcing: 'It's a Stripy Day'. The Beauty's is more abstract with just a smear of butter and a couple of crumbs, and Giles's is a still life of a tennis shoe. There are presents too.

'We bought them with Granny in Budgens,' explains Felix, wrapping one leg round the other and overbalancing in anticipation. He has given me a packet of chocolate cornflakes.

'How delicious, Felix, how did you know that I love these the most?'

He is terribly pleased with this reaction. 'Do you? That's really good. I chose them because they've got Space Trolls inside, and I wanted one.'

Giles kicks him; he howls.

'Shut up,' says Giles. 'You shouldn't give people things just because you want them.'

'Shut up yourself. You didn't even buy Mummy something in Budgens. You—'

Wave my arms and yell as forcefully as possible from trapped position beneath my tray. 'Come on, you two, let's not have a row. Let's see what Giles has given me.'

It is a false arm.

'It's meant to be like The Thing in *The Addams Family*,' says Giles, watching me keenly and trying to gauge my reaction. 'I got it in the shopping mall in Cambridge.'

The arm wears a white sleeve and likes to be draped out of pianos or car doors. Am nonplussed. Fortunately Giles has stopped looking at me. He has seized the arm and is demonstrating its skill at dangling from my knicker drawer. Following the success of this interlude, the arm is accompanied out of the room and around the house, until it is finally given some peace when it is posted through the letter box.

'Mum, will you take a photograph of the postman when he sees it?'

The Beauty gives me a pair of false eyelashes and a leather diary.

'How smart and kind. What a thoughtful—'

Am interrupted by the return of Felix. He picks up the diary.

'Oh, no! You can't have this, Mum. You'll be arrested. The Beauty stole it. In fact, she shoplifted it. What's the difference?' Felix pauses to glare at his sister.

'I'm not sure.'

'Well, anyway, Granny didn't notice it in the pushchair when we came out of the newspaper shop. It's a crime, and I said I'd take it back and I forgot. Will she be in trouble?'

He removes the stolen goods. Am very impressed by the high moral tone, but also disappointed; a new diary would be perfect. Perhaps I can sneak it back when Felix has forgotten about it again.

My mother meets me at the cinema with a green furry hot-water-bottle cover and a bunch of white roses made of satin and adorned with plastic dewdrops. David is with her. Immensely cheering, as Simon and Vivienne cannot come, and three are always better than two at dealing with Cromer.

'Happy Birthday, Venetia.' David kisses me and proffers a selection of gifts. 'I couldn't decide what to give you, so I brought all the things I had available.'

Not quite sure how to take this. There is a leopard-skin lead for Rags, who never has one, with a label saying, 'Love from Digger.' There is a scarf with poppies and anemones on it, and a glass scent bottle with a crystal stopper.

'Oh, David, how lovely. And how girlie.'

Eyes begin to smart with emotion and excitement. Suddenly realise what a thrill it is to receive girlie things, and how I have missed it. Hug him, accidentally dropping my hot-water-bottle cover into a puddle.

After the film (most satisfactory, being a costume drama with many horses, spirited heroines plus swashbuckling men, almost all of Georgette Heyer or Tolstovian quality), we scuttle down the High Street to the Indian, which apart from Le Moon, is the only restaurant to stay open beyond nine o'clock. Order Tiger beers and piles of poppadoms from a waiter who looks like a parrot with a curved nose and shaggy hair in a crest from his crown to his shoulders. Mouthwatering smells of grilling chicken and sauces seep from the kitchen and we eat all the poppadoms while admiring the disco decor of black velvet walls with hanging baskets of neon-green plastic plants and gold foil ceiling. David is wearing a grey shirt of extreme softness and loveliness, cut to emphasise broad shoulders. Cannot stop looking at it, coveting it and the notion of having someone to give it to. Wonder who gave it to him. Don't dare ask. We stay at the restaurant until one in the morning and drink quantities of Bailey's Irish Cream liqueur.

Driving my mother home, am engulfed in warm joy.

'This was an especially nice birthday,' I enthuse, but am met with a deep exhalation of breath. She is asleep in the back seat, propped up against The Beauty's throne, having refused to travel in the front because of my driving.

November 27th

Winter, as always, sets in as soon as the birthdays are over, and a sharp frost last night has left the hens' water bowl frozen and the car windscreen sparkly and groovy to look at but impossible to see through. Pour kettle of boiling water over it; very pleased with myself for remembering this practical tip. The piglets are going to the butcher today, so I cannot bear to be at home. We gave them apple crumble and fish fingers and macaroni cheese for their last supper. During this melancholy half-hour, one of the fruitcakes bit Giles, while a pink scraped the top layer of skin from my shin with its razor-sharp hoof, so their departure is not all bad.

Drop the boys at school and take The Beauty shopping in Norwich. Appalled to discover that Christmas is in full swing a mere twenty miles from my home, and all shops are decked with tinsel and piping carols. The Beauty has huge fun dancing along to 'Ding Dong Merrily' in the Marks & Spencer's ladies' changing room, where I try on and reject three depressing, matronly skirts, and finally select a knee-length pink felt one from the children's section. Marks & Spencer fourteen-year-old girls are the size of normal adults. Must be the delicious oven-ready meals. Buy many of these, especially the puddings. Supper with the boys tonight will be great, we shall have chicken Kiev with ready-washed new potatoes and chocolate bread-and-butter pudding.

'Mmmmmm. Yummy, yummy,' says The Beauty, who is most interested by the shopping and has climbed onto the conveyor belt to help me. Think about doing Christmas shopping, like everyone else, but am too daunted to begin. Have made no lists as yet, so am paralysed. The Beauty and I spend the afternoon in the toy shop testing different kitchen sets. She likes the most expensive one. It is an architect-designed cooker and surface set based on a highly fashionable restaurant, and has lots of organic-looking plastic veg on shelves and sheaves of black spaghetti. It also has heavenly miniature enamel implements, and a set of saucepans I could share with The Beauty. They would be big enough for boiling a bantam egg or making hot chocolate for one. Very practical. Very economical. Am so relieved that she doesn't like the soppy Cabbage Patch kitchen that I buy the architect-designed one for her. It costs more than I can believe; all the props are extra, but I am in too deep and just pay up. It will be delivered the week before Christmas. Hooray. One down, just a few more now. Pity it cost all my money.

Head for home, but pause at a groovy men's clothes shop, attracted by my favourite Willie Nelson track reaching its crescendo on the shop's sound system. A completely beautiful purple shirt beckons from the first rail. Simultaneously, The Beauty and I reach out and touch it.

'Aaah,' she says.

'Ooh,' I agree.

Buy it, and on the way home wonder why. Who can I give it to? Desmond, I suppose. What a waste. Maybe I can keep it myself.

November 29th

Sunday morning is spent arguing with the children. Their view of Christmas shopping is that I should take them to a shop, let them run riot and then pick up the tab. Mine is that they should choose very tiny, inexpensive items for everyone and pay for them with their own money. Cold War; no compromise is reached.

In despair, I make cheerful Blue Peter suggestion: 'I know, why don't you make a few things instead?' Giles is horizontal under the table, throwing tiny blobs of Blu-Tack at the underside of the tabletop above him. He drips sarcasm.

'Like what? I suppose you think it's easy to make a remote-control aeroplane which flies, or a size four rugby ball? You're on totally the wrong wicket, Mum.'

Pleased to know roughly what his slang means, and to note that 'wicket', popular when I was a child and in P. G. Wodehouse books, is making a comeback.

'No, I mean things like lavender bags and furry purses like we saw at that craft fair.' Felix takes the bait.

'Yes,' he says, already getting overexcited, 'we can do giraffe-skin frames, too. Mum's got some giraffe skin, haven't you?'

I nod, scanning my memory hastily to see if I can remember where I put the large fake-fur slices I bought last Christmas to make cuddly toys and did nothing with.

Felix continues, his tone now one of serious responsibility, 'But I don't think we should use the zebra skin because it's whole.'

Giles continues to kick furniture and look cross. We ignore him and assemble excellent items including glitter glue, fake fur, sequins, dyed feathers, gold spray and bubble wrap. These are irresistible. Before Felix has finished cutting his first strip of giraffe, Giles is at the table, expression now friendly and interested, demanding to be shown how to spray bubble wrap. Am able to enjoy fully the smug sense of being a Blue Peter kind of mother with Blue Peter children until I remember The Beauty. She has been occupied in silence, in the play-room, for some twenty minutes. Disaster. I have wronged her. She is in her tent with a Superman cape flung over her shoulders and a Red Indian headdress round her neck. On her head she has a suede cap with a foil hoe sticking out of the top, a relic from Felix's school play. Her tiny feet are wedged into the long toes of a pair of red velvet stilettos with one stiletto missing. When I look in, she is leaning towards a hand mirror dabbing at her face with a paintbrush.

'She's getting ready to go out and she's dressed up, just like you do, Mum,' laughs Felix.

The Beauty glances round at us and bats her eye-lashes before turning back to her toilette.

WINTER

December 1st

Postcard from Rose arrives with picture of a dolphin on it. 'Darling Venetia, you must have one of these new massages. It will make you feel like a dolphin. This is your late birthday token. Ring me to activate it and a pint-sized masseuse will arrive bearing table and swaddling gear. Prepare for meltdown.'

December 2nd

Do I want to feel like a dolphin?

December 4th

Am now an astral body and live on an astral plane where nothing matters and calm is deep and blue like the sea. Have been pummelled, kneaded, unravelled, unwound, stroked and filleted. Am more like an ear than a whole skeleton, being boneless now, and lacking any tension anywhere, so I could just slide through a wedding ring if anyone wanted me to. Thankfully, my mother is collecting the children and has The Beauty, for I am fit for nothing but silken sleep. Mmmmmm.

December 6th

Silken sleep was short-lived, but state of blue calm lasted forty-eight hours. It has now evaporated and been replaced by hysteria and also dogged determination. I have a puncture and I don't know how to fix it. More importantly, I do not want to find out how to fix it. I want someone else to do it. Am keen to master a variety of physical skills, including how to get rid of garden moles and how to syphon petrol, but not punctures. Have reached the age of thirty-five and had three children and, briefly, a husband, all without knowing how to change the tyre on a car. Anyway, I would be bound to do it wrong and the wheel would come off round a bend and cause a terrible accident.

Stand idiotically on the side of the road, next to a very smart triangle I found in the car boot. The triangle has an exclamation mark in the middle. Am sure that it makes me look efficient and in control. A silver car with blacked-in windows and throbbing music radiating from it stops. A greasy-haired creep gets out.

''Allo, sweetheart. Need rescuing, do ya?'

His neck is wider than his head, giving him the appearance of a gorilla. But not a friendly one. He leers and chews gum aggressively. Wish I had a big dog or a gun. The Beauty has taken charge inside the car, and stands on the driver's seat twiddling knobs and wiggling the steering wheel. Her lip trembles when the creep approaches, and tears well. I lean against the door, shielding her from him, and make a feeble excuse.

'I think I'll just wait a minute. Someone's coming to pick me up soon, anyway. I can manage. Thank you for stopping, but there's no need for you to wait, my friend will be here any minute.'

This is a big lie, but as I utter it, it becomes true. A throaty chugging sound heralds David's ambulance. It pulls up, menacingly close to the creep's car, the brakes squealing a protest like the fruitcake pigs.

David leans out, his face hard, angry, with his jaw clenched, and says to my would-be rescuer, 'OK, mate, thanks for your help but I'll sort this one out.'

Am most impressed by his aggressive stance as he swings out of his vehicle and moves over to stand protectively next to me and my puncture. Have to fight impulse to giggle weakly and hide head in his manly biceps. The creep narrows his eyes, rolls his jaw as if moving marbles in his mouth and evidently cannot think of anything cutting to say. He curses under his breath and spits his gum into the road before slamming himself back into his car and roaring off. Look to David to make fun of this interlude, but find he is grinding his teeth and wearing thunderous expression, not unlike that of thwarted creep, in fact.

'How can you be so stupid, Venetia? What if I hadn't come along? You are here on your own, in the middle of nowhere, with a baby. It's getting dark. Christ only knows what you've done with Giles and Felix, but presumably they're waiting for you somewhere. And don't even pretend that you know how to change that tyre. I know you don't and I'm going to show you now, so this cannot happen again.'

Mouth gapes, arms hang slack in astonishment and I keep quiet until he has finished and is scrabbling about in the boot looking for something. He doesn't find it, and slams the boot but starts rummaging in the Land Rover instead. Have an urge to vent my own spleen, and do so.

'I don't want to learn how to change a bloody tyre. That's what men are for. I would have easily got some-one to do it by now if you weren't standing here giving sanctimonious lectures. And actually the boys are with Vivienne and we're on our way to meet them and have tea.'

He misses most of this, as his head is in the bowels of the Land Rover.

'You need a jack first. Your car hasn't got one, which is peculiar. You must buy one.'

'I don't want one.'

'You will when you know what to do with it.'

'I don't want to know what to do with it.'

'Grow up.' The crisp delivery of these words leaves me smarting. David looks round to see why I am not answering back, and continues smoothly, passing me a weird-shaped bit of metal.

'Now I want you to do this yourself. This is the jack. Put the jack here behind the wheel and twist the handle clockwise. *I said clockwise. . .*'

On and on he goes, bossing me about as if I am five. The Beauty waves occasionally from her snug disco scene within the lopsided car, but is mainly oblivious to any humiliation and David's smug and patronising manner.

'. . . And you just check for one last time that each nut is tight before you put the hubcap back on.'

It is almost dark now, and my fingers are blunt and without feeling. I am cold, tired and depressed. David, on the other hand, appears overjoyed, and his former flint-like expression has given way to a wide grin.

'Well done. It wasn't so bad, was it? I'm really glad you made the effort, and I know you will be too. Next time it'll be so easy for you.'

His good cheer radiates through the dark and it is impossible to go on being cross. Instead I have a go at being graceful.

'It was very considerate of you to teach me how to change a puncture, and I really appreciate it.'

He laughs and climbs into his car, switching on the engine and letting it idle a little.

'I'm sure you don't. But you will. A single woman needs to be practical. I'll teach you now to split logs with an axe next.' He chugs away, missing a selection of filthy language which The Beauty copies.

'Oh, bugger off. Oh, bugger off. Bugger, bugger, bugger, HA HA!' she trills all the way to Vivienne's. There, just for good measure, she tries her new word on Simon. Finding him watching television, she homes in on him, patting his arm, smiling angelically and announcing, 'Oh, bugger,' in her breathiest voice. Simon's response is pleasing.

'That's really splendid, isn't it? Such a shame about the fog. Come and watch the local news, my dear.' He pats the seat next to him and The Beauty, sensing a kindred spirit, climbs on and becomes absorbed in the teatime news and weather.

December 8th

Sidney is ill. His coat stares and his eyes are dull. Dare say he has swallowed a fishbone or half a pheasant, but take him to the vet anyway, as work-avoidance exercise. It backfires. The journey is ghastly. We have no box, so he flits about the car miaowing and shedding hair. Finally subsides, emitting a menacing whine and flurrying hair, under my foot. Have to kick him to avoid crashing into a sugar-beet lorry. Vet gives him a pill, says, 'He's got worms,' and charges me £28. Wish I had Pet Plan, as recommended by Charles.

December 10th

Hurtling towards Christmas now, and am in deepest disgrace with Felix for not having the skill to make his costume for the nativity play. He is Joseph, and he has to sing a solo.

'All the other mothers are making costumes. They come to the school and sit in the library and sew and have coffee and stuff.' This outburst accompanies a session in the charity shop where I attempt to put together an Galilean carpenter's outfit scaled down to seven-year-old size; Felix refuses to have anything to do with me.

'I am not wearing that,' he hisses, when I hold up a matted purple knitted tunic.

I am reluctant to let so charming an item go without a fight: 'But it would look great over something long. Like a tabard.'

'I hate tabards. And I hate all this sort of thing.' He flings an expansive arm wide to include everything in the shop. Realise that I am not sure I know what a tabard is. Never mind. The big thing is to get out of the charity shop without either of us having a tantrum.

December 11th

Am at the sewing circle. Sewing. Badly. Try to rise above the frightfulness as Felix is very pleased with me, and skipped into school today making sure all his friends and their mums noticed his own immaculately behaved parent.

'Mummy's doing sewing today. She's making costumes,' he told Peregrine. Peregrine has a Roundhead haircut and is the most pampered boy in the school due to his mother having been forty-two and very rich when she had him, and because he is her only child after twenty years of trying.

'Tho what?' lisps poisonous Peregrine, 'my mum hath

been thewing ev'wy day and my coth-thume hath got sequinzth on it.'

Peregrine has been wildly miscast as the Angel Gabriel. His mother, Trisha, is a hell-cat, and is only attending the sewing circle to interfere in other people's work. Of course, she finished hers days ago, and it hangs on a rail at the end of the room, an example to us all, twinkling like something Gary Glitter might have worn in the seventies. She lords it over us for a while, then seizes my cloth and needle.

'That is not blanket stitch, Venetia. This is how you do it.'

As she hems the brown nylon, fashioning it, I hope, into a tabard, she sighs and glances at me contemptuously from beneath long, blue-mascaraed lashes. But what care I? She is my salvation, and makes the whole Joseph outfit for me. Hooray. Am now confident that Felix will be pleased with his costume for the play.

December 14th

Am sure that Christmas party invitations should be flooding in by now, and also seasonal cards to display on the mantelpiece, and if very popular, to hang on strings around the room. Today's post yields only the telephone bill and a children's gift catalogue. Resolve to do all my Christmas shopping right now from this catalogue. How splendid it will be in a minute, when I have chosen everything and dispatched the order. Getting along famously, and have just selected a Truth Machine for Charles, when I turn the page and recoil in horror. Utterly trashy, gaudy trembly letters announce Charles's clockwork coffin, updated since the one Felix had, but no less loathsome. A whole page is devoted to parading its virtues.

HEAVENLY PETTING ENTERPRISES
brings you memories to treasure when Poochy
passes on or Cheepy tweets his last. No pet will ever
leave you with our clockwork mini coffins. Pop a pinch of
your pet's ashes in through the plastic opening lid and you
have a personalised memento. It's as easy as that!
Wind the key and listen to evocative music,
chosen to bring your pet back to life.

Gasp at this brazen lie, then notice very small letters almost vanishing off the page: 'In your mind and heart, if not in person.'

This high treat costs £20. Charles is plumbing new depths. Telephone his answering machine to register disapproval, and get Helena instead.

'Hello, Venetia, how are you?'

'Fine, thanks.' God. I sound just like the children. Must do better.

'And how are you, Helena? When are the babies due?'

A long pause, then Helena's voice like acid down the line.

'I thought Charles had told you. They're due in ten days' time. On Christmas Eve. They're being induced so we don't have to wait until after the Christmas break.' She sounds as if she is talking about the arrival of a pair of curtains.

I babble back, 'Gosh, what a good idea. Bye, then.' Slam the telephone down and burst into tears. Must stop being so pathetic about all this. Is a shrink needed? Telephone Rose for guidance.

December 16th

Giles and Felix depart for school staggering beneath mountains of costumes and Rice Krispie cakes. Party season has begun for them with a vengeance, and after the dress rehearsal for the nativity play, Felix is going to a cast party, while Giles is doing the same after the choir's final carol service rehearsal in the chapel. Wave them off, propping The Beauty on the windowsill, and remain rooted for some time, not wishing to turn back towards the squalor of the breakfast table. Enchanting bird activity brings the yard to life. First, two bluetits swoop out from the eaves of the barn, and alight for a second to peck at the hen food Giles scattered earlier. They are joined by a chaffinch, rose pink and mauve and pretty as a flower, and a pair of yellow-hammers. A drab lady blackbird is next on the scene, and once she has tested the food, she calls to her mate, who swanks over, glorious in his glossy black plumage with show-off yellow beak. Wagtails, a gaudy cerise bullfinch and a group of greenfinches all gather too, and flutter low to scoop a morsel of food before lilting back up into the plum tree or into cosy nooks in the roof of the barn. The Beauty and I are enchanted. She keeps quite still, whispering 'Chicks,' delightedly every few minutes, sensing that to raise her voice will disperse them.

Tell the boys at bathtime that Daddy and Helena's babies will be there for Christmas. Have steeled myself for this moment and even bought special cereal with free trolls as a treat to give them in their pyjamas afterwards and so cheer them up.

No need. Felix, cocooned in a towel being an egg, is the only one to register that I have spoken. His voice is muffled, but as he slowly extends each limb, hatching from his towel shell, he answers, 'Yeah, I know. I'm making them a football team, but they'll have to share one because I haven't got time to colour in two. Will they like Arsenal? I'm not doing Cambridge United, they're sad.'

Giles, already in his pyjamas, is cuddling Rags in the bathroom armchair.

'Mum, Rags is really fat. I think she's got worms. Sidney had them, didn't he?'

'Let's give her a pink pill. I'm sure there's one left from last time I had them,' suggests Felix.

December 17th

My mother just pips Charles to the post, and her car hiccups and lurches up the drive in front of his. They exchange stilted greetings in the yard and The Beauty and I emerge before an embarrassing silence can set in. The Beauty is effusive in greeting her relations and blows kisses, keenly aware of the majestic effect she creates in her cherry-red velvet coat with ermine trim and her white fur hat. Charles salutes my cheek and opens the door of his car.

'I'm not going in that sports car,' shrills my mother. 'And neither is The Beauty. What's wrong with my car?'

Charles shrinks, clutching The Beauty awkwardly and shuddering.

'It stinks,' I reply, 'and Egor's in it and he's white. His hairs will go all over everyone's clothes and we need to look smart.'

My mother bridles at the hint of any criticism of Egor, who is drooling away inside the car and wagging his tail, delighted by the mention of his name. Charles deftly proffers a solution.

'Let's go in Venetia's car. It's got the child seat in it anyway.'

'All right, but I'm sitting in the front,' insists my mother.

Not surprisingly, we are late for Felix's nativity play, and are forced to sit in the front row because those are the only places left. This pleases Felix. A broad grin spreads beneath his matted-wool Joseph beard when he arrives on stage. I smile back, sniffing, having wept silently through his solo rendition of 'Away In A Manger', performed in darkness as the cast assembled. My mother, on the other side of Charles, is also much affected, and mops her face with a huge pink silk handkerchief. Charles glances at both of us, sighs, and tries, unsuccessfully, to look relaxed. None of us has a camera. Peregrine's mother leans over, fluttering her eyelashes (purple today) at Charles.

'Shall I make copies for you?' she whispers, pointing at her camera. Irritated, I pretend not to hear, but Charles accepts eagerly.

'How kind. Venetia appears to have forgotten to bring a camera.'

'There was nothing to stop you bringing one,' I hiss,

too loudly, as the Angel Peregrine twinkles across to deliver the good news to Mary.

'Sssshhhhh!' says Charles, enjoying my being in the wrong.

I seize an opportunity in a million.

'It's just like Helena's immaculate conception, isn't it?' Charles presses his lips together. If looks could kill. . . Ha ha. They can't.

'Oh, bugger and bye bye,' shouts The Beauty, jumping up as Felix leaves the centre of the stage to help some infant sheep find their positions. Dissolve into silent, stifled giggles. Shaking shoulders beyond Charles suggest that my mother has done the same.

Mince pies and coffee afterwards and Charles dissociates himself from us and works the room. He hands one of his cards to Peregrine's mother, and another to the headmistress. Overhear him offering to come and talk to the children.

'For of course they must prepare for grief, even at this age.'

'God, he makes me sick,' I snarl to my mother. 'In fact I'm glad he's having more children, it means he won't have to see mine so often.' Choke on a mince pie as an arm and a gentle hand rests round my waist for a moment. Turn to find David behind me, and am struck by the contrast between him with his red felt shirt and easy, wide smile and the many pale-faced, balding and besuited fathers in the room. He has Felix in tow and they are both eating tangerines.

'Hi, Venetia, I've just hauled this young star out from backstage; it's time to go to Giles's carol service, and Felix has promised to get me a seat in the gallery if I'm early, so I'm taking him now.' Hardly have time to kiss Joseph-I-mean-Felix, before they are gone.

'I suppose the children must have invited him,' muses my mother. 'Jolly nice of him to come.'

By the time we arrive at the chapel, it is dusk, and snow is falling as if in silent slow motion. Inside, the smell of wax and holly and oranges and expensive scent mingles with the excitement and expectation in the air, to create an immediate sense of Christmas. We find seats at the back, and can just make out David's red shirt next to Felix's small, craning head at the other end. The rustle of coats and murmur of voices subsides as the lights dim for the candlelit procession. A silver-voiced boy sings 'In the Bleak Midwinter', and sends a shiver up my spine. The service is uplifting and joyous, and as we queue to leave I am able to smile pleasantly at Charles and to introduce him to David.

'I think you may have met sometime at the house. Or maybe not,' I add.

Charles has not enjoyed his afternoon, although he did look pleased when Felix sang, and now slips Giles a fiver, saying, 'Use it for something fun for you and Felix. You did well.'

He turns to David and smiles briefly.

'Good of you to come,' he says, as if he had personally invited him, then looks at me. 'If you don't mind, Venetia, we should be going. I have to be in Cambridge in time for dinner.'

'Can we go with David and get fish and chips, please, Mum?' begs Giles.

'And a video,' adds Felix. 'You said we should see *Goldeneye* next. And David and Granny both really want to see it too. They said so.'

Bundle Charles into my car, hastily agreeing to everything in order to make my getaway without Charles learning too many of the slobbish details of our domestic life.

'That fellow seems very familiar,' he comments. 'Cosy set-up he's got with the boys. I should watch yourself there, Venetia.'

Am so angry that I cannot speak, so resort to Radio One to torture him for the ten-minute drive home.

December 20th

First buds of the hyacinths I planted and left in the airing cupboard have now opened, releasing a tide of bluebell scent through the house. Very thrilling, as I left them in the dark much longer than recommended and thought they might not recover in time for Christmas.

December 22nd

Excitement at fever pitch. Felix and The Beauty have taken every sock in the house and laid them in a line from the fireplace in the dining room up to their bedrooms. No one is allowed to wear any of them until they have chosen their Christmas stockings. Giles, who was given a personalised stocking with his name embroidered on it at birth, ignores the sock queue and continues to sew lavender bags and make giraffe-skin purses. Like any convert, he is far more zealous than those who always thought it a good idea to make a few presents. His mission is to avoid spending any of his own money on Christmas. Can't help admiring his resolution as I write the fifteenth cheque of the day, this one to the sewage man who has chosen this moment for his annual servicing of the cesspit.

December 23rd

According to Delia Smith, I am too late to start cooking Christmas dinner. I should have begun a month ago. Hate her smug line on preparing chestnut purée and getting up at seven a.m. to stuff the turkey and put it in the oven. Read her four essential shopping lists and realise that I am so inadequately equipped I may as well give up. Have no lattice cutter, no fuse wire or fuses, no spare set of Christmas-tree lights and no Tupperware. But I do have a Christmas cake, made by me and Felix a month ago (although Delia recommends three months, which would mean almost making it in the summer holidays). I have been spiking it with brandy every day, and am very proud of it. Giles fetches it from the larder and we peel off the layers of greaseproof paper to ice it. I can scarcely believe that we have made something so textbook.

'Let's do an arctic battle on it,' suggests Giles. Twenty minutes pass while four favourite Warhammers and three pink-haired trolls are placed in exact formation on the snowy royal icing.

We charge on through our pre-Christmas rituals, and go out to gather holly and mistletoe in the glittering bite of the frosty late afternoon, all bundled up in scarves and hats, boots and gloves. The children have red cheeks and bright sparkling eyes in an instant. Perfect, story-book afternoon, I think to myself, watching them dash to and fro as a vast pink sun descends to the horizon. Idyllic, and so much better than Delia's thirty-six-hour countdown to Christmas spent tied to the cooker. How I love my life in the country with my brood. It has all been worthwhile.

'Mummy, we haven't got a tree.' Felix hurls down a branch of holly in the lane and begins to howl. He's right. I have forgotten the Christmas tree. It is a disaster.

'Oh, God, how can I be so stupid? I knew I'd forgotten something. Quick, into the car, we'll go and find one at that roadside stall we saw yesterday. They had lots, don't worry.'

Felix sobs all the way and it begins to rain. Our heaps of holly will be soaked. We will not be able to decorate the house with it. The stall is packing up, and has no Christmas trees left over three feet tall.

'We can't have those, they're tiny,' screams Felix. 'The presents won't fit under them.'

I think of the mountain of unwrapped presents hidden in my study, the heap of washing-up in the sink, the forest of holly outside the back door and the unlaid and unlit fire in the drawing room. I, too, begin to weep. Giles pats my hand.

'Let's go and see if there are any at the garage, and if there aren't, let's ring David. He'll be able to find us one.'

Am very impressed by Giles's calm competence. Do exactly as he says, and moments later am sitting outside a telephone box while he makes a deal with David. He comes back to the car looking delighted.

'He's going to bring it round in an hour,' he says. 'It was really lucky, he said he was about to go out and then we wouldn't have got a tree at all.'

Felix maintains a distrustful silence until the tree is standing in its bucket next to the fireplace and David is testing the lights. Astonishingly, they work. Calm and good cheer return, and Felix begins sorting decorations and hanging them. The stress of the episode leaves me light-headed and heavy-limbed with exhaustion. A drink is called for. I offer one to David.

'Please stay and have a beer or a whisky or something. It was so brilliant of you to save us.'

'It's fine, it was easy.' David laughs it off, and turns to accept a pink sock The Beauty has brought him. Giles jumps onto the sofa arm next to me and whispers, 'He said I mustn't tell you, but David's given us his tree, and now he hasn't got one, so I think you should ask him to Christmas here.'

Am mortified to think of him in a house barren and empty of twinkliness for Christmas, but somehow balk at inviting him here. Can't face letting him in on the spectacle of us all in paper hats, and each wearing every item of clothing we are given on top of our Christmas Day outfits, in time-honoured family tradition. Will give him a present instead. Leave the room to rootle through my carrier bags. There is nothing suitable. I can't give him the orange nylon beard I bought for Desmond, or the snooker cue planned for Giles. Shuffle some more, and into my hands falls the delicious purple shirt. Perfect. Could have been made for him. He will look lovely in it.

Wrap it in a bit of wallpaper and return to the sitting room. Hiss at Giles, 'Let's give him this to say thank you,' but Giles doesn't hear; he has sidled over to where The Beauty and David are untangling a wooden apple from a tiny carved angel.

'We'd really like you to come here for Christmas Day, David,' he says, before I can stop him.

I interrupt, hoping to deflect him from answering and saying yes.

'Here. We've got you this.' I thrust the parcel at him.

Try to avoid his eye, but fail, and he is watching me intently, catching my expression of frozen embarrassment. He knows I don't want him to come. Oh, it's too awful. Maybe I do. Help. We're too badly behaved for strangers to cope with, and there's already Rose and Tristan. There won't be room. David is still looking at me, doubtless reading all these thoughts as they flit through my tiny, transparent brain. Am so embarrassed, and have flushed crimson; can feel it above my polo neck. Must look like a beetroot-head. David squeezes my hand, then coughs, giving himself time to choose his answer, and somehow manages to convey huge pleasure and no noticeable offence.

'No room at the inn,' he says lightly. 'But yours is the best offer I've had for Christmas, thank you, Giles, and all of you. I would love to, but I can't. I'm going to see my parents in Newmarket, so I'll open your present there. But thank you for asking me.'

I slump onto the sofa, relieved but a little deflated.

December 24th

Rose, Tristan and Theo burst into the house at a moment of high squalor. The Beauty has emptied a packet of icing sugar onto the kitchen floor and is making patterns with it, unnoticed because Rags has just given birth to a black puppy and is in the midst of squeezing a second one into the world.

'I thought she just had worms, Mummy, but she was pregnant. I think they're Digger's. How sweet. Black Russells. Can we keep them?'

Giles and Felix are ablaze with excitement, following me around, taking it in turns with the puppy, which they have wrapped in one of The Beauty's T-shirts. The second puppy is scarcely given a moment with its mother before it is tucked into one of those blasted socks which are still all over the house and not in any sock drawers. The telephone rings incessantly, the answerphone is bleeping and shouting in my study and a medley of Christmas carols plays in the sitting room, put on at breakfast time and now repeating for about the seventieth time.

‘Let’s call them Holly and Ivy,’ suggests Felix, as ‘The Running of the Deer’ warbles through the house.

‘Let’s call them The Ghost of Christmas Past and hope they’re just a bad dream,’ I mutter under my breath. I’ll kill David. I’ll kill Digger, the foul, sodding brute. Am now running on empty as far as goodwill goes.

‘Hello, darlings,’ says Rose, swooping all of us into her fragrant, silken embrace. Tears smart in my eyes. I have never been so pleased to see anyone in my life. Giles has ducked out of the collective hug to answer the telephone. He leaves it dangling and charges over to me, grinning.

‘Mum, Mum, it’s Dad. They’ve had the twins and they’re going to call them Holly and Ivy. It’s just like the puppies. It’s totally cool.’

Tristan gauges the situation as soon as he walks in, dumps the heap of expensively wrapped presents and interesting carrier bags he is carrying and reaches into one for a bottle. The cork cracks against the ceiling and rebounds into The Beauty’s icing sugar, creating a powder fountain. Doubled up with manic, hysterical laughter I manage to reach the telephone to congratulate Charles.

‘Well done. How lovely to have two little girls. Send Helena our love.’

Only when I get off the telephone do I realise that I truly am happy for Charles and Helena. I harbour not an ounce of bitter lemon about it, and while I can see that for them, their news is good, it is not half as engrossing as ours.

'Mum, Mum, look. She's just had another one. It's white and it's got legs about the size of a shrew. Let's call it Lowly.'

It is a positive relief to find there is no wood left in the stack by the fire. Peaceful ten minutes in the barn kicking logs is just what I need to restore equilibrium.

December 25th

'Gently lead those with young.' My mother cannot stop singing this reference to pregnant sheep from the *Messiah*. She is enchanted by the puppies, and likes Lowly best because he is not a Black Russell, and even at this early stage shows signs of having the chiselled profile and log-like physique of Egor.

'It is extraordinary that they can do that,' she muses.

'Do what, Granny?' asks Giles, lurking by the puppy basket taking photographs.

'Oh, you know, mating and stuff,' she replies vaguely. Giles is not easily put off.

'You mean have two different fathers for one litter of puppies?'

'Yes, darling.' She smiles fondly at him through lop-sided specs, relieved that he already understands.

'People can do it too,' continues Giles, with relentless logic. 'Or do Daddy's new babies count as another litter?'

My mother effects deafness and hurries towards the drinks tray. We drink toasts to all the young, including Holly and Ivy-Eff, as Tristan has christened the Cambridge twins. The toasts involve three bottles of champagne among Rose, Tristan, Desmond, my mother, The Gnome and me. We need the buffer of alcohol to be able to cope with the noisiest array of Christmas presents ever. The Beauty and Theo have a trumpet and a drum. Dreadful. They are laying waste to the architect-designed toy kitchen, and have posted a lot of black plastic spaghetti into the video recorder. It turns out that Tristan is in fact the architect who designed the kitchen.

'I could have got you that for free,' he says, and is kicked hard on the shins by Rose. She glares murderously at him.

'That is such an annoying thing to say.'

Worse than Theo and The Beauty's noise is that of the CD player Gawain has sent the boys, along with ten garage and house CDs. Hopes that they will not master the instructions are soon dashed. We cower for a while, then banish them to a bedroom.

'They'll come down when they're cold, and it won't

be for hours,' says my mother gleefully, pulling her chair closer to the fire and tipping a good measure of red wine into her glass. The Gnome is very overcome, and having chosen a small chair close to my mother with a good view of the Christmas tree, he sits in silence, smiling, but with a fat emotional tear strolling occasionally down his increasingly pink cheek. He usually spends Christmas Day alone with a nut roast in his caravan, but this year my mother insisted that he come here with her.

'I just couldn't bear the thought of his little face, woebegone at the window,' she explains.

The Gnome contributes a dish of lentils and some fifty-five per cent proof vodka which he makes into jellies with a packet of Rowntree's raspberry. We sample it before lunch, and it improves the cracker jokes no end. Felix's is the best, put to my mother who sits next to him.

'Granny, listen. How do hens dance?' Granny is puzzled.

'I don't know, you tell me, Felix.'

Felix shoots her a brimming look. 'Chick to chick,' he said triumphantly.

December 28th

Giles appears in my room at an ungodly hour, hair dishevelled, face lit with excitement.

'Mum, quick, look out of the window.'

It has snowed heavily in the night, and the garden is a chaste sheet of gleaming white, undulating slightly where lawn meets drive, but otherwise pure. 'I've woken Felix. Will you come and help us build a snowman?'

Giles is evidently in a hurry; he is eating bread and peanut butter and is already wrapped in three jerseys, a scarf and a pair of woolly gloves. His face is scarlet from two minutes in my warm bedroom.

'Out you go,' I propel him towards the door. 'I'll be there in a minute.'

The Beauty is convinced that the white floor show has been laid on especially for her, and dances on the doorstep, a genial gnomic figure in her bobble hat and glittering green wellies. She refuses to come out further, making blowing noises and shaking her head when coaxed. Instead she drags her deckchair onto the doorstep and climbs into it, hugely pleased with the spectacle of her mother and brothers rolling a vast white snowball in a shrinking spiral around the lawn. When the snowball is taller than Giles, we wedge it in the middle of the garden.

'It's got to be on a kind of rugby-ball tee,' explains

Giles, who is operations manager. 'Now for the head.' Another ball, another spiralling pattern on the broken-up snow.

'In art, at school, we have to make heads one-fifth the size of the body,' announces Felix. He inspects the ball doubtfully. 'Or maybe one-third for snowmen.'

Putting the head on the body requires Herculean strength, and is finally achieved by the brilliant placing of a plank onto the snowman's shoulders. I applaud the engineer.

'Well done, Giles, I would never have thought of that.'

Am dispatched into the house for an outfit. In the kitchen, The Beauty has been giving Rags some tips on mothering. Or maybe she is baby-snatching. The puppy Lowly has been removed from the basket with the other puppies, and is in The Beauty's pram, next to her dolly. Both are wrapped in napkins. Manage to prevent her from picking Ivy up by the tail, and swap Lowly for a toy rhino, hoping she will not notice the difference. We must make a gate to protect Rags and her children from The Beauty's nannying.

December 31st

Giles and Felix have gone to spend New Year with Charles and Helena and all-night television. They are very pleased not to be coming with me to my mother's party, chiefly because her television is very small and they might be made to join in with embarrassing dancing and singing. The Beauty has not been asked to Cambridge, but she will enjoy a bit of Granny's party until her bed-time. Accordingly, she arrives in Dalmatian pyjamas and dressing gown. My mother is similarly clad, but not with Dalmatians.

'I'm just going to change,' she says. 'Come and talk to Minna and Desmond.'

Follow her through the hall, and in the glare of the naked bulb there, notice something odd about her head.

'What have you done to your hair? Why is it purple?'

My mother dips her head and accelerates out of the hall and into the dining room.

'Because I dyed it. Actually, it's gone a bit wrong. It's more blue than I intended. I thought I'd read the instructions, but I missed out the gungy stuff, so I added it at the end.'

Minna and Desmond are snogging in the dining room. My mother squawks briskly and they separate, greet me, and continue with their job of laying the table. My mother hovers, moving candlesticks, fiddling with strands of ivy and trying to find a light for her cigarette. She can't face going to get dressed because she will have to dry her hair and it will be the colour of blueberries or worse.

'You know, I think it'll be a really wonderful colour when it's dry, and it'll look great with your blue velvet dress,' I say, thrusting her towards the stairs. 'Go on, or everyone will be here.'

'She's asked twenty people and there are only two chickens and some of The Gnome's lentils,' Desmond hisses, as soon as she leaves the room. 'They'll all get paralytic long before midnight.'

'I've brought some vol-au-vents,' soothes Minna. Desmond grimaces. 'Well you won't catch me eating them. I'm going to use up that ham and turkey we've still got right now and have a sandwich to keep me going.'

Minna rolls her eyes.

'He's always ravenous,' she says complacently. I wish I made someone feel ravenous all the time.

Desmond and I always become nostalgic in my mother's house. In fact Desmond seems unable ever to leave, and lives there in an impromptu fashion, insisting he is on his way back to London. Crammed with ephemera from our childhoods, including every clay or wood figure either of us ever made and brought home, and every macaroni-and-doily calendar, the house slopes and sags like the Moomintroll's residence. None of the doors shuts properly, and none of them has a key. My mother likes it like this, and although she keeps a bread knife beneath her mattress, she maintains it is for insurance purposes, and not because she is afraid.

Her friends, all aware of her doorkeeping policy, let themselves in, and we find a throng in the kitchen. The blue hair has worked a treat, and is now a heaped confection adorned with old silk roses, so tall that my mother has to curtsey at each doorway, as if in the court of Marie Antoinette. The only person taller than her hair is David, and his glamour in the shirt I gave him is astonishing. Had not expected it to have such a film star effect, and am quite overcome when he takes his jacket off and the shirt is on show.

'He's nice,' Minna whispers, as she passes drinks round. 'He's got such lovely broad shoulders. I like that in a man.'

'So much better in a man than in a glass of rum punch, for example,' agrees Desmond, who likes Minna to look at him alone. He is sporting a black eye this evening from a confrontation at the pub last night over whether Minna could be bought a drink by a man enamoured of her ankle chain. David leans against the mantelpiece with a rapacious woman called Verika.

'Tell me some things about wood and its uses,' I hear her ask him. God, the depths to which some people will sink. Especially Verika. She has been a friend of my mother's for ever; she was a famous model, or so she says, and always wears false eyelashes and a feather boa to hide the fact that her neck has turned to scrawn. Her skin is the colour and texture of a pickled walnut. She is very drunk and is trying to pick David up, making eyes at him and licking her rubber lips. Yuck. Nonplussed by the way she keeps bobbing her head and flicking her fringe about, he asks if she has a headache. She throws back her head, revealing perfect pearly teeth, and laughs loud and long. David keeps talking, but begins to shift nervously from foot to foot. Desmond and Minna, who have been sipping the rum punch as they circulate it, tumble over Egor and land on top of me on the sofa, giggling.

'Come on, Venetia. Find someone to dance with. Get David away from Verruca the Vampire and come with us. We've cleared the room next door and cranked up Mum's gramophone. Listen.'

Above swelling, rolling conversation, music swirls across the room. And David is pulling me to my feet, bowing and saying, 'Shall we dance?' Twirling, spinning, rock 'n' roll. As usual, Desmond is hurling his partner about the room. Luckily Minna only weighs about as much as a bunch of flowers, or he'd have a hernia. Am pleased I wore my floating tulip-red skirt and not the chic black trousers I had planned for a sophisticated and grown-up look. That idea was scuppered by The Beauty before we left home; ever the fashion leader, she clearly thought they were wrong for a party and dropped them into the bath, choosing a moment when I was concentrating on my make-up.

January 1st

It is dawn. Haven't gone to bed. Am delighted to be so advanced. Desmond, Minna, The Gnome, my mother and David are all still up too. Am feeling expansive and adoring. Adore them all. We toast the silver light of next year with sloe vodka. Then we toast Rags's puppies. David cannot stop laughing as my mother tells the story of all the Christmas Eve miracles. I smoke my twentieth cigarette of the night. Delicious. I haven't done anything this daring since before I had children.

January 2nd

Still hung-over. Thank God the boys aren't back until tomorrow. Light the fire, put on bedsocks and watch Marilyn Monroe films all afternoon with The Beauty and Minna. We eat a whole tin of Quality Street. David has taken Desmond to a football match. How wholesome men are.

January 4th

Dull grey sky and iron cold set in two days ago, and with no wind, or any form of weather at all. Can see no end to it. All the children are ill, chalk-faced with exhaustion and coughing like seasoned smokers. I can hardly do my jeans up, and can only wear one skirt with an elasticated waist because every other item of clothing is too tight. Also have a spot on my chin. It is the only totem of youth on a face otherwise careworn, dissipated and wrinkled. Too cold to try a face pack, so must put up with scaly, sallow skin and pensioner looks until the sun shines. Must rouse myself from torpor and try to persuade the children to write their thank-you letters. Wonder if I can still fake their handwriting? It would be so much easier to do it for them and skip the inevitable battle.

January 7th

Fatness peaks this morning, as I try to make myself respectable for first day of term and initial appearance in the school car park. Carefully ironed navy pinstripe trousers slide on with no trouble, although I do have to hold my breath to do them up. The effect is pleasing and businesslike until stooping over The Beauty to wedge her into her shoes. *Ping.* The button flies across the room, and my midriff, caught unawares, sags like a hammock. Can't find any safety pins, or a belt, so tie Rag's lead around the waist and untuck my shirt so it doesn't show. Why am I bothering? Who will care what I look like?

'Mum, Holly's pooed by the Aga and I trod in it.'

Felix limps into the hall, waving a shoe to which a chipolata of puppy shit is attached. Have to turn my face to the wall and force myself to take deep breaths to avert temper overflow.

School car park teems with clean cars and mothers who have had time to put make-up on and who have evidently been to health farms and also the Caribbean during the holidays. Trisha, mother of Peregrine, rushes over to me.

'Hello, Venetia, such a shame not to see you at Bronwyn's coffee morning. I was sure you'd be there, being so local. Did you forget?'

She blinks a hedge of emerald mascara at me and smiles.

'I wasn't asked,' I reply, hoping to sound disdainful and yet polite. She carries on blithely.

'It was such a hoot. She's having another one next week, and someone is coming to show us all some jewellery. Why don't you come, Venetia, it would do you good to get out a bit. I'll see if I can persuade Bronwyn to invite you, shall I? I'm sure one more wouldn't make much difference.'

God, how I loathe her. To my horror, I hear myself saying, 'Yes, that would be such fun, please do.'

January 8th

To Norwich, to purchase fun items in the sales and to find Felix some birthday presents. Wish I had been more organised with family planning and had given birth to him some other time, rather than just after Christmas when everyone is broke and it is difficult to muster energy for making more jellies. The sales are horrible, thronged people with sharp-edged bags barge into us and make The Beauty cry. Am about to brave the toy shop before lunch, in order to purchase Felix yet more bits of plastic to clog up the vacuum cleaner, when The Beauty squeals,

'Oooh, look!' and points, smiling across the crowd. The object of her attentions is tall and wears a plaid jacket and sheepskin-lined hat. Standing in front of the jewellery shop window is David. Amazing that The Beauty identified him, as his face is almost invisible between collar and hat, and there are far too many people milling about on the pavement.

'Venetia, what a surprise. This is hell, isn't it? Let's go and have some lunch. I owe you a treat as two of those puppies of yours seem to be Digger's. I dropped in and had a look at them this morning, but of course you were out. Here, I suppose.'

He swings The Beauty up onto his shoulders and leads me through a courtyard entrance I had never noticed before and into a restaurant. Enveloped in warmth and quiet, my senses invaded only by the murmur of conversation, the clink of glasses and the aroma of delicious food, I sigh with huge relief.

'What a treat. Will they mind The Beauty?'

'No, not at all. A friend of mine runs this place and he's got two kids of his own about her age. And I know that today's special is going to be fantastic – a tip from the chef.'

How wonderful: I don't even need to think about what to have. All decisions removed, my idea of bliss.

'Davey, Davey, give me your answer do,' sings The Beauty, nestling up to David. She thinks this song is his theme tune, to be sung whenever he appears, as if he is a Teletubby or similar. David sits her on his knee and posts bread into her mouth. She lolls against him, chewing dreamily for a few seconds, then, revived, sits up straight and bounces. Sip my wine and watch them, enjoying the picture they make, and happy not to have the ceaselessly moving Beauty on my knee for once.

Delicious lunch of lemon risotto and crunchy vegetables; hardly fattening at all. In fact quite possibly a Hay Diet lunch. So cheered by this thought that I have orange sorbet for pudding. A business lunch, as well as being slimming, as David is going to build a bunk bed for The Beauty and a safety zone for the puppies in the back of the hall. Am not sure if this is what he wants to be doing for the next few weeks, but when he hesitates, I just remind him that Digger's children need peace and space to grow up in. He agrees with alacrity.

'Of course they do. I'll just sort out a few things and be along next week.'

David's presence and the consumption of a bottle of Rioja over lunch eases the birthday shopping ordeal. We find a very excellent construction kit for Felix, with real cement and bricks. The Beauty buys a six-pack of trolls for him, and David chooses a projector with torch and clock. It comes in a complicated nylon suit and is for camping, I think. It is the kind of present I hate. I cannot make head or tail of its instructions, and become irritated.

'What's the point of giving him something no normal person can open?' I demand, just resisting to urge to stamp my foot. Am sure David is laughing at me, although there is not a quiver in his voice as he replies.

'Don't worry. I'll come and set it up with Felix. It really is very simple, you know. But you won't have to have anything to do with it at all.'

He can also help Felix build the little brick house. One look at the instructions, which include a section called, 'How to make floor plans to scale', has convinced me that I will have to retrain as an architect, or one of the three little pigs, to understand it. What a relief that The Beauty spotted David today.

January 10th

Cell-block-style cement skies and non-weather have given way to swirling sleet and hail. Cobwebs swing and flutter in the house, making sure that we cannot forget the draughts for a moment. I have taken to wearing three scarves, one around my waist, another to protect my neck and a third to keep my bottom warm. Odd how cold a bottom can get. I thought fat was supposed to insulate. Bronwyn telephones.

'I am sorry, Venetia, next week we simply haven't the

space for anyone else. But would you be interested in setting up your own Cabochon coffee mornings?'

'No. I'd rather die.' Oops. Not very graceful. Minus fifty brownie points, and Felix will be furious if he finds out. Take my mind off it with virtuous behaviour. Order packets of seeds from catalogue with no pictures and only Latin names. Jolly pleased with myself for coping with it. Cushion of smug deflates, however, when I add up the total and find I have spent £147. Try editing, but how can I get rid of any of these precious gems? My favourite is *Papaver somniferum*, Hen and Chickens, described thus in the catalogue.

> Flower-arrangers won't be able to wait to get their hands on this unusual strain of poppy, with its large, pale lilac flowers and curious seed-pod arrangement in which the central pod has arising from its base several little seed pods, giving the impression of a mother hen surrounded by her brood of chickens. The pods are very decorative when dyed and dried.

In fact, shall order two packets of this one, and create unique gifts for all next Christmas. Very pleased to have thought ahead for once.

January 14th

Felix is eight today. Lovely cosy breakfast with pancakes and chocolate topping is marred by frightful weather invading kitchen through the glazing bars. Torrents of icy water woosh onto the window sill, causing Felix's cards to curl up at the bottom. Roll up tea towels and balance them on window frames, then telephone David and ask him to bring a putty syringe when he comes and hope he is impressed with my expert knowledge. He says he is not coming until next week. This puts me in a filthy temper. Have to go outside and feed hens to recover and remind myself it is Felix's day.

Felix is much more excited by the troll six-pack and a PlayStation game given to him by Giles, than he is by my construction kit. Try not to mind, and get on with cake, which is to be in the shape of an Orc Chieftain and is to be the centrepiece of the party tea table tomorrow. Felix has chosen to throw a full-scale children's party, deeming that to have a couple of friends for the cinema is useless.

'I would hardly get any presents, Mum,' he explains, outraged that I can have made such a stupid suggestion.

January 15th

Arctic conditions prevail, and none of the ten children invited to the party has shut a single door since they arrived. Rather, they have opened them all, and a few windows, and are engaged in tramping quantities of mud and snow through the house. My mother and The Beauty are gathering objects to place on a tray for a memory game. The Beauty selects a lump of coal and a lavatory brush before tottering outside to join in the game of British Bulldogs on the lawn. My mother peels a lychee and adds it to the treasures on the tray, which include a scouring pad, a silver sugar shaker and a Boglin.

Grass-stained and flushed, the children troop inside as dark falls and more rain sets in. Lucille, a nasty piece of work from Felix's class, regards the tray with disgust.

'What horrible things,' she pipes. 'You have a really weird house, Felix.'

My mother grabs his wrist to prevent him from punching her, and winks.

'Lucille. You seem to know a lot,' says my mother in her best phoney-granny voice. 'Shut your eyes and let's see if you can guess what I am putting into your hand.'

Lucille adores the spotlight, and a mimsy smile plays around her lips as she obeys. My mother drops the lychee into her hand. Lucille freaks, and dashes out of the room yelling. My mother watches her go, her brows arched in surprise, then turns to Felix.

'Oh, dear,' she says, 'listen to Lucille's squeals.'

January 17th

Frozen mud and freeze-dried grass is the garden look at the moment, but the dreariness is broken on the edge of the wood, where a wintersweet is in full, fragrant flower. Go down there and close my eyes, inhaling deeply to absorb essence of vanilla and jasmine and wallflower all mixed together to make the unforgettable fragrance of wintersweet. Cut an armful and bring it into the hall, where the fragile flowers, like stars on black twigs, waft their scent through the house.

January 18th

Cannot believe that we are still only halfway through January. Am so fed up with winter that I went on a sunbed today while Vivienne took The Beauty swimming. Bliss to lie naked in the heat, and pretend to be in the Seychelles rather than Cromer Fitness Centre. Freckly afterwards, but not brown. Booked another straight away, then cancelled it for fear of becoming addicted and getting skin cancer.

January 20th

House almost uninhabitable now as David has finally started building Camelot-sized dwelling for the puppies. Far from keeping The Beauty out, he is tailoring it to her requirements. The twin turrets are her boudoir and kitchen, safe places for stashing jewels stolen from my dressing table and biscuits from the larder, as no one over three feet tall can get in. The puppies have a throne room in the castle keep, and The Beauty likes to crawl in and raise the drawbridge in order to spend quality time with them. The whole construction is larger than my bedroom, and sprawls through from the utility room into the hall and kitchen. Cannot see why David needs to have Smalls and his other henchmen here. All they do is make cups of tea and leave doors open.

January 21st

Retreat to bed for the afternoon to escape frenzied sawing and hammering and cup-of-tea-making. Force The Beauty to have a rest, and keep her quiet with a packet of raisins and another of Jelly Tots. Bed is splendid. Electric blanket, lots of pillows and the last pages of *Anna Karenina.* Am weeping over Anna's tragic destiny and comforting myself at the same time by stuffing Smarties into my mouth, when there is a knock on the door. Hide the Smarties, but cannot get out of bed as have taken off trousers, so cannot pretend to be hard at work, dusting or folding clothes. Opt for lying down flat, as if ill.

Quaver, 'Come in,' and David's head appears, his hair haloed with sawdust. We look at one another for an eternity.

'Can I turn the electricity off?' he says.

'Yes, do.' I keep my eyes half-closed, and hope mortification is not spreading pink across my cheeks. He tiptoes into the room, now keeping his eyes averted from my listless form. 'I'm sorry to bother you, but I need to get to the fuse box. Can I bring you anything? I think Smalls is making some tea. Or would you rather be left in peace?' he adds solicitously.

'I'm fine, just shut the door.' So unfair. Bloody hell. Why does the sodding fuse box have to be in my bedroom? David flicks a switch and I hear the answerphone click and bleep as dark and silence envelope the house. Groan atmospherically. David glances again at my slumped form.

'We'll keep the noise down, you rest,' he says kindly. 'You need to get your strength up.' He leaves the room laughing, I am sure. Turn over and see that the Smartie tube is not under the blanket at all, but next to me on the pillow. I am revealed as Bessie Bunter figure rather than glamorous consumptive type.

January 25th

Burns Night. My mother telephones and recites 'Wee sleekit timorous beestie' to Felix and Giles in turn. She wants them to learn it off by heart. They sound as if they are speaking in tongues, but Giles assures me, 'It's the proper Scottish accent for the poem. Robbie Burns used to talk like that. Granny said so.'

Anniversary of my divorce. Is it something to celebrate? Can't decide if it would be tasteless. Charles has no such qualms, but this is because he has forgotten all about it. He telephones briskly from the office. Minna puts us through, but chats for a moment first. She and Desmond have been to the Canary Islands to escape the weather here.

'Yeah, it was windy, but I managed a bit of topless most days, which isn't bad for January.'

She needs no prodding to talk about Charles's business.

'The clockwork coffins have generated ever such a lot of attention,' she tells me, 'and the demand for them is huge. I think Heavenly Petting could give up frying dead animals and move into the ghoulish gift market full time. I'll put you through to Mr Denny. Ask him.'

Charles does not want to talk about business, however. Nor about our divorci-versary.

'Venetia, hello. Helena's frantic that the twins should not be vaccinated. I say they should. She's pretty het up about it, so I said I'd ask you. What did you do about The Beauty?'

'Charles, you can't ask me to get involved in your decisions with Helena about your babies. I can't remember what I did about The Beauty, anyway. But she doesn't have a nut allergy.'

He is perplexed. 'Why should she have a nut allergy?'

'Oh, it's another thing people get very het up about. You'll soon see. Do you know what day it is?'

'Yes, of course I do. It's Burns Night.'

'Anything else?' I use my most dulcet tone, but it is ill received.

'Yes. Yesterday the twins were one month old, so as

you can imagine, I'm exhausted and not in the mood for playing calendar guessing games with you.'

Hang up, delighted to think of Charles being forced into unfamiliar, murky waters of babycare.

January 28th

Giles has refused to go and stay with Charles and Helena this weekend. I ask him if he is upset about the babies. He is sitting on his bed, looking tired, his shoulders sagging and his voice small and sad.

'It's not that. It's more difficult to explain.'

Hug him and sit closer on his bed, heart palpitating, awaiting awful traumatic revelation.

'Dad's house is different from here,' he says, diplomatically averting his eyes from the shredded newspaper stuck to my shoe, and the dark patches of cleared-up puppy pee on the carpet. 'And I feel homesick there, even though I'm with Dad. I'd just rather wait until everyone stops thinking about Holly and Ivy-Eff all the time.'

'All right then, I'll tell Dad. But remember, *never* call her Ivy-Eff when you're with Dad.'

Revived miraculously, Giles sits up. 'It's only so we know which ones we're talking about,' he cajoles, and then, in a much stronger voice, 'And can I have our Holly and Ivy up here? Felix and I are doing an episode of *Animal Hospital*. David's helping us and he's lending us his digital camcorder. Look, I've already got Lowly.'

He pulls back his duvet to reveal the slug-shaped dome of Lowly's belly as he lies on his back, paws beneath his chin, sound asleep on the pillow.

February 1st

Very cross-making day of being utterly ignored by everyone, even the puppies. The episode of *Animal Hospital* turns quickly and surreally into a tiny film for real television. House fills with gaffer tape, cables and huge fluffy brooms held upside down. All this equipment, and the stupid idea of putting the dogs and the children on the local news, comes from marvellous Marion, a so-called friend of David's who is a producer for the local television station. Try to get Giles to find out if marvellous Marion is David's girlfriend. Giles grins at me.

'I know she's not, because David said to me, "I bet your mum thinks Marion is my girlfriend."' Giles is silent for a moment, watching Marion's lithe frame leaning over to show David a shot she might use of the puppies' castle. 'But I think she'd like to be, don't you, Mum?'

'Honestly Giles, I am depressed by the coarse tone of your mind.'

'What about yours? You're the one who asked.'

All supremely irritating. David should not use my house as a pick-up joint for lissom journalists. Huh.

February 3rd

Letter from Charles announcing possible merger and subsequent flotation of Heavenly Petting with a pet shop chain. Visualise this as Noah's-ark-style manoeuvre, with rickety and antique animals sailing away with all Charles's money. In fact it means the opposite. Charles will become a squillionaire. Wonder if I will too. Hope so, but doubt it. Can't even remember how many shares I have. Resolve to become literate in pension schemes, life assurance and shares this year, and purchase the *Financial Times* in Aylsham. Spend a happy hour reading the classified advertisements and eating doughnuts at the kitchen table. The advertisements are top quality and include blissful-sounding holidays. Indulge in fantasies for a while, then flick through the headlines without seeing anything I need to know, and use the rest of the paper to line the puppies' castle keep. They look sweet nestled in the pink newsprint. Have a brilliant idea. Compose an advertisement to sell them and fax it to the FT classifieds. Most efficient morning.

February 6th

Charles collects the boys and takes them to Centre Parcs for the night. They are thrilled to have him to themselves, and all three of them drive off very animated, talking about what they will do first and whether they can go dry skiing. Wave them down the drive, scanning conscience to detect any lemon-faced feelings. There are none. This is what I wanted for them when Charles left. His twins have been a catalyst to change, and he is beginning to see the point of having Giles and Felix to himself. Not quite sure about The Beauty, but am convinced she will cope. Return to the kitchen to find her standing on the table surveying the wreckage of breakfast. Lips pursed, she shakes her head in disapproval.

'Tut tut tut,' she says, and, brandishing a dustpan brush, she begins to clear the table. Crockery catastrophe is averted by Sidney, who jumps onto the table to scavenge and distracts her. Sidney insinuates his way towards the butter dish. The Beauty joins him. Sidney shoots out a long pink tongue and achieves a slurp of butter. The

Beauty extends a dainty finger and dips its tip in, alongside Sidney's tongue.

'Mmmmmm, yummy yummy,' she smiles.

February 9th

Marvellous Marion telephones to ask if she can use the puppies' castle as a location for a children's programme.

'Which one?' Hold my breath, hoping and praying that she will say *Teletubbies*.

'It's called *Soppy Dog*. It's about a Cabbage Patch dog with learning difficulties, but a lovely, gentle, funny character.'

'Sounds ghastly,' I bark, and realising I sound like some old sergeant major, add, 'I mean, it sounds wonderful, and we'd love you to film it here. Will it be a series?'

'Yes, it will take about a week to shoot. Would ten thousand be all right?'

Just manage not to scream, but say airily, 'Ten's fine for that, yup.'

Put phone down and dance about, singing with joy. Must ask David to build some more things immediately. We will become like Shepperton Studios. Hooray. Rich, rich, rich. Must give David a cut, in fact, or go into business with him. Where *is* David? He is supposed to be here.

February 10th

Sudden landscaping interest has arisen today, because marvellous Marion has sent a lorry load of box-hedging plants to say thank you for *Soppy Dog*. Having no artistic flair myself, am flummoxed by all this evergreen twiggery. Telephone Rose.

'You must have a knot garden,' she says. 'I'll get Tristan to draw a plan and I'll fax it to you.'

Awful Zen fax arrives with absurd garden nothing like mine, having very straight lines, lots of tiny white chip gravel and smooth concrete paths. Look out of the study window at weed-strewn wilderness and become despondent. Take fax to David, who is in overdrive and is now creating a grotto in The Beauty's room. He is hammering and singing 'Sorrow' by David Bowie. It is one of my favourites. Stand behind him, listening, mesmerised by the rhythmic hammering and murmured song.

'The only thing I ever got from you was sorrow.'

He knows all the words, and carries on through the verses until Digger, curled on The Beauty's bed, notices me and thumps his tail. David turns his head and smiles a greeting. Have astonishing sensation of being quite naked with him looking at me. So powerful is this feeling that I find myself glancing down to make sure my jeans are still there. Start blabbering to hide my confusion.

'I wonder – I don't suppose – would you be interested? No. What I mean is, can you make a knot garden?'

He looks utterly blank. I pass the fax. He stares at it and then at me again. Fear I have offended him somehow.

'Don't worry. I'll just go and plant the trees any old how. It can't be hard.'

Rush outside in a chaos of irritation that David is not making the knot garden for me. Why am I so neurotic that I can't even have a conversation now without thinking I'm naked? Must change my life and get out more. Or not. Perhaps I am one of nature's hermits. David shouts out of the window at me.

'Sorry, I got the wrong end of the stick. Of course I'll make you a knot garden. Don't do any digging now. I'll draw a plan and do it for you. But I can't for a few days. So just leave it or you'll do your back in.'

'All right. I'll just do this row of plants before it's time to collect the boys,' I yell back, relieved that I no longer feel naked, and enjoying the hot physical exertion of the task. Once again have become a peasant from *Anna Karenina*. Dig a satisfactory square for my seventh tiny box plant, and am heaving taupe-coloured clay wodge into the wheelbarrow, when shooting pain cleaves my spine at the waist. Ping, just like a trouser button, except that instead of the midriff sagging, my vertebra has turned red hot and spiked. Stagger inside shrieking for help and collapse in agony on the kitchen floor.

February 12th

In bed officially now, with two Florence Nightingale attendants, one with purple hair, the other about two feet tall. Drug haze clears enough for me to identify them as my mother and The Beauty. Both have acquired starched aprons, red crosses and little hats like napkins. They flit and glide about my room, plumping cushions, tweaking the bowl of snowdrops and black hellebores and generally ministering. Have been given elephant tranquillisers or equivalent, so am in mad pink-edged, soft-focus world, and have no cares or responsibilities at all.

February 13th

Telephone interrupts fluffy thoughts. It is a minion from the Mo Loam Temple to Beauty.

'Mrs Denny, you have missed your appointment and must pay the full fee of a hundred and twenty pounds immediately. There is a waiting list here, you know.'

'But I've already paid a deposit,' I protest, still on cloud nine, but coming back to earth with a bump.

'This is immaterial,' drones the minion. 'Shall I book you another appointment to redeem your deposit, or shall we call it a day?'

'Do what you like.' Slam telephone down and weep for several minutes. The Beauty brings her kangaroo over to comfort me.

February 14th

Valentine's Day again. Am allowed to get up today, but can't be bothered. Self-pity has overtaken backache, thanks to wonder drugs, and I lie in bed with no prospect of being sent any cards and the future as a crippled old mother of three before me. Not even a beauty treatment glistens on the horizon. My mother is still installed, looking after the children. She will probably have to stay for ever. Through my bedroom door I hear muffled voices and pattering feet. The gravel crunches beneath car tyres, heralding the postman. Must get up. Pattering feet get louder and louder.

'Mum, Mum, even Rags has got a card. Felix hates his *again* this year. The Beauty's got two. Look, look.'

Quite absurd at my age to mind so much about Valentine's Day. I shall rise above it. But I want a card. Why has everyone except me got one?

The children swarm into the room, a bundle of envelopes coloured blue and pink and green like sugared almonds in their hands. Felix waves a duck-egg blue one.

It has tiny gold stars dusted across it, and it encapsulates everything that I love about stationery.

'Look, Mum. This one is for you,' he says. Giles has opened Rags's card and is reading it to her.

'Mummy, it says "Two out of three ain't bad." What does it mean?' Have no interest in cryptic canine messages.

'Oh, I expect it's from Digger. It must mean the puppies,' I suggest. Dress at top speed, staring at my card without opening it. Savouring the fact of having it. It is here. It is mine. It is, undoubtedly, a Valentine's Day card. How I have longed for this moment.

The boys depart, leaving twists of torn pastel paper, and charge downstairs to show my mother Rags's card and to see what The Beauty got. Hear them all clattering and shouting in the kitchen. Heart thuds madly as I approach the card. Feel exactly as I did when opening my A-level results, tight in the throat, my skin electric, my teeth clenched. Pick it up, turn it over, but am too overexcited to read the envelope, even though I know I should be poring over the postmark. Tear the envelope wide open. No card. This is terrible. No blooming effusions or lines of poetry. I wanted it to be Byron. I wanted someone to have chosen:

She walks in Beauty like the night
Of cloudless climes and starry skies;

And all that's best of dark and light
Meet in her aspect and her eyes

But no one has. A slip of paper falls out and onto the floor. Tears well and swim in my eyes as I pick it up.

Admired Venetia, look out of your window.

Thrilling, just thrilling. Rush to the window, fling open the curtains and look. There below, where I was digging in deepest mud a few days ago, is heaven. A tiny, intricate knot garden, gravel gleaming between the curves and swells of the hedging, and seats with backs like scallop shells at either end. Four slender trees stand among the box, their branches naked save for a thread of silver stars. The whole garden is not much bigger than my kitchen. It sparkles, still damp with morning dew; precious and perfect as a jewel.

The back door opens, and Giles and Felix, in wellingtons, charge into the yard, The Beauty riding piggyback on Giles's shoulders. They run through the orchard, scattering a trio of hens who are making a meal out of some worms in a molehill. The boys pause beneath my window and survey the knot garden critically.

The Beauty, sensing a celebration, claps, and shouts, 'Hooray.'

'Cool,' says Giles. 'He managed to get it finished in time after all.' Felix sits down on a bench.

'Mum will probably cry when she sees it,' he remarks. 'I would if I were her.'

'What do you mean? I think she'll really like it,' Giles is indignant.

'I mean that kind of crying she does when she's happy. You know, like at the school play.'

'Oh, yes. She will.' Both fall silent for a moment. 'Come on. Let's go inside. It's freezing.'

The first sun for days struggles through and dances on the leaves and stars and branches in my new garden. I lean in from the window and turn to go downstairs. David is on the threshold of my room.